Her hand la[nded on his] chest.

That was the m[oment she realized] exactly who he was. Clearly, she was a fan. His female admirers always wanted to touch.

"Aren't you cute," Boone said. "If you think it would help, I'll sign something for you and your daughter. Maybe this little encounter will turn the whole day around."

People used to tell him that all the time. They would profess their love for him and swear that meeting him was life altering. Boone Williams had that effect on people.

This little redhead cocked her head and seemed confused, however. Boone figured she was still trying to play like she didn't recognize him. It was a common ploy.

He gave her his trademark grin and lowered his voice, which had literally made women swoon. "You want me to sign something for you, pretty lady?"

The line between her eyebrows deepened. "Unless you're signing your name on a check, I'm not sure your signature is going to do me and my daughter much good, mister."

"Are you famous or something?" the daughter asked.

Dear Reader,

I am thrilled to be bringing you the second book in the Grace Note Records series. Boone Williams was a character introduced in the first book, who I was a little worried I wasn't going to be able to make very likable. As I began to write *Catch a Fallen Star*, he started to grow on me until he became one of my favorite heroes yet!

Everyone has good and bad moments in their lives, and we meet Boone when he's decided to try pulling himself out of the hole he's dug. It's never easy to accept when we're wrong, and for someone like Boone, who has had his head blown up thanks to his fame, it's even harder. Enter Ruby and her daughter, Violet. Sometimes people come into our lives whom we never expect to have much of an impact, but they surprise us. Ruby and Violet do that for Boone.

I hope you enjoy this story and open your heart to Boone, who isn't perfect by any means. But he's working on it!

Visit me on Facebook and Twitter (@vastine7) or on my website, www.amyvastine.com.

xoxo,

Amy Vastine

HEARTWARMING

Catch a Fallen Star

—

Amy Vastine

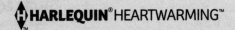

Recycling programs
for this product may
not exist in your area.

ISBN-13: 978-0-373-36815-0

Catch a Fallen Star

Copyright © 2016 by Amy Vastine

This edition published by arrangement with Harlequin Books S.A.

For questions and comments about the quality of this book, please contact us at CustomerService@Harlequin.com.

Printed in U.S.A.

www.Harlequin.com

Amy Vastine has been plotting stories in her head for as long as she can remember. An eternal optimist, she studied social work, hoping to teach others how to find their silver lining. Now she enjoys creating happily-ever-afters for all to read. Amy lives outside Chicago with her high school sweetheart turned husband, three fun-loving children and their sweet but mischievous puppy dog. Visit her at www.amyvastine.com.

Books by Amy Vastine

Harlequin Heartwarming

The Girl He Used to Love
The Hardest Fight
The Best Laid Plans
The Better Man
The Weather Girl

To my darling teenage daughter, Alyssa. I hope you read this someday and can laugh at the bits of you I may have written into Violet. I hope you know I love you dearly even though your eye-rolling is now documented for all to see.

Acknowledgments

To my book-club friends who helped me name many of the characters of this book. You guys are the best!

CHAPTER ONE

"WHAT IN THE name of all that is holy is this?" Boone Williams stood in front of the shiny silver Airstream trailer with his hands on his hips. He'd slept in a lot of strange places while touring the country, but this had to be a joke.

"This is your new home away from home," Dean said, flashing the used-car-salesman grin he thought worked on everyone.

Dean Presley was the head of Boone's record label, Grace Note Records, and the one who had convinced Boone to come down here to small-town Grass Lake. He had promised the perfect Tennessee retreat. A place with all the comforts of home and none of the stress. It was supposed to be top-notch, somewhere the rich and famous like Boone could reconnect with the music.

"You've got to be kidding me," Boone grumbled. This was a trailer in the middle of a horse farm. The pungent smell of manure did battle with the overwhelming scent of hay that made his nose itch. This was no vacation home. This was a nightmare.

"Don't judge until you see the inside. It's not the Four Seasons, but you'd be amazed at what we fit into this little space."

"I knew there wasn't a Four Seasons in this Podunk town, but I'm sure there have to be accommodations a little more fitting for someone like me."

"Boone—"

"I have twenty-five number-one singles, I've won three Grammys and ten Country Artist Awards, and I was named America's favorite male country music artist at the People's Choice Awards…four times. I'm pretty sure I deserve better than this."

Dean sighed, mimicking Boone's stance. He closed his eyes for a moment and his smile faded. "I hate to remind you that you also haven't had a record out in five years. Instead, you've had two DUIs and a few other run-ins with the law that you were fortunate to get out of because of who you are. The last time you attended the CAAs, you were asked not to return because you shoved an assistant producer backstage. And right now, the only thing you'd win if people voted would be favorite tabloid star. I'm pretty sure this place is exactly what you need."

Every dose of reality was like a hot poker in the gut. Dean was right, but that didn't mean Boone wanted to hear it. Dean opened the door to the Airstream, and Boone stomped up the stairs and inside.

It wasn't the worst place he'd ever had to stay, but not at all what he had expected. He had grown accustomed to his life of luxury. The pillow with the words *Welcome Home* stitched across it mocked him from the beige couch in the front. A basket of cookies and a bottle of sparkling water sat on the little dinette in the kitchen area. In the back was the bedroom, complete with a full-size bed and one tiny nightstand. Boone threw his suitcase on the bed.

"Faith stocked the kitchen with some basics, but I can take you into town to pick up groceries or any incidentals you might have forgotten," Dean offered. "I can also show you around the barn and introduce you to the horses whenever you're ready. We can save the studio tour for tomorrow."

Studio tour? The studio was apparently also on this godforsaken farm. The likelihood that Boone would be impressed was low. Not that he had anything to record. The words still weren't coming. The music had dried up when he'd dried out.

"How many horses are there?"

"We've got three right now."

"That's not very many."

"We lost one back in May," Dean explained. "Faith's been taking her time looking for a new one. Therapy horses aren't easy to come by. They're special. Not every horse can work as one. Faith drove up to Nashville this morning to check out a filly a friend of hers has for sale. Maybe we'll have four in a few short days."

Faith was Dean's fiancée and the one who ran the farm where Boone was now trapped. It was supposedly a therapeutic horse farm called Helping Hooves. Boone wasn't sure how horses could help someone like him. Of course, the humans who had tried hadn't had much success, either.

Maybe he was a hopeless case. The failure his father had always believed he would be.

Suddenly the already tight quarters began to feel even more claustrophobic. The walls closed in, and Boone began to panic. Soon there wouldn't be enough air for both of them.

"Let's go meet the horses," he said, pushing past Dean to get to the door. At least he knew the animals wouldn't ask him about his divorce or when his next album was coming out. They wouldn't remind him of how far he had fallen.

THE AFTERNOON SUN shone bright in a cloudless sky as Dean led Boone to the stables. Boone rubbed the back of his neck, cursing himself for not grabbing a hat.

A red sedan that hadn't been there when Boone arrived was parked near the barn. An uneasy feeling came over him. He did not want to deal with the public just yet.

"Just to be clear, I'm not signing any autographs or doing any meet and greets while I'm here."

Dean glanced over his shoulder with what strongly resembled a smirk. "We're definitely on the same page about that. You aren't exactly what I'd call fan-friendly at the moment."

"What's that supposed to mean?" Boone nudged him from behind. Dean's business partner was usually the one who acted like Boone was incapable of being nice. Maybe Dean believed that to be true.

The real truth was that if Boone wanted to, he could charm the pants off anyone. All he was saying was he didn't want to, not that he couldn't. There was a big difference.

"I mean you're here to focus on you and the music, not make new friends."

The two men stepped into the stables just as a teen girl with dark hair and ripped-up jeans began her tirade.

"I knew you would tell him! This is my time with the horses, and now he's going to make me talk about things I don't want to talk about! Why do you hate me so much?"

A man dressed in jeans and a flannel shirt—presumably the "he" who was going to make the girl talk about whatever it was she clearly did not want to talk about—stepped between the angry young lady and whoever had made her so furious.

"No one is going to make you talk about anything you don't want to talk about, Violet. That's our deal, remember?"

"You say that, Jesse, but you always get me to spill my guts even when I don't want to."

The girl reminded Boone of another indignant teenager who loved horses. His daughter, Emmy, was fourteen and, likely thanks mostly to her mother, hadn't answered his calls or replied to any of his text messages in months.

"Please give me a break," an exasperated redhead said as she pushed her way around the man named Jesse. "I can't take this drama. Jesse is your social worker. He should know when things happen so you two can process through it. Lord knows you don't want to talk to me about it."

"Why would I talk to you? You don't want

to hear about my *drama*. I bet you wish you could ditch me just like Dad did."

The mother's head fell back as she let out a growl of frustration. Boone took a step toward the door. They were obviously intruding on a very personal conversation.

Jesse noticed them then. "Dean." He made his way over while mother and daughter glared in their direction—another all too familiar sight.

"Sorry, Jesse." Dean also began to back-pedal. "We'll come back. I didn't realize you had a session scheduled."

"No, I'm going to go," the redhead said. "Violet's right. This is her time with the horses, not our time to fight. We should save that for home."

"Ruby..." Jesse spun back around. "We should use this as an opportunity to work on your communication."

"I am pretty sure you could spend the rest of your life helping us with our communication. I can afford only an hour of your time, so I am going to leave." She gave Dean an apologetic grimace. "Sorry for the...whatever this was, Dean."

"Don't be sorry. We really can come back. Maybe you should stay and talk this out with Jesse and Violet."

"And keep your friend here from getting the

grand tour? No way." Her hand landed solidly on Boone's chest. That was the moment he realized she knew exactly who he was. Clearly she was a fan. For some reason, his female admirers always wanted to touch.

"Aren't you cute," Boone said, ready to prove to Dean that he could be nice. "If you think it would help, I'll sign something for you and your daughter. Maybe this little encounter will turn the whole day around."

People used to tell him that all the time. They would profess their love for him and swear that meeting him was life altering. Fans often told him that getting his autograph or their picture taken with him was the best moment of their lives, even better than the day they got married or gave birth to their children. Boone Williams had that effect on people.

This little redhead cocked her head and seemed confused, however. Boone figured she was still trying to play like she didn't recognize him. It was a common ploy. Fans sometimes tried acting unaware of who he was at first in the hope it would put him more at ease around them.

He gave her his trademark grin and lowered his voice, which had literally made women swoon. "You want me to sign something for you, pretty lady?"

See? He could be nice.

The line between the woman's eyebrows deepened. "Unless you're signing your name on a check that's going to pay for about a hundred more sessions with Jesse, I'm not sure your signature is going to do me and my daughter much good, mister."

With that, she was gone.

"Are you famous or something?" the girl asked, arms crossed tightly in front of her.

He thought he was. He sure used to be. Lately, however, he'd been famous for all the wrong reasons.

"Violet Wynn, this is Boone Williams." Dean paused for her to react. She didn't, so he continued, "He's a very famous singer at my record label. He's going to be staying here for a few weeks to work with the horses and maybe write some new music."

That was a big maybe.

"Welcome to the farm, Boone. I'm Jesse Keyes." He held out his hand to shake. "We're happy to have you here."

"Jesse says that to everyone," Violet said behind him.

Jesse took a deep breath. Turning, he suggested to the girl, "Why don't you go in the tack room and get things ready while I grab Sassy?"

"It's true. You do say that to everybody. You're one of those nice people who goes around saying nice things to everyone you meet. I just thought he should know so he doesn't start offering to sign things for you, too."

Dean coughed a laugh into his fist. Jesse seemed to be fighting a smile as Violet took off in the other direction. "Not surprising she gets along best with the horse named Sassy, is it?" he asked Boone.

"Not surprising in the least." Boone glanced around at the stables. How had his life come to this—hiding on a horse farm in the middle of small-town Tennessee where people didn't even know who he was? This was not the way things were supposed to be.

He had to get his career back, and fast, or fame would be nothing but a faded memory. And if he wasn't famous, what was the point of all those years of hard work and sacrifice? Boone had given everything he had to his career. Without it, he was nothing.

CHAPTER TWO

IF RUBY HAD her way, she would eradicate the world of men. Maybe not all men, just the ones who didn't give a damn about their children and the ones who thought they could fix the world's problems by smiling and offering... their signatures.

Okay, the signature part was still weird. Why anyone would think writing his name on something could make this horrible day better, she'd never understand.

With an hour to kill and an ex-husband she'd also like to kill, Ruby figured the safest place for her was under the watchful eye of her best friend.

Holly Davis was editor of the *Grass Lake Gazette*. The *Gazette* was published on Thursdays and had a distribution of a whopping 2,600 people. Holly certainly didn't need to work on a Saturday, but she often put in more hours on the weekend when her husband could be home to watch their three kids.

The small-town newspaper was housed on

the top floor of the tallest building along Main Street. Ruby decided walking up the six flights of stairs would help her burn off some of the adrenaline that seemed still to be coursing through her veins.

Sure enough, the door to the *Gazette* was unlocked when she reached the top. Holly sat at her desk with a pen in her mouth.

"I know you come here for peace and quiet, but I need to spend some time with someone who likes me," Ruby said, slightly out of breath.

Holly removed the pen and stuck it in the bun on top of her head. Her round face and large blue eyes gave her a childlike appearance, such a stark contrast to the streaks of gray in her dark brown hair. "I love you," she corrected Ruby. "Who doesn't love you?"

"I'll give you a hint. She's about this tall and is a professional eye roller."

"How is my favorite thirteen-year-old?"

"She's a pain in my butt." Violet had a way of perfectly pushing Ruby's buttons. She somehow managed to make her mom feel bad for her and infuriated by her at the same time. And whatever the problem was, it was always Ruby's fault.

Never mind the fact that what had sparked the whole meltdown today was that Levi had once again canceled his visit with his daughter. Never mind that he'd spent months promising to take Violet to California for a long weekend. They were supposed to go to Disneyland and see the Hollywood sign. Only, Levi called last night with yet another lame excuse for why he couldn't follow through.

"She loves you," Holly said. "She's starting puberty. It's natural for her to clash with her mother. It's her destiny to fight you on everything until she's grown and on her own. Then she'll think you're the wisest person in the world."

Ruby dropped into an empty office chair. "Ha! I hope I live that long."

Jesse had once explained that it was safer for Violet to be angry with Ruby because she could trust that her mother would always be there. If she were to lash out at her dad, he might cut and run for good. Even the occasional phone call was better than nothing, so Violet couldn't express her frustration to the real cause of all her angst.

Sometimes being the responsible and reliable parent really stank.

"When I was Violet's age, I used to tell people I was adopted because I didn't want them to think I was related to anyone in my family."

"Holly!" Ruby leaned back and put her feet

up on the desk. "That's terrible. Your family could not have been that bad."

"Oh, that's nothing compared to what my younger sister did. My parents deserved a medal for surviving our teens."

Ruby knew all about pushing parents to their limits. Her own mother could have written a book about the things Ruby had done at Violet's age. What was happening now was most definitely karma.

"I don't need a medal. I'd be happy simply to get one day without her sighing or telling me I don't understand. Don't worry. I won't hold my breath, I promise."

"Good, because that could take a very long time."

Even though Holly had three boys who still let their mom tuck them in at night and asked for extra kisses before they could fall asleep, her opinion still fed Ruby's fear that she and Violet would never find common ground. Especially when Violet's father constantly played games with her emotions.

"Tell me something good. What amazing things are happening in Grass Lake this week?"

Holly rubbed her hands together and giggled like she had when they were roommates in college and had a secret to tell. She leaned forward, putting her elbows on her cluttered desk. "Grass Lake is about to be put on the map."

Ruby raised an eyebrow. "How so?"

Holly's blue eyes somehow got bigger. "We have a celebrity in town. A megastar."

"What kind of celebrity? A movie star?"

"Not someone from Hollywood. Someone from Nashville."

Ruby's interest diminished significantly with that revelation. Country music wasn't her thing. Never had been, even though Levi loved it. She was more of a progressive rock kind of girl.

"Nashville stars are not mega."

"Oh, I know a whole lot of people who would disagree. Boone Williams is easily one of the biggest names in country music. He's right up there with the likes of Johnny Cash and Willie Nelson."

Boone Williams. Ruby knew the name. She'd have to live under a rock to not have heard of him. He'd been married to some other country singer and made a mess of his life a few years back. Ruby couldn't picture him, though. A quick Google search would remedy that.

As she typed his name into her phone, Holly added, "In fact, he's staying over at the Stratton farm. You have a decent shot of laying eyes on him when you're there with Violet."

Oh, Ruby had laid eyes on him. In the images on her screen, he resembled more of a rugged cowboy than the average Joe he'd seemed to be in the barn. Not that he was average-looking by any means. His piercing blue eyes had caught her attention, as had his rock-hard chest. Of course, then he had opened his mouth.

"I definitely saw him there."

Holly nearly fell out of her chair. "You met Boone Williams? Did you talk to him? Did he talk to you? Did you ask him for an autograph?"

Ruby wanted to laugh out loud at the last question. He had been offering her an autograph because he thought he was as famous as Holly did. His ego was incredible, but perhaps a bit more understandable now that she knew who he was.

"Had I known you were such a fan, I would have taken him up on his offer to sign something to make up for the horrendous argument I was having with my dear daughter when he stumbled upon us."

"He what?"

"I guess that's how he rolls. Whenever he sees pain and suffering, he offers to sign his name on a piece of paper so all the troubles will be forgotten." Ruby placed a hand over her heart. "He's such a giver, a true hero. Just think if he used his amazing powers of peace-keeping in the Middle East or North Korea."

Boone, ego and all, was similar to the other men Ruby had known in her life. They thought they could charm their way out of anything and women should simply be grateful for their existence. They certainly didn't have to be responsible or deal with the messy parts of life. They never truly cared about anyone's feelings but their own.

"Are you telling me you didn't get his autograph?"

Ruby found her friend's disappointment a tad disturbing. "Holly, are you not hearing me? Perhaps the sarcasm distracted you from what I said. The guy thought giving me his autograph would make up for the fact that my daughter thinks I hate her. That it would make that little girl forget her father is a lying deadbeat. His delusions of grandeur are ridiculous."

"Cut the guy some slack. He's used to people knocking each other over to get a look at him," Holly said in his defense. "Maybe we can get him to agree to do an interview for the paper."

"We? I have nothing to do with this. I deliver babies, not the news." Ruby had moved to Grass Lake because Sadie Greenville decided that after sixty years as a midwife it was time to retire. She had offered Ruby her office space and her handful of patients.

Refusing to give up, Holly reminded her, "You do a great job with the column."

Ruby had also inherited Sadie's monthly advice column at the *Gazette*. Ruby was now responsible for enlightening the town on how to be a good parent. She was waiting for someone to call her out as a fraud.

"Not the same thing," Ruby argued.

Holly folded her hands together and started with those puppy-dog eyes. "Pleeeease. You have a reason to go to the farm. I only need you to see if he'd be willing to sit down with me. You wouldn't have to do the interview."

"I go to the farm because my kid is falling apart thanks to the fact that her dad doesn't care about her."

"Oh, man." Sympathy quickly replaced the pleading look in Holly's eye. "I know things haven't been easy, but I thought they were getting better since you moved here."

That was true, but as long as Levi was still in the picture, things would never be okay. His constant indifference was the reason Ruby had agreed to take over for Sadie. She had an excellent reputation, and that meant a viable business for her successor. Once Ruby made enough money to hire a lawyer, she planned to file for full custody and take off to Seattle to be near her older sister.

"Coming here was the best decision I've made in a long time." Ruby tried to smile for her friend's sake. She didn't want Holly's pity.

"Jon and I knew this community was exactly what you needed. And I, selfishly, love having you so close."

It had been Holly who had convinced her to come to Grass Lake. Sadie had delivered Holly's boys and wrote the parenting column for the *Gazette*, so when Holly found out she wanted to turn everything over to another midwife, she suggested Ruby. Holly even rented her mother-in-law's house to Ruby dirt cheap.

Friends like Holly came along once in a lifetime.

"I don't know about an interview, but I bet I can get Boone Williams's autograph when I go back to pick up Violet."

Holly grinned from ear to ear. "I'll take it. But maybe slip in that I'd love to do an interview. My sister will be absolutely Wicked-Witch-green with envy if I tell her I'm going to sit down with Boone Williams."

Holly's sister wouldn't envy her at all if they both knew what Boone was really like, but Ruby would try to give him the benefit of the doubt. Perhaps he wasn't good with first impressions.

JESSE AND VIOLET were leading one of the horses around the paddock when Ruby returned to Helping Hooves. She noticed the content smile on her daughter's face as she spoke with her social worker.

Ruby's heart ached the way it always did when she thought about how Violet would feel if she had a father who actually participated in his daughter's life. It was so depressing; she couldn't dwell in that thought for too long.

Slamming the car door shut garnered the attention of both of them. Violet's smile quickly disappeared, and Ruby's heart took another stomping.

Someday she'll like me.

Teenagers weren't supposed to like their parents, and parents weren't supposed to be their teens' friends. In a few years, her daughter would thank her for being a parent and not a friend. Ruby had been given all that advice and then some as Violet approached this wretched age. It didn't always ease the pain of her daughter's constant rejection, though.

"Why do you always have to show up so

early?" Violet complained. "I still have to clean Sassy up before I can go."

Ruby took a deep breath and reminded herself not to be offended by her daughter's tone. "I can wait. No worries."

"Why don't you let your mom know what you accomplished today?" Jesse prompted.

There was a small glimmer of pride in Violet's eyes. "I got Sassy to perform a flying lead change."

"Really?" Ruby tried to show the right amount of enthusiasm. Violet hated too much and resented too little. "That's awesome."

"Do you even know what that means, Mom?"

Ruby had no idea, since she had little to no experience with horses, but she wasn't about to admit it. "Yeah, of course."

Violet seemed unconvinced. Jesse saved the day. "Violet's doing a great job of getting Sassy to change her lead legs. I think the two of them are going to do really well at the horse show in a couple of weeks. Do you want to join us in the tack room, Ruby?"

The look on Violet's face made it clear she did not want her mother to come with them. The last thing Ruby needed was to agitate her bear of a daughter.

"I need to touch base with Dean about something," Ruby said, throwing a thumb over her shoulder. "But I'll meet you in there in a few minutes."

Violet's visible relief was yet another punch in the stomach.

"All right, we'll chat when you get back," Jesse said.

Ruby headed toward the main house. She'd probably have to go through Dean to land Holly an interview with Boone Williams. He ran his record company from somewhere on the property.

As she climbed the porch steps, the sound of someone screaming bloody murder made her pause. Someone was not happy and was letting the heavens know about it. Fearing someone was hurt, she followed the porch around to see what was wrong.

Boone stood in the yard and was doing his best impression of a woman in the throes of childbirth. He puffed his chest out and let his head fall back as he roared at the sky. He took a deep breath and relaxed his shoulders. When he opened his eyes, his gaze fell squarely on Ruby.

Feeling as if she had been caught snooping instead of doing a welfare check, she took a step back and tripped over a rocking chair that seemed to have appeared out of nowhere.

Ruby fell on her behind and felt a sharp pain in her wrist as she attempted to break her fall.

Those stormy blue eyes that had blown her over were now glaring at her through the slats of the porch railing. He somehow managed to look angrier than he had a moment ago.

"Unbelievable," he growled.

CHAPTER THREE

BOONE WAS NEVER truly alone. Lonely, yes. Alone, never. There were always plenty of people around. Some of them had a job to do. Most wanted something from him. He hadn't figured out where this redheaded mystery fit in.

"Did you hurt yourself?" he asked even though the grimace on her face told him she had.

She inspected her wrist, wincing as she rolled it around. "Yes."

"Good." Boone headed back toward his trailer. That was what she got for spying on him.

"Good?" she shouted from the porch.

This was exactly the kind of thing Boone was trying to avoid by coming to this place. He hated all the prying eyes and straining ears back in Nashville. Everyone wanted in his business.

"You've got a lot of nerve, you know that?" The nosy redhead wasn't finished interrupting his scream therapy.

Boone stopped and turned as she came barreling after him. He really shouldn't have been mad. It wasn't like the therapy he was testing out helped ease any of the frustration he felt. He was beginning to think every doctor/psychologist/psychiatrist/social worker he'd seen in the past few years was a quack.

That didn't mean he'd cut this intruder any slack, though. "*I* have a lot of nerve? You're the one snooping around," he accused her.

Her face was flushed as she held her injured wrist against her chest. "Snooping? You sounded like you were being murdered! Excuse me for caring enough to make sure you weren't dying."

"Nobody's dying. Even you and your poor little wrist will live."

Her eyes narrowed. "You should really get those issues checked out. Whatever your problem is, it's bad."

This woman sure was something. "The only problem I have is that you seem to think I owe you something because you tripped over your own two feet."

"I tripped over a rocking chair, thank you very much." She smoothed her hair and tugged on the hem of her shirt. There was a bit of insecurity under all that tough talk. "Next time I hear you screaming, I'll be sure to let whatever's eating you have at it."

"Perfect," he replied, hating himself for noticing the cute way her eyebrow was cocked. Fine, she was attractive, but he was not interested.

She stared hard at him before spinning on her heel and taking off. Boone sighed with relief, but she stopped and came back at him. She apparently was never going to leave him alone.

"You know, I have a friend who works for the *Grass Lake Gazette*, and I almost feel like it's my duty to tell her to warn the good people of this town to steer clear of Helping Hooves so they don't find out the almighty Boone Williams is an enormous jerk."

"So you *do* recognize me." He knew it. She had almost fooled him earlier in the barn. Then the rest of what she'd said settled in. "Wait, who works for the paper?" It figured she was also in cahoots with one of his least favorite groups of people—the press.

Instead of answering, she stormed off. He followed her for no good reason other than that she had made him lose his mind.

"I'm here to get away from the media," he said, trying his best to catch her. "I don't need anyone publishing anything about me."

She was not only irritating but also incredibly fast. She made it to the barn before he could reach her.

"Did you hear me?" When he touched her arm, she whipped around and swatted at him.

"We have this thing called freedom of the press here in this country. Journalists can write about anything they want."

"I know they can. I got people writing baloney about me every day."

"Well, maybe you should think before you act and people wouldn't have so many salacious things to write."

Boone felt his temperature rise. "You know nothing about me."

"Oh my gosh, Mom! Stop making a scene." The woman's daughter stood outside one of the stalls with her hands on her hips, staring them both down.

"Stay out of this, Violet."

"Stay out of this, kid," Boone said at the same time.

"Don't tell my daughter what to do," the woman snapped.

She confounded him. "We said the exact same thing."

Thankfully she looked a bit chagrined. "Just don't talk to her."

"I don't want to talk to either of you. I want you to leave me alone. Is that really too much to ask?"

She softened for a moment. Maybe it was

because her daughter was watching. Maybe she'd finally realized she was being completely unreasonable. "No, it's not. I'll leave you alone and you leave me and my daughter alone and I think we'll both be happy."

"Absolutely." Boone could not agree more. Alone. That was all he wanted to be.

AFTER THE DISASTER of day one on the farm, Boone hid out in his trailer most of the next two days. This seemed to bug Dean, who was determined to get Boone out and about. It had started with a simple dinner invitation that Boone had quickly refused. Next up, Dean had encouraged some time with the horses…and Jesse, the resident shrink. That wasn't happening.

Boone knew what Dean was up to. He thought that if Boone talked to this Jesse guy, he'd step into the studio and record a platinum single. Music didn't work like that. At least not good music.

By Tuesday afternoon, Boone was sick of the trailer and annoyed with himself for being curious if and when the spunky redhead might return with her daughter. It wasn't like him to be preoccupied with anything other than when he was getting his next drink. Maybe it was his sobriety that had changed things, but it sure felt like the fire in that woman's eyes had consumed him.

Maybe his problem was starvation. When Dean had said his fiancée had stocked the kitchen with some basics, he'd meant the bare minimum to keep a person alive: some bread, peanut butter and jelly, a half gallon of milk, a box of macaroni and cheese, gummy bears and a bag of barbecue potato chips. Dean had obviously shared a list of Boone's tour hospitality requests with Faith. These might have been all his favorite comfort foods, but Boone needed something a bit more substantial.

"I want to go to town and buy some groceries," he said when Dean stopped by to extend another dinner invitation.

"Great!" Dean's eyes lit up. "Let's go. I can show you around and we can check out Main Street."

"I don't need a tour guide. I need a car."

"We can take Faith's truck."

"You're not understanding me. If I go into town with you, I can't get in and out unnoticed. I want to get groceries, not do a meet and greet with everyone on Main Street."

Dean didn't seem too keen on this plan, but Boone wasn't going to do this any other way. Dean mulled it over for a minute and then offered to go get the keys.

Luckily there weren't enough streets in this small town for Boone to get lost. He found the local grocery store and filled his cart with all the things that made his stomach growl. With the bill of his baseball cap pulled down, he managed to avoid eye contact with the other shoppers until a familiar voice caught his attention.

"Oh my gosh, you are so annoying."

"You're trying to chicken out. I knew you would."

"I'm not chickening out of anything."

Boone lifted his head and his gaze fell directly on the queen of teenage angst. He glanced around to make sure the girl's mother wasn't nearby. Ruby was the last person he wanted to bump into during this little excursion. He made a quick detour down the last aisle before Violet spotted him.

He hoped the kid was here with only her friend and not her mother. Just the thought of Ruby made his blood boil. It bugged him that this woman had so easily gotten under his skin. It shouldn't matter that she was pretty and petite, just his type. Or that she had the face of an angel. She was the devil in disguise, threatening to send the press after him. He began to contemplate the idea of taking Dean's truck and driving home to Nashville.

"Could you help me?" a dark-haired woman

asked him. She immediately reminded Boone of his nana. She was well put-together and small in stature. Her bright red lipstick was meticulously applied. "For some reason they put my husband's favorite bottle of wine on the highest shelf."

Boone realized in that moment that he had landed himself in the aisle with nothing but beer and wine. His stomach growled louder than it had the entire shopping trip, and his mouth felt drier than a desert. There was only one thing that could quench this particular thirst.

He could smell it now—the hoppy beer and the fruity notes in the merlots. He could almost feel the bubbles of the champagne on his tongue. Given his physical reaction, it was amazing his body hadn't led him to this aisle the second he set foot in the store. It was either fate testing his sobriety or the devil begging him to give it up.

"Are you all right?" the woman asked, giving him a peculiar look.

Boone snapped out of his daze. Embarrassed, he shook his head. "Which one?" His voice was rough, like he hadn't spoken in years.

"That one right there." She pointed.

With shaky hands, Boone reached up and

grabbed the bottle that had eluded the poor woman. He knew how it felt to have what you wanted most just out of reach.

"Thank you," the woman said, waiting patiently for him to hand it over.

Boone couldn't turn it over just yet. He wanted to feel the glass in his hands, take in the weight of the liquid held inside. What he wouldn't give to open it up and take one tiny sip. He could handle one sip. That wouldn't really be cheating. One sip wouldn't get him drunk.

"My husband swears he needs one drink a night to fall asleep. I think that's just an excuse to have one drink a night."

Boone would never stop at a sip. He wouldn't stop at one drink. He'd finish the whole bottle and start on another before he knew what hit him. He handed the wine to the woman and, without a word, pushed his cart out of the aisle and as far away from temptation as possible.

He was still trying to control his thoughts while he waited in the checkout line. The young woman in front of him had a handful of coupons and was taking her sweet time sorting through them to find the ones she could apply to her purchase.

Out of the corner of his eye, he spotted Violet and her friend hanging around the display of lighters near one of the empty checkout lanes. They seemed quite interested in what the employees were doing and where they were looking. Violet put a lighter in her pocket and started for the door. Boone noticed that the guy by customer service who was almost certainly the store manager saw the same thing. He could only imagine how much trouble the kid would get into with a mother like Ruby. He deserted his cart and got to Violet right before the manager confronted her.

He threw an arm over her shoulders and turned her back toward the checkout. "There you are, kiddo. I thought I lost you."

Violet turned white as a ghost. "What are you doing?"

"Saving your butt," he whispered. "Wanna hand over that lighter you were trying to lift so that Mr. Manager over there doesn't call the police or, worse, your mom?"

Violet glanced over her shoulder at the man who was glaring in their direction.

"He didn't see anything," she argued weakly.

"You want to risk it?" Boone lifted his arm and motioned for her to head back toward the exit.

Violet thought about it for less than a second and dug the lighter out of her pocket. She set it in Boone's waiting palm. "Whatever," she mumbled.

"What was that?" He cupped his ear with his hand. "Thank you? Is that what I heard? Thank you for saving me?"

"Thank you for embarrassing me in front of my friend. How about that?"

The other girl was long gone. She must have figured Violet was caught and didn't want to go down with a sinking ship. "You need better friends, kid."

"Maybe you can come to school with me and offer to sign things for everybody. I bet that will make me super popular."

"Why am I helping you again?"

"Beats me," Violet said with a shrug.

Coupon Lady finally finished checking out, and the clerk welcomed Boone to Valu-Save. Her wide-rimmed glasses looked like they were straight out of the 1980s.

"We decided we don't need this," he said, handing the clerk the lighter.

"Oh, wow. Thanks for nothing," Violet grumbled.

"I can't think of one thing you'd need that for that doesn't end with you getting in even more trouble. You'll definitely thank me for that later."

"Oh my gosh, you sound exactly like my mother."

There was little chance that was a good thing. Not to mention he had absolutely nothing in common with that woman other than their mutual desire to have nothing to do with one another. "Speaking of your mother, let's keep this little rescue mission to ourselves, okay?"

Violet covered her heart with her hand and gasped like a world-class actress. "You want me to lie to my mother?"

The clerk glanced up at them, causing her to ring one item up twice. She looked away and corrected her error.

"I would never ask you to lie to your mother," Boone said through gritted teeth. "All I'm saying is that not telling her every detail of your day is probably pretty normal for you. This should perhaps be one of those things you keep to yourself."

"Boy, you really better start talking to Jesse. You are in worse shape than I am."

She had no idea.

CHAPTER FOUR

"I THOUGHT YOU were hanging out with Stacy," Ruby said from her spot at the dining room table as Violet charged through the front door and took the stairs two at a time. There was no reply except the slamming of her bedroom door.

"One of these days I am going to take that door off its hinges!" She meant it this time. Ruby didn't care what Jesse had said about Violet needing privacy. If she couldn't treat their house with respect, then she would have to suffer the consequences.

Ruby stood and stretched her arms above her head. She'd spent the past hour organizing her schedule for the coming weeks. There were two women in Wilcox County due to give birth in the next month with Ruby's assistance. She had to make sure she was ready when those calls came in.

The sound of angry girl music filtered downstairs. Jesse's voice in Ruby's head told her to go check on Violet, to offer an ear and not a lecture. She took a deep breath and headed upstairs. She knocked on the door but got no answer.

"Vi, can I come in?" She tried turning the knob before getting the okay, but the door was locked. "What did I say about locking the door? Open it. Now."

An increase in the music's volume was Violet's only response. Ruby inhaled deeply, trying to rein in her emotions. Jesse had once reminded her that when she lost her cool, it gave Violet an excuse to lose hers.

"I will leave you alone, but I need you to unlock the door and respect my rules."

Ruby waited until she heard the soft click of the lock releasing. She resisted the temptation to push the door open, pressing her ear to the door instead. She hoped for an invitation to come in, imagined sitting on Violet's bed and hearing all about what had happened to make her so upset.

"You can go away now," Violet said from the other side.

Ruby straightened and bit her lip. It didn't matter if there was a door or not. Violet wasn't going to let her in.

"I'm going to start dinner. And you *will* be eating," she said before Violet could protest that she wasn't hungry.

Their dinner options were limited. Ruby had neglected certain chores this week, like grocery shopping. Cooking had never been one of her strengths, and living in Nashville had given her plenty of good reasons to eat out. There were several restaurants in the city Ruby missed like dear friends.

She scavenged some ham that still smelled edible and some cheese from the deli drawer. With any luck there would be four slices left of the bread she bought a week ago. If Violet gave her any grief, Ruby would serve her the heel.

While the frying pan heated up, Ruby found one apple in the refrigerator and half a can of Pringles in the pantry. Ruby's mother had always been a stickler about serving a proper dinner, which consisted of a meat/protein, a starch, a vegetable and a fruit. Everyone was expected to eat everything, no exceptions. It didn't matter that Ruby hated brussels sprouts or that her sister gagged whenever a banana was near.

Violet had never known such horror. Too bad she didn't appreciate how cool her mom was.

Ruby grilled up two sandwiches and cut up the apple. Before she could call Violet down to eat, there was a knock on the front door.

"Hey, Ruby." Mary Ellen Kingston lived

next door and had twin daughters who were almost two. Ruby envied how put-together she always was. Her blond hair never failed to look like she'd just left the salon. She always wore some cute little sundress and strappy leather sandals that required buckling.

When Violet was two, Ruby had been lucky to get out of the house wearing clothes that weren't covered in something Violet had wiped on or thrown at her. And if her shoes didn't slip on, she went barefoot.

"How are you tonight, Mary Ellen?"

"Good. We're on our way home from gymnastics. The girls and I have had a busy day. In fact, we were shopping at Valu-Save earlier and—" her voice dropped lower "—I don't want to come off like I'm minding your business, but I feel like I need to tell you what I saw there."

The uneasy feeling in Ruby's stomach told her Mary Ellen wasn't here to share information about a sale on orange juice. "What did you see?

"Well, Violet was there with her friend, but I noticed her later in the checkout lane with a man I didn't recognize. I think he might have bought her something. She walked out of the store with him. I think he was trying to get her to go in his truck, but she kept on walking.

Not that I would have let her go with him, of course," she added.

Mary Ellen glanced back at her minivan parked in Ruby's driveway. Her angelic twins were probably strapped inside, waiting patiently for their mother to return. They would never talk to strangers when they were older, or break any rules. Or shut their mom out of their lives.

"I swear I would have stopped her if she had made a different decision. I just thought you should know. We gotta look out for one another, being neighbors and all, right?"

"Right." Ruby didn't know what else to say as her heart beat out of control. She thanked Mary Ellen for her concern and shut the door.

For about a year after deciding to leave Levi, every communication Ruby had with her mother contained some reminder of the damage divorce did to children. Children raised by their mothers were ten times more likely to be physically hurt or murdered. Seventy percent of long-term prison inmates were from broken homes. Children from two-parent homes were happier, healthier and better-adjusted.

Ruby hadn't needed scientific studies to tell her what divorce did to children. Her father had walked out of her life when she was seven years old. He hadn't even tried to pretend he cared like Levi did with Violet. Ruby knew better than anyone the cost of a failed marriage and how the children paid the price.

Given Violet's tendency to make trouble, Ruby always figured she needed to be more worried about her daughter ending up in jail than becoming someone's victim. But the thought of Violet almost getting into some strange man's truck caused tears to prick at the corners of her eyes.

This time she raced upstairs and didn't bother knocking. Violet was on her bed and sat up when Ruby burst in.

"Mom! Seriously, leave."

"Who was the man you were talking to at Valu-Save?"

"What?"

"Don't play games with me, Violet." Ruby clenched her fists to keep her hands from shaking. "Mrs. Kingston saw you and someone who isn't from around here standing in line together. She said he bought you something and tried to get you to come into his truck. What happened?"

Violet rolled her eyes, and she flopped back on her bed, phone in hand. "Oh my gosh," she said with an exasperated sigh. "People need to mind their own business."

Ruby sat on the bed and blinked back her

tears. "Honey, there are dangerous people in the world, even in small towns like this one."

"I know, Mom. I don't need you to lecture me about stranger danger. I got it. You can leave now," she said, going back to her phone.

"Vi." Ruby snatched the smartphone from Violet's hands. She would not be dismissed. "Do you have any idea what I would do if something happened to you? You are all I have in this world."

For a moment, Ruby thought she saw a flicker of remorse in her daughter's eyes. It was quickly replaced with familiar annoyance.

"Nothing is going to happen to me. Stacy dared me to steal a lighter so she could smoke these cigarettes she snagged from her mom's purse, but that guy from Helping Hooves who thinks he's famous caught me and made me stand in line with him because he said the manager saw me, too. He wouldn't even buy me the lighter. He's so lame."

"Boone Williams was the man in the store?"

"I don't remember his name because he's old. And not cool. Can I have my phone back now?"

Ruby felt relieved and enraged at the same time. Thankfully some creepy pedophile hadn't attempted to lure Violet into his car. However, Boone had interjected himself into Violet's life without any thought to how his actions might affect Ruby's ability to parent her troubled teen.

"I will be holding on to this until I can think of a more appropriate consequence for attempted shoplifting," she replied, standing up and slipping the phone into the back pocket of her jeans. "And tonight at dinner, we will be discussing all the reasons someone your age shouldn't take up smoking."

"Oh my gosh! Are you serious? I didn't say I was going to smoke."

Ruby paid her no mind as she headed for the door. "Dinner's ready, by the way."

"I shouldn't have told you anything. Boone was right. I should have kept the whole thing between him and me."

That, on the other hand, got Ruby's attention. She spun back around. "He told you not to tell me?"

Violet rolled over and curled into a ball. "I'm never telling you anything ever again."

The heat of her anger crept up Ruby's neck and burned her cheeks. Violet didn't have to tell her anything. Ruby would confront the supposed adult in this scenario. Of course, that was if she didn't knock him out instead.

CHAPTER FIVE

STARING AT EMMY'S number on his phone, Boone contemplated what he could say on her voice mail today that might make her finally call him back. He paced the inside of the Airstream and fought the anxiety that made his palms sweat.

He pressed the button to call. Four rings and there she was.

"Hi, this is Emmy." She giggled, and Boone's heart swelled, then dropped. "Leave me a message or text me and I'll get back to you."

Boone cleared his throat and waited for the beep. "Hey, Em. It's Dad. I, ah, I'm trying to remember the name of that horse you used to ride when you took lessons at Tressman's. You know, the all-black one? They've got a beautiful black gelding here named Renegade. Cool name, huh?" This had to work. Nothing he'd said in the past few months had earned him a response. He hoped her love of horses might convince her to reply this time. "Well, if you remember that horse's name, give me a call

back. I miss you, honey. I hope we can talk
soon."

He hung up and slid his phone into his back
pocket. The knot in his stomach stayed tied
tight. Boone could perform in front of thou-
sands without an ounce of fear, but his daughter made him more anxious than a long-tailed
cat in a room full of rocking chairs.

His nerves eased and gave way to his anger.
He was a grown man groveling for a minute
of his child's attention. It was pathetic. There
was no way he could keep this up. What was
the point of leaving message after message if
she wanted nothing to do with him? This was
all her mother's fault.

Maybe the best thing to do was to give
Emmy what she wanted. Maybe he should
leave her alone. That would sure make his ex
happy. But that was as good a reason as any
not to give up. He wouldn't decide today.

The lack of space inside the trailer was giving him a headache. Boone pushed the door
open, and it almost knocked Faith over. The
woman jumped back.

"Sorry about that," he said, stepping out and
taking a deep gulp of fresh air.

Faith ran a hand through her thick brown
hair. "Getting out of the way is one of my
many talents, thanks to years of working with

horses. You only have to get kicked once to know you don't want it to happen again."

"What can I do for you, Miss Faith?"

"I'm here to invite you to dinner again. My fiancé hasn't had much success getting you to accept, so I'm here to personally invite you."

"That's mighty kind of you, but I just got back from the grocery store with plenty of food."

The sun sat low in the sky, hovering over the Airstream like a giant egg yolk. Faith squinted up at him. "You've been staying on *my* property for four days. I understand you're a private man, but when someone graciously opens their doors for you and you make excuses not to come in, it feels a bit like a personal rebuff."

Boone's mother would have slapped the back of his head for being so rude. It had been so easy to say no to Dean, he hadn't thought about the message he had sent to the actual hostess.

"I never intended to offend you. I'm not very good company, that's all. I was trying to spare you the trouble."

"It's no trouble," she said surely. "We'll see you in an hour for dinner."

He watched her walk away, not giving him any chance to decline her invitation this time. He appreciated her straightforwardness, though. Sharing one meal couldn't be that bad, as long as Dean didn't bring up getting in the recording studio. Boone would need to set clear ground rules, and number one was no business talk at the dinner table.

BOONE TUGGED THE collar of his button-down shirt. Dinner attire wasn't specified, so he went with a dress shirt and jeans—the best of both worlds. Knocking on the door, he prayed this get-together wasn't a bad idea.

"Come on in," Dean said, pushing open the screen door for his guest. "Whatever Faith is cooking smells so good, you'll regret not taking us up on this offer earlier."

"Your fiancée's definitely more persuasive than you are. You might want to consider hiring her to make all your deals from now on."

Dean laughed as he led Boone inside. "No one knows how hard it is to say no to that woman more than I do."

Faith came out of the kitchen, wiping her hands on the pink apron tied around her waist. "Glad you could make it, Boone. Can I get you something to drink?"

A whiskey on the rocks would be nice. It had been hard not to think about how a drink would taste since he held the wine bottle in his hands. He could feel the burn and missed the way it would make his head fuzzy. It muted the feelings that often felt too big to carry around sober.

"Thank you, but I'm fine."

"We have sweet tea," she offered with a smile.

Not exactly what he needed to quench this thirst. "Maybe with dinner."

A chocolate Lab flew down the stairs, followed by a young man whistling like today was nothing but a good day. "Well, I'll be," he said as he hit the last step. "I can't believe Boone Williams is standing in my living room."

"Our living room," Faith corrected him. "Boone, this is my brother, Sawyer."

"Sawyer's new to the label," Dean said. "He's got a hit single out right now, so we had him start recording his debut album this week, which is why you haven't seen him around. You remember what those days were like."

The two men shook hands and exchanged pleasantries. Dean's future brother-in-law reminded Boone of a younger version of himself—cool, confident and completely unaware of how the business wouldn't think twice about chewing him up and spitting him out.

"If you wanted to drop in and take a listen one of these days, I'm sure Sawyer wouldn't mind." Boone hadn't even been in the house five minutes and Dean had set another trap to get him in the studio.

"Mind?" Sawyer echoed. "I'd be honored."

"We'll see," Boone replied halfheartedly.

"What did I say about no Grace Note talk during dinner?" Faith asked Dean.

Dean wrapped an arm around her waist and kissed her temple. "I'm not eating dinner yet, so this doesn't count. But I promise to be good the rest of the evening."

Their display of affection, although small, still caused Boone's chest to tighten. There had been a time in his marriage when he'd held Sara like that, when they had actually cared about one another. Sometimes it seemed unbelievable that what they'd had could have unraveled so thoroughly.

"Well, I was about to tell you dinner's ready," Faith said. "Why don't you show our guest to the dining room?"

Just as they started to move, there was a knock at the front door. Sawyer hung back to answer it. Boone was pulling his chair out when he heard a familiar voice. Ruby wanted to know where she could find Boone, and it was clear her daughter wasn't as good at keeping secrets as he had hoped. Ruby didn't sound like she was there to thank him for keeping Violet out of jail.

"Is that Ruby?" Dean asked.

"You guys have a back door I can use?" Boone asked, pushing his chair back in.

"What did you do?"

"I didn't do anything. That woman's got problems. Problems I don't need."

Dean didn't look convinced. "Faith's clients are like family. I wouldn't say anything like that in front of her."

"You wouldn't say what in front of me?" Faith asked, carrying in a steaming casserole dish.

Dean and Boone exchanged a look, but they were saved by Sawyer.

"Ruby Wynn is outside. She says she needs a minute with Boone."

"Ruby wants to talk to Boone?" Faith set the food on the table and wiped her bangs from her face. "Do you need a midwife for something?"

The only thing Boone needed was a way out of this, but there was no way to avoid this confrontation. He could run back to his trailer and call it a night, but now that he not only smelled dinner but also could see it, there was no way he was missing out on this meal.

"I'm kidding," Faith said. "You probably don't even know what she does for a living. She's not a fan, is she?"

"They met the other day when Violet was

here," Dean explained. "I don't think she knew who Boone was."

Boone shot Dean a look. He didn't need to be reminded. "I'll be right back."

Ruby had her back to the door as she leaned over the porch railing. She righted herself and spun around at the sound of the creaky screen door.

"Porch spying again?" he asked, knowing it would get a rise out of her.

He could certainly see that fire in her eyes. "I thought we had an agreement."

"Yet here you are keeping me from the delicious dinner that's waiting for me inside."

She took a step toward him. Her proximity was unsettling, mainly because there was something about it that he liked. "Maybe I wasn't clear, but staying away from me includes staying away from my daughter. She told me what you did today, and I don't appreciate your meddling."

"If by meddling you mean keeping your daughter from getting arrested for shoplifting…" Boone barked a laugh.

"You're not funny."

He wasn't trying to be funny. He was just as annoyed as she was. "I have no idea what you're so hot about—I did her a favor. But I'll be happy to let the police deal with your kid next time."

"It's obvious you don't know what it takes to parent a teenager."

Boone bristled at her assumption. "You don't know anything about me and my parenting."

She seemed to take pause. "You're right. We don't know anything about one another, and I thought we wanted to keep it that way."

"I do." Like Boone had told Dean, he didn't need or want Ruby's problems. Her kid was entertaining, but not enough to put up with this kind of nonsense.

"Then I'd really appreciate it if you didn't do Violet any more favors. She's going through some tough stuff." She bit her bottom lip and wrung her hands. "Her dad isn't really involved in her life. I am doing my best, but sometimes my best isn't enough. We come here to work with Jesse, and some days I think it's helping, and then days like today make me think no matter what I do, I can't make things right for her…"

Boone stood silent as Ruby dumped all of her parenting fears like a pile of dirty laundry right at his feet. Her worry and insecurity were palpable. The empathy he felt in return was unexpected, but her emotions were so similar to the ones he wrestled with every day. Parenting was a lot tougher than he'd ever imagined, and it was nice to know other people struggled to get it right.

Ruby leaned against the railing. Her vulnerability was so much more attractive than her anger. "I'm sorry. None of this matters to you."

"Don't apologize." He stepped closer. He wouldn't touch her no matter how much his fingers were itching to. "I get it. I have a teenager, too. You might not believe me, but I know how it feels to wonder if you're doing this parenting thing right or not. And I'm sorry for making things harder for you today. I really thought stopping her from stealing was doing the right thing."

"It probably was," she relented with a sigh. "The bigger issue was conspiring with her not to tell me. I can't help her if I don't know what's going on. Hearing it from you would have been better than from my neighbor, who thought you were trying to kidnap my daughter, by the way."

"Kidnapping? Seriously?" People were unbelievable.

"One thing you need to learn about a small town is that someone is always watching." Ruby smiled, and it sure looked good on her. "Trust me—it's not my favorite part, either."

"Maybe we have more in common than we first thought."

"We should start over." She held out a hand. "I'm Ruby Wynn—midwife, Worst Mother of the Year according to my daughter, and Tennessee's biggest Pink Floyd fan. Welcome to Grass Lake."

"You're a Pink Floyd fan? No wonder you had no idea who I was." Boone shook her hand. "Boone Williams—Grammy Award winner, incredibly handsome country music superstar and not exactly the most humble guy in the world."

"I might have noticed that," she said with a laugh.

They were still holding hands, but she didn't seem to mind and, much to Boone's surprise, neither did he. She had beautiful green eyes and cheeks that looked naturally pink.

"This went a lot better than I thought it would," he said, letting her go.

Ruby's gaze dropped to her hand and then went back up to him. "Yeah, well, I should let you get back to your dinner. Have a good night."

"You, too." Boone watched her go down the steps and walk to her car. The last thing he expected was to have compassion for the woman who'd made him want to pull his hair out a few days ago. "Hey!" he shouted to get her attention. "You can't be the worst mom in the world. Your kid might be a pain, but she's brave and has a sense of humor that makes her interesting."

"Interesting's good?"

Boone didn't have to think twice. Violet wasn't the only interesting one in the family. "Always."

CHAPTER SIX

VIOLET DIDN'T TALK to Ruby for two days. The silent treatment finally came to an end when she needed something. So typical.

"One of my flip-flops broke. I need new ones. Can you take me to get another pair?"

"Oh my goodness, she speaks!"

Violet rolled her eyes and folded her arms across her chest. "Are you done?"

"Are you?" Ruby looked up from her laptop.

"Forget it. I'll ask Dad." Violet turned to go.

Good luck with that, Ruby thought but didn't say aloud. She hit Print on her laptop so she had the documents she needed for her next patient. "I can take you in about an hour, but you'll have to come with me to check on one of my mommies-to-be."

"Fine," Violet said, climbing the stairs back to her room, where she had been holed up since the attempted shoplifting incident. The child was so stubborn; she could argue with a wall... and win.

"Knock, knock," Holly said, opening the

front door and popping her head in. "Can I come in?"

"You're my landlord." Ruby shut her laptop. "Of course you can."

Holly dropped her purse on the floor and flopped down next to Ruby on the couch. "Jon's sister took the boys to the lake to go swimming, and I have a whole hour of me time."

"So you came here for wine or chocolate?"

"Chocolate. My four-year-old patted my belly last night and asked me if there was a baby in there. If I have to endure looking as though I'm eating for two, I might as well enjoy it."

Ruby couldn't keep from giggling. "Oh, come on. It was probably just wishful thinking on his part. Zander's always saying he wants a baby sister."

"Well, he can keep wishing if he wants to, but my baby-making days are over."

Ruby went to the kitchen and grabbed two chocolate chip cookies she had made the day before in a failed attempt at luring Violet out of her room. She handed one to Holly and took a bite of the other.

"They weren't both for me and my pretend baby?" Holly whined as Ruby sat back down.

Ruby elbowed her friend playfully in the

side. "At least your children talk to you and ask questions about how you're doing."

"Vi's at it again, huh? What did you do this time?" Holly asked before devouring her cookie and snatching Ruby's half-eaten one from her hand.

"I grounded her from all electronic devices for one week. You would think it was a fate worse than death."

"How long could you live without your phone?" Holly challenged her.

"I use my phone for work. It's a necessary evil."

It was Holly's turn to laugh. "Keep telling yourself that. I saw your new high score on Jelly Chains posted to Facebook. Was that for work?"

Ruby gave her another elbow.

"Speaking of work," Holly continued. "Any chance you asked Boone Williams about that interview?"

Hearing his name sent a strange tingle through Ruby's body. Ever since they'd made amends on the Strattons' front porch, she couldn't stop thinking about the way he had looked at her and tried to make her feel better about her shortcomings as a mother.

"I'm not too sure he's a big fan of the press."

"Oh, please. I'm hardly the press. We're a

tiny paper, eager to hear what the other half thinks of our humble hometown."

Ruby smiled. "Boone and humble definitely don't mix."

"So you asked him and he flat out said no?"

"I mentioned I had a friend at the *Gazette*, and he made it clear he wasn't interested in being interviewed." Ruby left out the part where she had threatened to have Holly write a scathing article on his bad behavior.

"Did you at least get him to sign something for me?"

Ruby cringed. "I forgot," she said, making Holly frown. "But I will the next time I see him. Violet's got a session over there tomorrow."

"Maybe I could come with you. If he meets me, he'll like me and want to do the interview."

"I'm not sure that's a good idea." The foundation of Boone and Ruby's truce wasn't the strongest. Bringing "the press" would likely cause some strain.

A couple of days ago, Ruby wouldn't have cared. But Boone had shown her something she absolutely hadn't been expecting—compassion. He had also made her believe his intentions were to help and not make things harder on her when he intervened with Violet.

"What's that look?" Holly snapped Ruby out of her thoughts.

"What look?"

"That's the look you got the first time you saw Levi ride a bull at the rodeo," Holly accused her.

Ruby shook her head. "No way. I have no idea what you're talking about."

The first time she had seen Levi, she'd been a naive twenty-year-old with absolutely no idea what she wanted in life. Falling for a cute bull rider had seemed like a perfectly rebellious thing to do. It was a stupid crush that had turned into a horrible marriage that ended in an even worse divorce.

Ruby did *not* have a crush on Boone Williams. And she certainly wasn't some naive kid without a clue. Ruby knew exactly what she wanted, and it had nothing to do with getting involved with a man who clearly had more issues than she did.

"You stared into those blue eyes and got Booned, didn't you?"

"Excuse me?"

"Booned. It's what happens when Boone Williams makes you fall in love with one look."

Ruby let out a sarcastic chuckle. "I did not fall in love in Boone Williams. In fact, his first impression was terrible."

"And then he gazed into your eyes and you

were Booned. It's okay. You can admit it. He's the hottest guy over thirty-five I have ever seen."

"Holly, I was not Booned. He was a total jerk that day I stopped by your office. Then he caught Violet shoplifting, and instead of telling me what happened, he told her to keep quiet about it." Ruby went on to share her embarrassing conversation with Mary Ellen and her confrontation with Boone. "In the end, he apologized for not telling me and we parted on friendly terms. At no time did he Boone me with his eyes. I swear."

"I can't believe he cared enough to look out for our little Violet. That is the sweetest thing I have ever heard."

"That's your takeaway from this story?" The woman was hopeless. Ruby had always trusted Holly to be a levelheaded, reasonable person, and here she was acting like a love-struck teenager.

"I think the boys and I would like to come with you to the farm tomorrow. They think the horses are cool. And I want to see for myself that you can resist Boone Williams the way you say you can."

Hopeless and impossible. Holly was almost as stubborn as Violet, and that was saying something. "Fine. I can't stop you from showing up at Helping Hooves, but I am not hunting down Boone while I'm there."

"Don't worry." Her best friend smiled. "Leave that to me."

THE NEXT DAY, Ruby's stomach was in knots. Holly brought the boys over for lunch and couldn't be talked out of following Ruby and Violet to Helping Hooves.

She prayed Boone would be nowhere to be seen and there would be no way for Holly to get to him. She didn't want him to think she'd ignored what he'd said about interviews. His mistrust of the media was clear.

"Did Dad text you to get the information on the horse show yet?" Violet asked.

Ruby's worries about Boone quickly shifted to the familiar worries regarding Levi. "I haven't heard from him, but I'll call him tonight and remind him to check the email I sent him last week."

"Make sure you don't start a fight. He won't show up if you make him mad."

That was what Violet always believed when Levi ditched out on her. It was always Ruby's fault. Violet's defense mechanism was to believe her mother must have said or done something to set her dad off. She refused to see his selfish and manipulative behavior for what it was.

Not that Ruby could blame her. Who would want to believe their father was such a class A jerk? Ruby had never liked to admit her own dad was one.

"You guys aren't going to stay the whole time, are you?" Violet asked as they pulled into the parking area.

"Probably not. Holly is hoping to meet Boone, but I'm sure he's—"

She was going to say *not around*, except there he was, leaning against the paddock fence. Dressed in dark blue jeans and a red plaid button-down, he fit right in. His black cowboy hat shaded those blue eyes, but that didn't stop them from taking Ruby's breath away when he turned his gaze on her.

"Oh, he's going to love having a real fan. Maybe she'll let him sign something and his life can be complete," Violet quipped as she opened the door.

Ruby eased out of the car and hoped she didn't blush when he tipped his hat at her. She could only imagine what Holly would say.

"Boone and I were just talking about you two," Jesse said. Ruby hadn't even noticed he had been standing there.

"Whatever he told you happened at Valu-Save is probably a lie," Violet said.

"He didn't tell me anything about Valu-

Save, but I hope you will, now that I know there's something to tell," Jesse said with a grin only he could get away with when dealing with Violet.

Ruby enjoyed the rush of relief. Thankfully Violet had ratted herself out, and she wouldn't have to be the bearer of bad news to Jesse this time. When she glanced at Boone, he was smiling back at her like he thought she had been smiling at him. She hadn't been. She wanted to explain she had only been reacting to her good fortune and look away, but she was caught like a rabbit in a snare.

The slamming of car doors finally jarred her loose. Holly lifted Henry, her youngest, out of his car seat. The two-year-old pointed at the black horse in the paddock with an expression of pure joy on his face.

"Boone was just telling me he's pretty familiar with some of the horse shows and riding competitions around Nashville," Jesse said. "His daughter rides, so I thought Violet could show him what she can do on Sassy and get some feedback."

"That would be nice of you," Ruby said, her lips still curled up in that stupid smile she really needed to get rid of before Holly noticed. "My friend and her boys are here to watch a little, too. I hope that's okay, Jesse."

"As long as it's okay with Violet."

"Whatever," Violet replied with a shrug. "More people means less serious talk."

Holly sidled up to Ruby. "What beautiful horses! The boys want to know what the black one's name is."

"That's Renegade," Jesse answered, stepping forward. Boone seemed happy to hide behind him.

Jesse named the other two horses and introduced himself, as well. He did not mention Boone, which meant Ruby would have to. Hopefully Holly wouldn't do anything embarrassing or lead with a request for an interview. But Ruby didn't think Boone could Boone her so badly that she'd make a fool of herself.

"Holly is a big country music fan. I hope it's okay that I brought her by. I promise she won't throw herself at you or anything, Boone. At least not while she's holding Henry."

Boone was hesitant but inched forward. "Well, I'm surprised someone like you is friends with someone who knows who I am. I thought maybe you only hung out with progressive rock types," he teased.

"I'll have you know I'm a very open-minded friend. I do not judge based on musical preference. Unless they tell me something crazy, like boy bands are more musically significant than Pink Floyd. Then we can't be friends."

The grin on Boone's face exposed his straight white teeth. "The New Kids got nothing on Roger Waters."

"I knew you were smarter than you looked," Ruby replied with a grin of her own.

"Booned," Holly said in a cough. Ruby felt her cheeks heat up. "Don't listen to a word this woman has to say about music, Boone. If she gave country music a chance, she'd love it."

Boone's attention shifted to Holly. "You sound like a woman who has her head on straight. You're a big fan of my work?"

"The biggest, but I'm not the only one here in Grass Lake. We have a ton of Boone Williams fans. I'm editor in chief of the *Grass Lake Gazette*, so I have my finger on the pulse of this town, and I would love to interview you about how you like it here so far."

Boone's smile faded. His whole body seemed to tense and his jaw ticked. Holly had done it. With one foolish confession, she had gotten him to put his wall back up.

"Well, that's mighty interesting," he said, backing away. "But I'm not doing any press while I'm here. You ladies take care. Jesse, I'm going to have to take a pass on helping out today."

Ruby chased after him as soon as he took off. She caught him behind the Strattons' house. "Come on, don't be like this."

He stopped and turned around. "Is this all some sort of game to you?"

"No! I swear I didn't bring her here to start trouble. We cleared the air, remember?"

"I thought so until I realized you brought a reporter here to snoop into my life."

Ruby blew out a frustrated breath. "She edits the *Grass Lake Gazette*. It's a small-town paper, not a gossip magazine. The most scintillating thing they've ever written about was when Grace Reilly's roses beat Joyce Newberry's in the Grass Lake Garden Contest. Relax."

"Don't tell me to relax. Until you've had your face on every magazine known to man with headlines that are bald-faced lies, I have no reason to trust your advice on which reporters are safe to talk to or not."

"I don't know any reporters other than Holly, but I know Holly like I know my family. She's a good person with honest intentions. There is not one malicious bone in her body."

"I'm not doing an interview. I thought I'd made that clear."

"Well, don't punish Violet because you're mad at me. Please." It wasn't like Ruby to beg, but she felt like it was the only thing that might change his mind.

"I'd have to care about you to be mad at you," he said. His words sent a chill through Ruby that she hadn't felt in a long time. They stared wordlessly at one another for a full thirty seconds before he continued his retreat to wherever he planned to hide from the world he was so sure was out to get him.

CHAPTER SEVEN

BOONE HAD HIS mind made up about Ruby Wynn. The woman was nothing but trouble. She pushed his buttons and flashed him those smiles. He never knew which way was up with her, and he didn't have the energy to figure it out.

"Boone, I need your help," Jesse said as he knocked on the door of the Airstream. "I promise the coast is clear."

Boone was still on the fence about Jesse. He seemed like a nice guy, but he wanted inside Boone's head for sure. The man could have all the good intentions in the world; it didn't mean he would be good at actually helping Boone through this struggle.

Boone pushed the door open. "I'm a little busy. You sure you need my help?"

"Busy hiding in the trailer? Come on. We need to get a stall ready for a new horse. Faith went to pick it up, and I told her we'd be ready when she got back."

"Don't you have volunteers for this kind of stuff?"

"You are a volunteer. Wasn't that the point of you coming here? Do some work, clear your head? Nothing clears a head like physical labor. Here…" Jesse tossed him a pair of work gloves. "You'll need these."

Boone stepped back inside and grabbed his hat. Jesse didn't appear to be a man who took no for an answer. As they walked to the barn, Boone noticed Ruby's car was gone, along with her friend's. They probably left right away when they didn't get what they came for. Everyone wanted a piece of him. He didn't know why he'd thought Ruby was any different.

"Let's sweep this stall out before we lay down some fresh straw," Jesse said, handing Boone a broom.

Jesse did all the talking as they got to work. He shared information about the new horse and how excited he was to train it with Faith's help. Jesse clearly had a passion for the animals.

"How exactly did you become a social-worker-slash-riding-instructor-slash-horse-trainer? I didn't know there were colleges giving away degrees in that."

Jesse stopped working and rested both hands on the top of the broom handle. "Well, I grew up with horses. We had a ranch about forty miles from here. I loved it. I think horses are the most amazing animals on the planet."

Boone kept sweeping as his curiosity got the best of him. "So why get a degree in social work?"

"That story's a little bit more complicated. Did you notice I said we *had* a horse ranch? My dad was a good man, but he had a gambling addiction. It cost him and my mother everything they had spent their lives working for. The bank foreclosed on the ranch on my sixteenth birthday. All the money I thought my parents had put away for me to go to college was gone. We had to move in with my grandparents. My parents split about a year later."

Boone froze. He wasn't expecting Jesse to share something so personal.

"Ever since then, I've been fascinated by the power of addiction," Jesse explained. "How could a decent man who loved his family let his life fall apart? How did betting on a horse race or a football game become more important than putting food on the table? My father would tell you it wasn't more important, but he couldn't stop himself. Losing was painful, but when he won, he claimed there was no feeling like it. He had to chase it. That's how I fell into social work."

The weight of his own shame made Boone weak in the knees. He leaned against the wall for support. Somewhere along the line in his life, alcohol had become more important than everything else—his marriage, his career, his daughter. It wasn't more important, but Boone couldn't stop. His body literally craved it, even after all these months of sobriety.

Jesse pushed his broom around. "Thanks to scholarships, loans and working any job I could get, I managed to pay my way through college and graduate school. I learned everything I could about addiction and treatment. I believe that people can overcome their addictions with the right tools and a lot of determination. I tried to convince my dad to get help, but he was too stubborn and proud. Three months before I graduated with my master's degree, he died, carrying more debt than I had at the time."

"That's quite a story," Boone said.

"What doesn't kill you makes you stronger, my mom used to say."

"It's like this place was made for you."

"That's exactly how I feel." Jesse smiled, and the wrinkles around his eyes appeared. "I like to imagine my dad had something to do with it. I think he'd be happy to see me doing something I love while helping people like him at the same time."

"You think you can help someone like me?" Boone asked, unsure if he really wanted to hear the answer.

"I can help anyone who wants it badly enough and is willing to work hard. There's no miracle cure for addiction. It's not easy, and you have to be willing to fight it the rest of your life. Some people have the strength to do that and some don't."

This wasn't a new message. No one ever gave Boone any guarantees. All the doctors and counselors liked to remind him that he was in control of his treatment. Jesse was the first one to make him almost believe it.

"I might be a lost cause."

Jesse pressed his lips together while he seemed to consider that self-assessment. "If that's what you truly believe, then what are you doing here mucking stalls with me?"

It was an excellent question. Boone didn't want to die with a million regrets. He wanted his daughter to answer the phone when he called. He wanted to shake the feeling that everyone was waiting for him to fail. "I don't want to be one."

Jesse put a hand on Boone's shoulder. "Then you don't have to be."

THE TWO MEN had the stall ready to go when Faith returned home with the newest member of the Helping Hooves family. The blue roan filly was a beauty. Her head was dark like her mane and tail, but her body was a bluish gray.

"Isn't she gorgeous?" Faith asked once she'd backed her out of the trailer. She tried to lead her toward the barn. The horse had other ideas. She wasn't going anywhere.

Jesse snickered at her struggle. "She's got a little stubborn streak, huh?"

Faith had the patience of a saint. She stayed calm and encouraged the horse to come along. "We've got our work cut out for us, but she's going to be something special. I know it."

"What's her name?" Boone asked.

"They called her Willow."

Boone stepped closer, and Willow pulled on her lead to back away. "Hey there, sweet Willow," he said, running a hand down the side of her neck to calm her. "You are a pretty girl, aren't you?"

"You want to try?" Faith asked, offering him the lead.

Boone took the rope and kept talking to the horse. She seemed to like his attention and took a step forward when he moved toward the barn.

"Well, look at that. I think we have ourselves a horse whisperer," Jesse said to Faith.

"Or another Boone Williams fan," Faith joked.

Boone led the horse into the barn. She immediately went to the water and took a drink.

Jesse stood outside the stall. "I may have found the perfect job for you."

"Dare I ask what?"

"How do you feel about helping us train Willow to do some therapy?"

"I don't know what that means, but I wouldn't mind working with this lovely lady." Boone held some alfalfa hay out for Willow, and she took it without hesitation.

"We need to talk about something first," Jesse said, making Boone's stomach turn. He liked the horse-training Jesse better than Jesse the social worker.

Faith took that as her cue to go. "I'm going to clean out the trailer. I'll check in with you later, Jesse. Good to see you again, Boone."

Boone could have sworn the stall walls moved inward. His heart beat faster, almost painfully. "What do we need to talk about?"

"I need to know what's up with you and Ruby Wynn."

That was not the issue Boone assumed he wanted to discuss. "What does Ruby have to do with me helping you with this horse?"

"Holly threatened your sense of privacy. I get that. What I don't understand is why that impacted your relationship with Ruby and your willingness to help Violet."

"Ruby knew I wasn't interested in being interviewed, and she still brought that reporter here," Boone answered. His anger reignited. "That woman is a beautiful disaster, and I'm not going to let her bring me down."

"It was Ruby's fault you felt anxious, so as punishment you wouldn't watch Violet ride. Do I have that right?"

The way Jesse said it made Boone sound like a child. "It's not that simple. I wasn't punishing anyone. I needed to walk away because I was frustrated."

"And when you're frustrated, escaping is the easiest thing to do?"

Boone's agitation increased. He could feel his muscles tense and his blood race through his veins. "No, the easiest thing to do is scream and yell, but that's gotten me in trouble, and I was trying not to make a scene. What does this have to do with Willow?"

"First, this horse is going to frustrate you. Screaming at her isn't going to help. You already know that. Walking away isn't going to help me. I need to know that you're willing to try some other strategies."

"Sure," Boone replied gruffly. A stubborn horse wasn't anything like a stubborn woman. He could manage his frustrations with the horse because it wasn't going to be personal. He could do this. He wanted to do this. He imagined Emmy answering the phone to hear all about his work with Willow.

"The other issue is, I promised Violet I would let her help with the new horse. You can't join the team if that's going to be a problem for you."

The wind was quickly taken from Boone's sails. Of course Ruby would ruin this for him...unless he didn't let her.

"I've got no issue with the kid. I don't have to work with her mother. So what's the problem?"

"Violet doesn't need to get caught in the middle of two more people who don't see eye to eye. She can't be someone you use to show Ruby you're frustrated."

Was that what he had done? Inadvertently, yes. He had needed to get as far away from the reporter as possible. He hadn't thought about how his refusal to stick around to watch Violet ride would affect her. The only person he wanted to hurt was Ruby.

"The kid won't be put in the middle. I didn't mean to do that, and it won't happen again."

Jesse clapped his hands. "Then we start tomorrow."

CHAPTER EIGHT

"ARE YOU SURE you want to spend the rest of your summer at Helping Hooves, volunteering?" Ruby wanted to make sure Violet really understood what she was committing to. She couldn't admit she didn't want Violet to do it because it meant Ruby would have to drive her there and pick her up several days a week. Each visit was a potential run-in with Boone, a man she'd had the displeasure of knowing for all of a week.

"Oh my gosh, Mom. Jesse is going to show me how to train a therapy horse. Maybe Faith will let me work with her like the high school girls do."

Not surprising Violet wanted to be like the high schoolers. She was thirteen going on eighteen. There was no way Ruby was going to convince her daughter this was a bad idea. She was much too excited.

"I guess that means yes, you want to do it. What time did he say you needed to be there?"

"Nine. Eat your breakfast faster. I don't want

to be late." Violet snatched a blueberry muffin off the table and headed back upstairs to finish getting ready.

Ruby should have known Violet was serious about this when she was up and moving before eleven. All Ruby could do now was accept that there would eventually be some sort of awkward face-to-face with Boone.

Letting Holly come along had been the worst idea ever. Boone had proved to be exactly like Levi. Her ex-husband loved to blow everything out of proportion and didn't care about anyone except for himself.

"Let's go, Mom!" Violet shouted from the front door.

Ruby stood up and grabbed her purse. The things she did for this child. Although this time, she hoped Boone was there when she arrived, so she could get the awkwardness out of the way.

Her prayers were answered. Boone and Jesse were standing outside the barn when she drove into the farm. They watched the car pull in, and surprisingly Boone didn't run off.

"Don't get out of the car, Mom. Come back at eleven and wait in the car for me."

Apparently Ruby wasn't the only one worried about what would happen when she had to confront Boone again. "I'm not going to embarrass you, I promise."

"Yeah, I totally trust you." Violet's sarcasm was not Ruby's favorite. "Please stay in the car."

Ruby did as Violet asked. There was no reason for her to start trouble with an angry teenager *and* an angry country star. She didn't avert her eyes when Boone stared her down, though. She held his gaze until he was the one to look away. It was a small victory, but a victory all the same.

She drove home, determined to push all thoughts of Boone out of her mind. It was impossible that she could be under some strange spell like Holly claimed. Maybe he was a bit intriguing and quite handsome, but he was also stubborn and mean. His negative traits outweighed the positives.

Ruby's phone rang just as she pulled into her driveway. Levi's name appeared on the screen. Given a choice, she would have preferred fighting with Boone to fighting with Levi, but she wasn't lucky enough to choose.

"Hello?"

"Ruby? I thought I was calling Violet's phone."

No, he didn't. He had pulled this trick a time or two, especially when he had bad news to share with Violet but didn't want to be the one who had to tell her.

"Violet is at the horse farm. Should I have her call you when she's done?"

"Oh, I thought she'd be sleeping. Does she have an early-morning lesson?"

Ruby took a deep breath to keep her frustration from spilling over. She got out of her car and headed inside. "She's volunteering there now. They got a new horse, and she's learning how to train it to do therapy."

"Wow. Good for her! What kind of horse is it?"

There was no need for all this small talk. "What do you want, Levi? Do you want me to have her call you when she gets done?"

"No, no, no," Levi insisted. "I was just calling about that email you sent with the info on Violet's horse show. Next weekend is kind of a busy one for me—"

Ruby lost what was left of her patience and cut him off. "Don't you dare back out. You know how important this is to her. She has worked really hard, and she wants you to see what she can do. Your opinion matters to her."

Violet was dying for her father's approval. Levi was a bull rider. He wasn't a huge star but made a decent living doing it. Violet thought riding was the way to prove to him that she was worthy of his attention.

"I didn't say I wasn't coming. I just need you to know that there's a possibility I might only be able to drop by for part of it. I have a life, you know?"

He had a life? Ruby was about to hang up but stopped herself. If she turned this into a fight, he would tell Violet he hadn't come because of what her mother did or said.

"I know you have a life. You also have a daughter. I trust you'll do the right thing."

"Of course you try to make me feel bad," Levi complained. "I'm doing the best I can, Ruby. Sorry I'm not perfect like you."

Ruby tried not to laugh. "I'm far from perfect, but I am here. Every day. Trying to do what's best for her."

"You're the one who moved out of Nashville. You're the one who thought you could do this on your own. That's not my fault."

Levi loved to blame that one on her. As if he was such a big help when they were living within the city limits. Even then, Ruby was raising Violet on her own.

"You do what you have to do. I hope you make it to the competition. Vi really wants you to be there."

Levi wouldn't let it go. He wanted a fight

even if she wasn't going to give him one. "You act like I said I wasn't coming. I called to say I *was* coming but wouldn't be able to stay the whole time. You love to make me the bad guy, don't you?"

"I'm not calling you a bad guy. I will let her know that you'll be there."

"Well, if you're going to be like this, I'm not sure if I will. I don't deserve to be treated this way."

Ruby sat down at the kitchen table and propped her head on her hand. Classic Levi. He instigated the argument and imagined insults she might have thought but didn't say aloud. It would be all her fault when he didn't show up to the competition, and Violet would believe it.

"What if I promise not to say a word? Will you come then?"

"You don't have to say anything to make me feel judged. You say plenty with one of your dirty looks."

"I promise not to give you any dirty looks or say anything that could be construed as an insult. Please come," she begged.

"I'll think about it. As much as I want to go to support our daughter, I don't know if I can trust you."

"I hope you will." She wanted to tell him to

put Violet first for once but figured he'd take it the wrong way. Someone was on the other line. "I have to go, Levi. One of my patients is calling."

"Right," he said before hanging up.

Ruby wanted to scream, but there really was a patient calling. Iris Downing was thirty-nine weeks pregnant and had called last night about some back pain. Today her contractions were coming every ten minutes. She'd been timing them for almost an hour.

It was time to go to work. A baby would be born today, and it was Ruby's job to see to it that the delivery went smoothly. Mrs. Downing would be in charge of smoothing out the bumps for the little boy or girl after that. Hopefully she'd be better at it than Ruby was.

CHAPTER NINE

BOONE AND VIOLET watched Jesse try to get Willow to follow his lead without much success. The horse wasn't just stubborn. She was completely unmanageable.

"I think she's laughing at him," Violet said.

The horse whinnied and pulled Jesse backward. Boone chuckled. "She's definitely laughing at him."

"I don't think she's going to be a very good therapy horse. I think she *needs* therapy."

Boone laughed harder. "You might be right about that, kid."

Violet's phone chimed in her back pocket. She pulled it out and started typing a reply to someone at the speed of light. Boone had never seen fingers move that fast. She waited for a reply and sent off another message like lightning. The next reply caused her to growl and type even faster.

"Everything okay over there?"

"My mom seriously hates me."

Boone wondered why kids always thought

that. Why did they think not getting their way meant their parents didn't care about them? Had he been like that as a kid? He didn't think so.

"What's the problem? She tell you she isn't going to buy you the new Jordan O'Neil record?" Girls Violet's age all had a thing for the young pop star.

"Um, no. Ew. I don't listen to Jordan O'Neil. Do I look like that kind of girl? If I do, please kill me now."

So dramatic. Boone shook his head. "I have no idea what those kinds of girl look like. You seem like you're the right age to listen to someone like him. Don't you follow him and all the other cute boys in the teenybopper magazines?"

Violet's nose scrunched up as she side-eyed him. "Seriously? No one says *teenybopper*. That's not even a thing anymore. It's not 1950, old man."

Boone held up his hands in defeat. "Sorry, Miss Smarty-Pants. I'm not up-to-date on all the lingo."

"No one says *lingo* or *smarty-pants*. You should stop talking," she said as she shot off another text message.

If this was what Ruby had to put up with every day, he was beginning to feel bad for her. "Are you going to tell me what your mom's done that's got you all upset or not?"

"She says she can't come get me on time because someone decided to go into labor. And she's not sure she can find someone to drive me home."

"Oh yeah, she totally hates you," Boone said with a roll of his eyes. He could tell her stories about his childhood that would give her some serious perspective on what a mean and nasty parent was like. "And the nerve of that lady to decide to go into labor when you have plans. So rude."

Violet shot him a look. "You're not funny."

"I'm hilarious. And I'll bet I can give you a ride home when you're done here."

"You'd do that?"

"If we can find someone to lend us a car."

"Are you for real? You're offering to drive me home, but you don't have a car?"

Boone shrugged. "Dean wanted to trap me here until I make him the album he's been waiting for."

"You are so weird."

He nudged her with his elbow. "Tell your mom we'll find a way to get you home."

She somehow typed that into her phone in half a second and slipped the device back into her pocket. "Maybe I can ride Willow home.

I'd probably have more luck doing that than Jesse's having getting her to walk in a circle."

Boone watched as Jesse tried to coax the horse to take a step forward. Dean was more likely to get an album out of Boone than Jesse was to get that horse to move where he wanted her.

"Maybe I should show him how it's done. She likes me."

"Oh, really? Did she ask for your autograph?" Violet said with a smirk.

"Never going to let me live that down, are you?"

Violet shook her head.

Boone crossed the paddock to where Willow was holding Jesse hostage. "Can I try?"

Jesse seemed reluctant to give up the rope. "This can take hours or sometimes days. Every horse is different, but they all learn eventually."

"What if she doesn't want to learn?" Violet asked.

The horse turned away and tried to pull Jesse along with her. He dug his heels in and tried to tug her back. "She'll learn. They all do. You want to get her to look at you and understand what the rope is for."

"Can I try now?" Boone asked again.

Jesse handed him the thick lead rope. The horse took notice of the new man in charge and began running around. Boone could see the anxiety in her eyes. He let her run and move, get out that nervous energy.

He made some kissing noises in an attempt to get her to come check him out. He gave the rope a gentle tug in his direction. "Come here, pretty girl."

"Does that line usually work for you?" Violet teased.

"Watch and learn, kid." Boone got Willow to look at him and met her halfway. He spoke quietly to her and gave her long neck a rub. After a few minutes, Boone had Willow under control. "And that's how you teach a horse to lead," he said proudly.

JESSE HAD A therapy session with someone after their training with Willow ended. He offered to let Boone borrow his car to give Violet a ride home.

"Mind if I watch Violet ride Sassy for a little bit first?" Boone asked, feeling generous.

One side of Jesse's mouth lifted. "I think that would be real nice of you."

"Come on, kid," he said to Violet. "Let's get Sassy saddled up."

"Are you sure you don't have other plans?" She sincerely sounded concerned.

"No plans except for the ones I'm avoiding."

"Cool," she replied. "Thanks."

For the next hour, Boone watched Violet complete all the Western riding tests with ease. She was an excellent rider for someone who was fairly new to the scene.

"Do you always ride Sassy, or have you ridden other horses here for your classes?"

"I tried riding Renegade a couple of times, but he's a little bit harder to control. He's faster, and I think I get freaked out."

"It doesn't hurt to ride other horses. You and Sassy are awesome together, but riding other horses teaches you to adjust quickly and deal with different situations."

Violet unlatched her helmet. "That makes sense."

Boone checked his watch. "I don't know about you, but I am starving. You want to grab some lunch before I take you home?"

"You paying?"

"I have to drive and pay for you?"

"I'm a kid. I can't drive and I have no money."

"Excuses." Boone gave her a playful shove. "We could see if Jesse will lend us twenty bucks and his car."

"That's a plan, but I thought you were rich and famous. Have you been lying to me this whole time?"

He narrowed his eyes. "No, I am richer and

more famous than you could ever dream of being."

"Then stop giving me a hard time and buy me lunch, old man."

This kid was something else.

Violet picked the restaurant, since she was familiar with the town. The Cup and Spoon Diner didn't look like much, but Violet swore the food was good. Boone decided she didn't rave about too many things, so it must be true. They sat down in one of the booths and perused the menu.

"What's good?"

"Anything breakfast, the bacon guacamole burger, the double cheeseburger, the chicken fingers, all of the salads."

"So pretty much everything."

Violet nodded. "Pretty much."

The waitress came over dressed in a bright yellow uniform with a name tag that read Heidi. Her white-blond hair was pulled back in a ponytail, and she couldn't have been older than twenty-five. She greeted Violet like she was a regular. That look in her eye told him she recognized him as someone she should know as well but couldn't place yet. She took their drink orders and thankfully let them be.

"So what are you avoiding?" Violet asked as she put her menu away.

Boone looked over his menu at her. "Huh?"

"You said you had no plans except the ones you would be avoiding."

He was surprised she'd taken note of that. "Remember when I said I was being trapped there to record a new album? I'm pretty much avoiding everything that has to do with that."

"You don't want to write any more albums?" Violet pulled out a sugar packet and ripped it open so she could dip her finger in it. She reminded him of Emmy. His daughter had the biggest sweet tooth.

"I would love to write another album, but I don't know if I've got one in me. I guess you could say I have something like writer's block."

"How hard is it to write country music? Sing about a truck and a girl in cutoff jean shorts and you've got a number-one hit."

Boone nearly choked on his water. "Oh, that's all I have to do, huh?"

"Yep. Stop making it so complicated."

He shook his head. "You're a piece of work, you know that?"

"That's what my mom always says, but I don't think she means it like that's a good thing."

"Why do you always give your mom such a

hard time? Is there some teenage rule book that says you have to drive your parents crazy?"

Violet shifted in her seat and tucked her hair behind her ears. "I don't always give my mom a hard time. She gives *me* a hard time. She's so embarrassing when she does things like letting Mrs. Davis come with us to Helping Hooves and making you all mad."

"She didn't make me mad," he protested in vain.

"Yeah, right. That's why you took off." Violet rolled her eyes. "She does it to my dad all the time, too. She ticks him off and he leaves or doesn't show up places. I don't get why she can't be normal and stop ruining my life."

That seemed like an awfully harsh assessment. Boone found himself feeling bad for Ruby once again. "I'm pretty sure she's not trying to ruin your life."

"Why are you taking her side? I thought you hated her."

"I don't hate her. I barely know your mom," Boone said. He wanted to stay neutral, but that wasn't working. Besides the physical attraction he couldn't deny, there was something about Ruby that tugged at his heartstrings. "It's possible that I might have overreacted to some small-town newspaper editor asking for a fluff piece for a paper that's probably distributed to a few hundred people. Your mom isn't so bad."

"My mom's not bad. She just doesn't get me. She wants me to be this perfect kid. But that's not me. I mess up. I don't like to wear dresses or go to Jordan O'Neil concerts. I like wearing black and being alone in my room. I like horses more than I like people."

"I don't like people, either," Boone confessed.

Violet smiled. The waitress returned with their drinks and took their lunch orders. Boone went with the burger, while Violet asked for the chocolate chip pancakes with a side of bacon and sausage. She also wanted hash browns and extra syrup. Heidi, the waitress, had definitely figured out who he was while she was getting their drinks. She hovered a little bit longer than needed and giggled when he said everything was good and she could go now.

"Has your mother not been feeding you?" he asked Violet as Heidi walked away.

"I told you, everything here is good. And since you're so rich and famous, I figured you could afford to buy me all my favorites."

"Piece of work."

Violet was right about the food. The service was fast and the food was hot and delicious. Violet had devoured her bacon and was pouring syrup on her pancakes when her phone rang.

"Seriously?" she groaned. "My mother has the worst timing."

She answered the call and told Ruby where she was and who she was with. Boone got the sense that Ruby had been worried.

"I'll be home soon, Mom. Chill." She paused to listen to her mom's reply. "Okay, bye."

"Everything all right?"

"My mom's home. She freaked out because I wasn't there when I told her I was getting a ride. I swear she's paranoid about me getting kidnapped."

"Trust me, anyone who kidnapped you would be trying to return you as soon as possible."

"Ha-ha," she said, stabbing her fork into a big bite of pancakes. Her smile told him she found it a little funny.

CHAPTER TEN

RUBY PACED THE front hall with her wallet in her hand. Thanks to Violet's disappearing act, she was too anxious to sit. How in the world had her child convinced Boone to take her to lunch? Every time she thought she was done with that man, he popped back up. She peeked out the window. No sign of them yet. They couldn't eat forever. She resumed her pacing.

The sound of a car sent her racing for the door. She pulled it open and stood on the front porch with her arms crossed over her chest. Boone and Violet were both laughing as he shut the car off. Why was he turning off the car? Did he think she was going to invite him in? Why would he want to stay?

"I think you should write a song about how you broke her heart. Country songs are always about that," Violet said as she climbed out.

"I thought all country songs were about trucks and girls in cutoff shorts," Boone said with a grin a mile wide.

"Most, not all," Violet clarified. "You need some heartbreak and beer drinking songs, too."

Boone's smile fell. "Right."

"Looks like you two had fun," Ruby said. "Did you thank Mr. Williams for lunch and giving you a ride?"

"No, you taught me nothing about manners. I'm the rudest kid in the world." Violet's sarcasm was worse than her eye rolls.

"She thanked me more than once," Boone answered, coming up the walk. "There's a polite young lady under all that Violetness."

His words made Ruby smile. "Thank you for bringing her home. What do I owe you for her lunch?" She opened her wallet.

Boone shook his head. "Nothing. You don't have to pay me back. Getting lunch was my idea."

"Oh my gosh, Mom. He's, like, a millionaire. Why do you do this to me?" Violet pushed open the door and went inside. "I need to give Boone the information on the horse show. Where's all that stuff?"

"On the kitchen table." Ruby felt the burn in her cheeks as Boone joined her on the porch. "Are you sure I can't reimburse you? I don't want her to think that just because you have money, you should spend it on her."

"Really, it's fine," he assured her.

"It's just, your money should be spent on people you care about, so…" She couldn't resist throwing that in there. Even though there was no good reason for it, his words had hurt her feelings yesterday.

Boone's smile returned. "Boy, it's a good thing neither one of us holds a grudge."

"I'm not holding a grudge. You have no reason to care about us. We're nobody to someone like you."

"I don't usually apologize for my bad behavior because most of the time I don't care who I hurt, but I was out of line with you yesterday. I'm also aware that I might have overreacted to your newspaper friend's presence."

Was Boone Williams apologizing to her a second time? Ruby wondered if she should pinch herself to make sure it was true. She tried to hold back her grin. "You totally overreacted."

He scratched the back of his neck. His dark blue T-shirt was pulled tight across his chest. Ruby had to force herself not to stare, but she didn't want to look into those eyes, either. Holly had made her paranoid.

Boone wouldn't let her focus on his feet. He used a finger to lift her chin so they made eye contact. "But will you admit that you knew I wouldn't want to do an interview?"

Ruby's mouth went dry, and his touch made

her skin tingle. Those eyes of his locked her in place. "I tried to warn her, but she's almost as stubborn as Violet is."

"Impossible." He slipped his hands into his back pockets as if he needed to keep them away from her.

"You're right. No one's as stubborn as Violet."

"Why are you two talking about me?" Violet poked her head outside. "This is why I have no manners. Are you going to make him stand outside or invite him in? Gosh, Mom," she huffed.

Ruby took a step back and waved him in. "After you."

He walked past her, brushing against her ever so slightly but enough to make her knees a little wobbly. *He's not nice, he's not nice, he's not nice*, she tried to remind herself. She had a classic case of bad-boy-itis. It was a chronic disease, really. When was she going to have this kind of physical attraction to some nice guy who never raised his voice and wore khaki to work? She followed him inside and noticed how Boone's jeans fit him so right. Mr. Nice Guy in khaki didn't stand a chance against those blue jeans.

"It's called the Bayview Classic. Have you heard of it?" Violet asked, handing Boone the paperwork for the upcoming show.

"I think my daughter rode there last year.

I can't remember for sure, though. Last year wasn't a good year for me."

"I'll bet Jesse would be cool with you coming. You know, if you wanted to," Violet added.

"I don't know. You gave me all these great song ideas. I could be busy writing about how I missed out on my one true love at the Cup and Spoon Diner."

Violet laughed at their inside joke, and Ruby's heart swelled at the sight of her daughter happy for the first time in what felt like forever. "Make sure to add in how hard it was to walk away because she was wearing Daisy Dukes."

"But she wouldn't ride in my truck." Boone's and Violet's giggles filled the room.

"What am I missing here?" Ruby asked, wanting in on the fun.

"Your daughter thought our waitress had a crush on me."

"Please. Mom, tell me she didn't have a crush. She brought over a piece of pie." Violet pretended to be the waitress, her eyelashes fluttering out of control. "'If I give you this piece of pie, can I get a picture with you? I used to dream about you coming in here, and this is the pie I served you.'" She stuck her tongue out and pretended to gag herself. "So gross."

"She was a fan," Boone said with a shrug.

"Who wanted you to ask her to marry you

because she gave you a free slice of pie? It happened. In her dream. So weird." Violet shook her head in disgust.

Boone laughed. "There's a song in there somewhere."

Ruby was so happy to see this lighter side of Violet, she couldn't stop grinning like a fool. "Let me guess. Was it Heidi?"

"Yep," Violet said. "I think she would have kept us there all day if I hadn't faked a coughing fit and begged Boone to take me home so I could get my inhaler."

"I thought you were serious for a minute," Boone interjected.

"So gullible." Violet's phone chimed and she checked it. "Thanks again for lunch and the ride. See ya tomorrow." She didn't even wait for Boone to reply. She flew upstairs, and the sound of her door closing echoed through the house.

"That girl is quite the actress," Boone said, handing the paperwork back to Ruby. "Has she ever used her powers for good on a real stage?"

"No, but that's not a bad idea. Maybe I'll encourage her to look into that when school starts." Ruby had been pushing Violet to get involved in something more social than horseback riding. Perhaps the drama club was exactly what she needed. "Maybe if I tell her it was your idea, she'll actually give it a shot."

Boone nodded. "Kids are funny. I don't know why they think their parents aren't like all the other adults in the world."

"We are a million times more clueless. Didn't you get that memo?"

"I'm pretty sure teenagers don't even know what a memo is. They probably sent it out via social media and I missed it."

It was annoying how he could be so darn charming. Ruby couldn't forget there was a nasty side to him, too. If she gave in to the charmer, Lord only knew what trouble she'd get herself into.

"Your daughter rides in these shows?" She held up the papers.

"She loves it. She's got a nice collection of blue ribbons."

"Violet would freak out if she won a blue ribbon."

"She's very good, given her experience level. She should do well."

As hard as she tried not to get sucked in, she found it impossible not to fall into easy conversation. She invited him to sit and got him some lemonade. Boone told her all about their morning with the new horse at Helping Hooves. She told him all about her special delivery.

"It was Iris's third child, so he practically delivered himself. I felt like I was really only there to document time and date of birth."

"I can't imagine women having babies anywhere but in a hospital. Mind you, I've only seen one baby born in my life, but it was enough to know I don't want that mess on my living room rug or my expensive bed."

Ruby stopped herself from rolling her eyes like Violet. "We plan for the mess. It isn't like I tell her to lie down wherever she is and push. It's all very sanitary. But sometimes hospitals are the way to go."

"Where was Violet born?" he asked, taking a sip of his lemonade but never breaking eye contact.

"Violet was born in a hospital. She's been difficult since birth, if you can believe that. There were issues with her kidneys in utero, and I couldn't take the risk that we wouldn't have access to everything we needed after she was born."

"She's all good now?"

Ruby was surprised he was interested enough to ask. "She is. Trouble, but healthy as a horse."

Boone's phone rang. He apologized and pulled it out to answer it. "I didn't run away to Nashville, Dean. I promise." He winked at Ruby, and she suddenly felt very warm. "Oh, man. I totally lost track of time. Tell Jesse I'll be back in a couple of minutes. I'm leaving right now." Boone stood and hung up his phone. "I have Jesse's car and the man would like to go home, so I better head back."

Ruby saw him out. "Thanks again for bringing my daughter home. In my line of work, there are never any set hours. Babies come when babies want to come."

"No problem. Violet's a good kid. Deep down. Just got to get under all that sarcasm and teen angst." Boone knew her pretty well for having spent only a few hours with her.

He stepped out onto the porch. "Have a good night, Ruby."

This felt oddly familiar. "You, too."

"Hey, neighbor!" Mary Ellen shouted from the sidewalk. She was dressed for a run, her twins strapped in snug as bugs in their double-wide jogging stroller.

"Hi, Mary Ellen." Ruby gave her a wave.

For some reason, that was taken as an invitation to come over for a chat. She pushed the stroller up the driveway. "I'm sorry, but are you Boone Williams?"

Now she recognized him.

"I am," Boone said before glancing at his phone. "But I'm on my way out."

Mary Ellen pretended not to hear. "I heard

a rumor you were in town. I can't believe it's true. I'm a huge fan."

"Thanks, but—"

"And here you are at Ruby's." She smiled, but it was obvious the whole thing completely perplexed her.

"He was dropping Violet off," Ruby said. "Not kidnapping her, like you thought last time."

Mary Ellen's eyes bulged, and her enormous stroller blocked Boone's path to his car. "That was you at Valu-Save? Oh my, it *was* you! I can't believe I didn't notice."

"That was me. I really have to go. I'll see you tomorrow, Ruby. Nice to meet you, Ruby's neighbor." He waited for her to move, but she didn't.

"How do you guys know each other, if you don't mind my asking?"

"I do mind. I need to get going. Could you…" Boone motioned for her to move her stroller.

"Oh! I'm so sorry." Mary Ellen finally took the hint. "Like I said, I'm a big fan. I guess I'm a little starstruck. I didn't know Ruby had such famous friends."

Boone didn't reply. He went to the car and climbed in. He gave Ruby a wave that was enthusiastically returned by Mary Ellen, then drove off.

Mary Ellen turned to Ruby. "You have been holding out on me, Ruby Wynn. I need to know right now how you know Boone Williams! We've been neighbors for months, and you neglected to tell me you're friends with someone so famous?"

They weren't friends. They were barely acquaintances. But something told Ruby not to tell Mary Ellen that. It seemed better to let her believe anything was possible.

"Just think what else I haven't told you. Have a nice run, Mary Ellen!"

Mary Ellen's jaw nearly hit the ground. Ruby slipped back inside and shut the door before dissolving into laughter.

CHAPTER ELEVEN

"I NEED A CAR. I don't care how you get me one. I need one." Boone had stopped to chat with Dean before heading to his trailer for the night.

"I thought the idea of coming here was to stay here. On the farm. And in the studio."

The studio. Boone smiled, thinking about the crazy song ideas Violet had come up with today at lunch. All her country music clichés were pretty funny. If only writing real songs was that simple.

"I'll get in your studio when you get me a car. I don't care if you have to have my agent drive mine down here for me. I need one."

Dean's eagerness lit him up. It was like Boone had waved a steak in front of a hungry lion. "I'll see what I can do if you really mean it about coming by the studio."

"You'll find out when you get me a car," Boone replied as he jogged down the steps.

"You'd better mean it, Boone!" Dean shouted after him.

Inside the trailer, it was quiet and surprisingly comfortable after a long day. Boone was beginning to think this place wasn't so bad. He would almost describe today as fun. An image of Ruby smiling up at him when he'd apologized and her cheeks turning pink when he'd tipped her chin up flashed through his mind.

He shook his head, hoping the action would rid it of ideas like that. Thinking about Ruby was dangerous business. Her kid was hilarious, though. Spending time with her felt so natural. So different from every exchange he'd had with his own teenager over the past few years.

He pulled out his phone and psyched himself up to call Emmy. He had left her a message about Willow yesterday and hoped she would answer today. If he could somehow relate to Violet, he should be able to do it with his own kid.

He pressed her number and held his breath. Four rings and right to voice mail. The disappointment was overwhelming. "Hey, Em. It's Dad. I was really hoping to talk to you. Maybe you could call me back. You can call me anytime during the day or night. I'll pick up. I really miss you." His voice cracked and he almost hung up. He swallowed the lump in his throat and tried to sound as upbeat as possible. "I can't wait to hear from you."

There was nothing in the world worse than

being rejected. It didn't matter who was doing the rejecting most times, but when it was someone you wanted in your life so very much, it was soul-crushing.

Boone decided there was only one thing he could do. He pulled up Sara's number. She would probably decline his call, but if there was even the smallest possibility it would lead to him talking to Emmy, he had to do it.

The phone rang twice before she picked up. "Did someone die?"

"Hello to you, too, Sara."

"Why are you calling me, Boone?" She sounded as irritated as Boone felt.

"I've been calling Em for months and she never answers and never calls back. If you are influencing her to ignore me, I am asking that you stop."

Sara laughed and didn't bother to hide it. "I don't have to tell Emmy Lou to ignore your calls. You did a great job of alienating her yourself."

Boone inhaled deeply. The breathing exercises he'd been taught weren't helping the way they were supposed to. "I made some mistakes. I've gone through the program, and I am trying to make amends with my daughter. It would help if you were a tiny bit more supportive of that."

"I am not going to make her do anything she doesn't want to do. She's fourteen and old enough to make her own choices, and she has chosen not to talk to you. You reap what you sow, Boone."

This plan to get Sara to help had completely backfired. "Thanks for nothing." He hung up and opened the door to the trailer. He tossed the phone as far as he could fling it.

Maybe giving up was the only answer. It was either that or head back over to Valu-Save and buy all the wine in the place. Good thing he didn't have a car.

Yet.

THE NEXT MORNING, Boone found his phone in the grass. The battery had died, but otherwise it had survived the night. He put it in his pocket and went to meet Jesse and Violet for their training session with Willow.

Jesse was grooming the horse in the tack room. Helping Hooves had a beautiful horse barn. It was well maintained, showing how important the horses were to them.

"Morning," Jesse greeted him. "The horse whisperer has arrived. Ready for another day of learning to lead?"

"There's nothing I would rather be doing this morning."

Jesse stopped brushing to give Boone a once-over. "That didn't sound too sincere. I'm hearing some frustration before the training has even begun. Is the trigger here or somewhere else?"

Oh, the trigger was far, far away. All the way on the other side of Nashville. In a gorgeous house on ten acres of land. Sara had probably woken up this morning patting herself on the back for telling Boone off last night.

"It's not here. I'll get over it once the coffee kicks in."

"Family, friend or foe?" Jesse asked.

"Former family, current foe."

"Besides waiting on the caffeine to make you feel better, what strategy are you using to manage this frustration?"

Boone took the brush from Jesse and began grooming Willow. "I don't know. I'm here. I'm trying to work it off, I guess."

"Physical activity is a good strategy. Anything else?"

"I'm talking to you, aren't I?" Boone didn't know what else Jesse wanted from him. He was doing his best to hold it together. He needed a distraction so he wouldn't sit in his trailer, thinking about how badly things had gone with Sara last night and how much he wanted to drive into town for a drink.

"Using your resources. Another good choice. What relaxes you, helps calm you down when you're feeling agitated?"

"Vodka tonics were my drink of choice. They always calmed me down."

Jesse asked him a few questions about his urges and his recent thoughts about alcohol. Boone promised him he had no intention of falling off the wagon.

"No one ever plans to have a setback. They happen. What other things calm you besides the things that you are addicted to?"

Boone ran the brush over Willow's back. "Music, I guess."

"You play guitar, right?" Jesse asked. Boone nodded. "Did you bring your guitar with you from Nashville?"

"Dean expects me to write an album while I'm here. Of course I brought my guitar. Problem is, there's no music in me. I'm dry." There was nothing left in his well of creativity.

"I'm not thinking you should play for Dean. I'm thinking you should play for *you*. Don't worry about writing something new. Play something you love. Maybe something you wrote, but maybe something someone else wrote. Just play."

Boone hadn't played for himself in a very long time. He tried to imagine what it would

be like just to play and not to think about what
the product would sound like in the end. Music
had become something that was bought and
sold and was no longer an expression of how
he felt.

"Not sure it'll work, partner."

"You try it and get back to me," Jesse said,
untying Willow's lead. "Let's go wait for Violet outside."

That was way too easy. Jesse wasn't going
to ask him what he was mad about or pry into
his history with his ex-wife. What kind of social worker was this guy?

"That's it? You don't want to dig deeper?"

Jesse cocked his head. "Do you want me to
dig deeper?"

"Absolutely not."

"I figured, which is why I didn't."

Boone was beginning to like Jesse more and
more. When they got outside, Ruby had just
parked, and Violet got out of the car. Ruby
waved from the driver's seat but stayed put.
She made him smile, and that was impressive
on a day like today.

"Stop staring at my mom," Violet said as she
approached. "Creeper."

Boone's focus shifted to the younger and
much more annoying of the Wynn ladies.

"Good morning to you, too, Violet. I see you took your smart-aleck pills this morning."

"Wow, you do know it's the twenty-first century, right? I'm not sure calling someone a smart aleck has been a thing for, like, forty years."

Jesse shook his head at the two of them. "Wow, you sure are two peas in a pod."

Violet covered her face with her hands and let out a groan.

"What? What did I say?" Jesse asked Boone.

"You just outed yourself as a shriveled-up pea in my outdated pod." Boone gave him a pat on the back. "You've officially lost all your cool and hip points with her."

After a more productive training session than the day before, Boone worked with Violet and Renegade on some of the Western horsemanship tests. Ruby showed up and watched them from outside the arena.

"Your upper body is out of position, and you're moving your legs to compensate," Boone said. "It makes you feel off balance, and you'll fall if you don't correct your positioning. Don't hunch over—focus on your posture."

"He makes me nervous."

"He's no different than Sassy. He will follow

your lead. Don't get sloppy on him or he'll get sloppy on you."

Violet tried again and held her position. Boone applauded her efforts before making his way over to Ruby.

"You're an accomplished singer *and* a riding instructor? Overachiever, huh?"

"That's just the tip of the iceberg. I'm a man of many talents."

Ruby's eyebrows lifted. "Of course you are."

Boone couldn't help but smirk. He looked back at Violet. "She's going to do great this weekend. I can't wait to see her compete."

"So you're coming to the show?"

He wondered if her question meant she didn't think he should. Maybe he was overstepping his bounds. "Is that a problem?"

"No," Ruby said, shaking her head. "She'd be over the moon. She went from thinking you were lame to listening to some of your music last night. Don't tell her I told you that. She doesn't know I heard."

Boone was relieved it wasn't an issue and shocked to hear Violet had given him a listen. "Uh-oh. You're going to have a country and Western lover in your house. How will you handle that, Miss Prog Rock?"

"My love is unconditional. She is free to listen to anything that doesn't have swearwords, racist language or references to sex, drugs or violence against women. Other than that, she can listen to anything."

She was cute even when she was being an overprotective mother. "I will keep that in mind when I write my next album."

"Is that why you're here? To record some new music?"

That was a good question. Boone wasn't sure if it was possible. He was here because there weren't any other options. Dean wasn't going to let him sit around his house in Nashville, sulking about the disaster his life had become or drinking himself numb so he could get through each day.

"That was the plan when Dean arranged this little getaway. I needed out of Nashville. The horses were supposed to offer some distraction. Truth is, I haven't even stepped foot in the studio yet."

"You should. How cool is it that there's a recording studio right here?" Ruby blushed. "It's probably not that exciting to someone who's been in a studio before. I forget you've already recorded a million albums."

"Ten, but thanks for that life goal," he said with a crooked grin. "Why don't you and Violet come with me? Dean said I could drop in whenever."

Ruby didn't hesitate to take him up on the offer. They got Violet off the horse and sent Renegade out to play with his friends in the field. Boone didn't really know what to expect. He couldn't imagine the studio was too state-of-the-art. He also didn't know if Sawyer was in there working or not.

The double-wide trailer was situated behind the farmhouse. Dean had said it replaced an old equipment shed. Boone hoped there would be no one inside but was quickly disappointed.

Dean and Wyatt, a producer Boone was familiar with, sat at the controls while Sawyer sang in the sound booth. Dean's eyeballs almost popped out of his head when he realized Boone had come in. Boone wouldn't have been surprised if he kicked Sawyer out of the booth and locked Boone in there until he sang something.

"Hey, guys, welcome!" Dean greeted them with handshakes and hugs. "I'm glad you came to check this place out. It's about time," he said to Boone.

"Ruby wanted to see what a recording studio looked like. I told her this wasn't what I was used to, but actually—" he scanned the equipment "—I'm more impressed than I thought I would be."

Wyatt pressed a button. "Let's try it again.

You sound like you're thinking about a million things other than what the song's about."

"I'm not thinking about anything but making it sound good," Sawyer replied.

"Well, it's not working. Think about something else."

The exchange reminded Boone of feedback he'd gotten over the years. When he was new to the business, he did everything the producer asked of him. As he got older and wiser, he learned to trust his own instincts. This time, Wyatt was right. Sawyer was holding back. There was something missing.

"I think we need to call it a day, Dean," Wyatt said while Sawyer tried again with little positive result. "He's sung this part thirty times, and I can't get him to relax enough to do it right."

"Let him try a couple more times," Dean said. "He'll get it. He has an audience now— he loves an audience."

Boone knew the feeling. Performing was a million times better than recording music. As much as Boone enjoyed the creative process of writing a song, performing it was the reason he'd gotten into this business in the first place.

Sawyer gave it a go three more times before Boone decided it was time to say something. He squeezed in between Dean and Wyatt and pressed the button for the intercom. "What's this song about?"

Sawyer stared back through the glass walls. "It's about chasing fireflies."

Boone tipped his chin to his chest and gave Sawyer his best impression of an annoyed Violet. "What's it really about? Figuratively, not literally."

"Missing someone. Hanging on to the one good memory you have and wondering if that's enough."

"How bad do you miss that person?"

"I don't," Sawyer snapped back. "It's a song, not real life."

Yeah, right. Just like Boone's song about the backyard swing wasn't about his dad. "How bad does the person in the song miss that person?"

He shrugged. "I guess a lot. He just doesn't realize how bad because he's still remembering something good."

"But he will realize eventually. He's gonna be hurting something bad as soon as he knows all he has left is that memory. It's going to rip his heart out, and he's going to wonder if the hole will ever heal. Imagine feeling like that when you're singing. Think about the words that are coming out of your mouth. Don't focus on your pitch or making sure everything sounds perfect. Feel it. If you feel it, we'll feel it in here, and that song will be a hit."

He let go of the button and waited for the music to start. Sawyer closed his eyes and didn't sing a word the first time around. Wyatt cued it back up, and when Sawyer sang, he didn't just sing a melody; he spilled his guts out in front of all of them. The whole room went silent. Boone glanced back and caught Ruby wiping tears off her cheek. Violet's eyes were also watery. That spoke volumes.

He pressed the button. "Well done, kid."

Dean grabbed Boone by both shoulders and gave him a friendly shake. "That was incredible. See, I knew getting you in here would spark something. You know music, Boone. Next time, it's going to be you in there."

Boone wished he believed that. Knowing music and creating it were two very different things. Letting himself feel that intensely wasn't something he could do without wanting to numb it all away with some whiskey or two bottles of merlot. Feeling was the scariest part of this whole thing.

When he thought about how he had wanted to wrap his arms around Ruby when he'd caught her crying, he knew music wasn't the only thing that could rip him into tiny pieces.

CHAPTER TWELVE

"ARE YOU SURE you gave Dad the right address?" Violet was on her tiptoes, searching the crowd for Levi.

The knot in Ruby's stomach grew bigger. He wasn't going to show. He was so predictable. "He said he might not be able to come for the whole thing. Maybe he's planning on getting here when the competition part starts."

"Does he even know what class I'm in?"

"Do you want me to text him?" Ruby offered.

"No, don't. He'll get mad at you for checking on him, and he won't come at all. I'll text him after warm-ups."

Jesse returned from registering Violet and Sassy at the check-in. He pinned Violet's number to her back. "Why don't we take Sassy for a walk and get her comfortable?" he suggested.

"Are you sure Boone is coming?" Violet asked. She wrung her hands and paced a bit alongside Sassy's trailer.

Violet's anxiety was definitely rubbing off on Ruby. She felt like throwing up. If Boone and Levi didn't show, it wouldn't matter if Violet won a blue ribbon. She'd be so disappointed; the whole experience would be ruined.

"He got grabbed up by Dean and Sawyer right as we were packing up, but he said he'd meet us here. He's got time," Jesse reassured her. "So does your dad."

Thank God for Jesse. At least one man in Violet's life came through for her when she needed him. The two of them backed Sassy out of the trailer and took her for a quick walk around the grounds. Ruby offered to take the tack to Sassy's stall, allowing her to fret openly.

She texted Levi, even though Violet had said not to. She was only going to make sure he remembered.

Got lucky with the weather today for Violet's show. She's super excited and can't wait to see you.

There was no way he could take a comment about the weather the wrong way. But he could ignore it, which was exactly what he did.

Holly, Jon and the boys planned to be there to support Violet but weren't due for another hour. Ruby had to remind herself that Violet would have the best cheering section no matter what. If Boone and Levi blew her off, the rest of them would simply have to be louder and prouder.

Jesse and Violet returned. Ruby noticed the disappointment on Violet's face when no one else was waiting for them. Jesse offered to help her saddle Sassy up and get her looking pretty.

Violet didn't look too shabby herself. She had picked out a purple shirt for her show outfit, and it was nice to see her in something other than head-to-toe black. Not that she didn't still have on plenty of her favorite color. Her riding pants, boots and helmet were all black, but the shirt was what made her stand out today.

"You okay?" Jesse asked Ruby once they got Sassy ready.

Violet was hand-feeding the horse some hay, occupying them both for the moment.

"I love how much she loves horses."

"Sassy loves her back. She brings out the best in Violet. They're a good team."

Hearing that tore Ruby in two. There were times she feared taking Violet away from Nashville had done more harm than good. Seeing her with Sassy completely washed that worry away. At the same time, knowing Violet was bonding with this horse and her coach made

Ruby question if she was doing the right thing by making plans to leave Tennessee altogether.

She checked her phone. No reply from Levi and only twenty minutes until the competition began. If Levi didn't show and Violet ended up crushed, Ruby wouldn't have to question her decision to start over in Seattle.

"He'll show," Jesse said.

"I don't think he will."

"He promised me," Jesse said surely.

"Levi promised you?" Ruby scrunched her nose in confusion.

"Levi? Boone. I thought we were talking about Boone."

Laughter bubbled up and out of her. "I thought you were conspiring with my ex-husband behind my back."

"Never," Jesse assured her.

All of a sudden, Violet's entire face lit up. "You made it!"

Ruby couldn't believe Levi had actually showed. She turned around to find not Levi but Boone approaching.

"I said I'd be here. Did you doubt me?"

"I was worried you got mobbed by all your fans in the parking lot," Violet teased. "You could have been stuck there signing autographs all day."

"Ha-ha," he said, giving Sassy a pat. "Everyone looks good. You ready to ride?"

"Do you doubt me?" Violet tossed back at him.

"Not for a second, kid. You're going to do great."

The confidence boost Boone gave her was priceless. Ruby wanted to throw her arms around him and kiss that smug face. It didn't hurt that he looked even more handsome than usual. He had on a dark blue plaid shirt with the sleeves rolled and pushed up to his elbows. His sunglasses and cowboy hat would ideally give him some anonymity today.

Jesse suggested they head over to the ring for warm-ups. The closer it got to competition time, the more nervous Ruby felt. Levi still hadn't answered her text and was nowhere to be seen. Holly and family arrived, and thankfully no requests for interviews were made this time.

There were a dozen riders in Violet's class. With everyone in the ring, Violet was doing a good job of not getting caught in the more crowded areas.

Boone sat down next to Ruby in the bleachers. He grabbed her hand. "You seem more anxious than she is. Take a deep breath."

Ruby stared down at their conjoined hands.

His touch might have helped her forget her worries for Violet but did nothing to stop her heart from racing. She didn't dare glance to her right to find out how far Holly's jaw had dropped.

"She grew up going to rodeo shows every weekend. My ex is a bull rider. Violet wanted to do barrel racing so she could be a part of the shows her dad was in. She took some beginner riding lessons in Nashville but thought it was boring when all she did was ride a horse around in a circle."

"That sounds like Violet."

"She wanted to learn to barrel race. Period. She didn't understand that she had to start at the beginning, not the end. But Helping Hooves changed everything for her. Jesse talked her into Western horsemanship and she was hooked. I want her to do well so she sticks with it."

"She's having fun out there," Holly noted. "Don't worry so much."

At least Violet didn't seem to be searching the stands for Levi. She'd even smiled the last time she passed by her cheering squad.

"I really want to thank you all for coming," Ruby said. "It means a lot to her."

"Any word from Levi?" Holly asked.

Ruby simply shook her head. Thankfully

Boone's presence seemed to be enough for Violet. Ruby wasn't sure how to feel about that.

"Did he say he was coming?" Boone asked.

"He said that he would try, but that I need to remember he has a life."

Holly groaned. "He's such a jerk."

"Mommy said a bad word!" her six-year-old accused her.

"You should not say it to your brothers or your friends, Trevor, but Mommy can say it about people who are mean to Ms. Ruby and Violet."

Boone let go of Ruby's hand and scratched the back of his splotchy red neck. "It's not easy to be the odd man out at something like this."

"Are you seriously defending him?" Holly asked.

"I'm not defending anyone. I'm just saying if I was him and I knew I had to come join a group of people who obviously think I'm a bad guy, I wouldn't be racing over here, either."

That sounded exactly like he was defending Levi. Ruby wanted to argue that Violet was more important than Levi's need to feel comfortable. Maybe if he didn't act like such a jerk, he wouldn't feel bad being around Ruby and her friends.

The steward called for the end of warm-ups. The competition was ready to begin. Jesse went down to have one more chat with Violet, and Ruby pulled out her phone to give Levi one more chance.

Competition is starting. We're in the stands.

He wouldn't answer because he wasn't here. He wasn't coming, and Ruby couldn't find it in her heart to understand why he would let Violet down like this.

Violet rode Sassy like a champ. She had the loudest cheering section and ended up winning second place. Holly got to high-five Boone and would probably never wash her hand again. Ruby was so proud of Violet not only for placing but also for being a good sport. Violet had a history of thinking that if she wasn't first, she was last and whoever placed ahead of her was a cheat. Today, Ruby watched her clap for the blue ribbon winner with a smile on her face.

"Oh my gosh, let me see that ribbon!" Ruby said when they got done taking the five hundred pictures she needed to memorialize the event properly.

"It's not that big a deal, Mom." There was that familiar attitude.

"Yes, it is," Boone countered. "A lot of kids don't place at their first competitions. Some don't place at their second, third or fourth. This is a very big deal, kid. Be proud."

"It's not like I won a Grammy."

"Well, no one expects you to be as awesome as me. I'm extraordinary. You're above average. Still something to be proud of."

Violet's smile melted Ruby's heart. Boone had a way with her that not many others did.

They headed back to the trailer to untack Sassy and get her loaded up. Holly's boys were getting tired, and Jon carried little Henry to the car while Holly and the two older boys hung back to say goodbye.

"So now that we're friends, Boone, any chance you'd change your mind about that interview?"

Ruby wanted to tackle her best friend right then and there. She threatened to ruin the first good day Ruby'd had in a really long time. But Boone's response surprised her.

"I'll make you a deal," he said, not appearing the least bit ruffled by her question. "I'll do an interview, but I trust only Ruby to do it."

"What?" Holly and Ruby exclaimed at the same time.

"I don't know anything about conducting interviews," Ruby said.

"She doesn't like country music. She's not

even a fan," Holly said, clearly hoping that would sway him.

"That's why she's perfect for the job. She's not part of the media, and she doesn't really know anything about me or my past. Those are my conditions. Take it or leave it."

"I write an advice column for the paper. I am a member of the press," Ruby said, hoping that would deter him.

"Fine," Holly conceded. "She can do it."

Ruby didn't like this idea one bit. "Wait, don't I get a say in this?"

"Sure," Boone said. "If you don't want to do it, then there's no interview."

"She'll do it," Holly said. She wouldn't let Ruby say anything. "You'll do it."

She wasn't going to do it, but there was no reason to start a fight in the middle of a horse show. Holly left believing she had secured an exclusive interview with Boone for the *Gazette*.

Violet and Jesse loaded Sassy into the trailer. Boone promised to be right back and ran to his car. The first question Ruby would ask him if they did do this interview was why he had to look so good in those jeans.

Boone returned with a huge gift bag overflowing with rainbow-colored tissue paper. He handed the bag to Violet.

"Don't say I didn't think you were going to

win something. I came prepared for a celebration."

Violet dug inside the bag and pulled out a picture frame. She frowned at Boone, who was already chuckling.

"What? You don't like it?" he said through his laughter.

Violet held up the frame so Ruby could see the picture it held. It was an eight-by-ten head shot of Boone signed to Violet with all his love. Jesse and Ruby couldn't help but laugh, as well.

"There'd better be something else in this bag," Violet threatened with a scowl.

"What more could you possibly want?" Boone asked before cracking up again.

Violet fought a smile and shook her head. She could act mad all she wanted, but Ruby knew she thought it was just as funny as they did.

In the car on the way home, Ruby felt like she'd better get one thing out of the way before Violet went to her room and shut down all communication for the night.

"I'm sorry your dad didn't make it."

Violet shrugged and stared out the window. "No biggie. I want him to come next time when I win first place. Second place is nothing."

Ruby hated that she was discounting what

an accomplishment today was because Levi hadn't been there to tell her second place was phenomenal.

"I don't think it's nothing. Neither did the Davises or Jesse or Boone."

Violet was holding the framed picture of Boone's face along with her ribbon. "Yeah, but we can't really trust Boone's judgment. The man thinks his autograph is magical."

Given the way Violet was smiling down at it, maybe it was.

CHAPTER THIRTEEN

Monday morning, Boone walked down to the arena after eating some breakfast. Faith and girls a few years older than Violet were leading Winston the horse and a little boy with braces on his legs around to different hoops. The little boy would throw a ball through and move on to the next.

Jesse had told him to meet him here at ten, and it was a quarter to. Boone stood behind the fence and watched the therapy session. The boy's dad cheered him on as they returned to the mounting ramp.

Father and son high-fived, and Boone's chest tightened. He didn't have enough of that kind of memories with Emmy. Sure, he'd gone to some of her horse shows and watched her do her riding lessons here and there. But his music had kept him away so much in the beginning, and his drinking ruined the times he was home later on.

"Look who's ready to go," Jesse said, coming up from behind.

"I figured I would get out here early so Dean couldn't intercept me this time."

Jesse leaned against the fence. "But you were hanging out in the studio last week, right?"

"I've listened to Sawyer in the studio and offered a couple suggestions. I have not been in there doing any of my own stuff." It was safer that way. Sawyer's emotions didn't overwhelm Boone.

"Have you tried playing for yourself yet?"

Boone's guitar was still in its case. He hadn't even touched it since he hid it in one of the storage compartments in the Airstream.

"I've thought about it but haven't mustered up the courage yet."

"Why do you need courage to play music if it's something that you think relaxes you?"

"Music is like therapy. It might feel like a huge release after you do it, but you have to psych yourself up for the pain first."

Jesse nodded. "Okay, I get it. So it makes you feel, and feelings are something you've been trying to avoid."

"I really hate feeling."

"Not all feelings have to be bad," Jesse argued. "How did you feel the other day when Violet got second place?"

"I was happy for her. It was nice to spend

the day doing something so normal, but it's the good times like Saturday that make the bad that much worse."

Jesse gave him his full attention. "Why is that?"

"I came back here that night and was alone. My daughter won't answer my calls or texts. The only people who get in touch with me are people who work for me—like my agent—or who want something from me—like Dean."

"Spending the day with friends, people who care about one another and support each other, reminded you of how that's missing in your life." Jesse summarized it nicely.

Being with Ruby and Violet made Boone feel good. Too good. Late at night, thoughts of Ruby and those green eyes did battle with his desire for a drink to see which one could keep him awake.

"And being drunk lets me forget I feel lonely. I can wake up in the morning feeling sick instead of sad." Being honest about the alcohol was easier to admit than his feelings for Ruby.

"Is that how you feel this morning?"

Boone shrugged one shoulder. "I don't know how I feel. I guess I'm excited to work with Willow today." And by the possibility of seeing Ruby.

"Having a purpose definitely helps. Yesterday was probably tough if you spent the whole day alone."

Boone had spent nearly the whole day in bed. He figured staying under the covers kept him out of the nearest bar or Valu-Save's liquor aisle. It also stopped him from making a fool of himself and showing up on Ruby's doorstep, asking for some of her time. Even though some of her time was all he could think about lately.

"You two going to stand around all morning, or are we going to teach Willow how to do her job?" Violet stood a few feet away, cross-armed and impatient.

She made Boone smile. Hanging out with Violet was another plus for today. She gave him a hard time, but he knew she respected him no matter what her smart mouth said. Being around her made him feel like a dad even if he wasn't hers.

"You're the one who's late," he said to her. "We've been waiting forever."

"I'm not late." She checked her phone. "Jesse said ten."

Jesse let her off the hook. "He's teasing you."

"You're such a bully," she told Boone. "Do you always pick on innocent little kids?"

"When I see one, I'll let you know." He pulled on her ponytail as he walked past her to the barn. "Come on, kid. Let's get Willow."

Willow was in a mood today. She would let Boone lead her around, but teaching her to stop was a whole different story.

"The idea is to use the arena corners to help teach her when we want her to stop," Jesse explained to Violet. "We want her to feel like the wall at the corner is closing in front of her. Just before she walks into that trap, Boone needs to turn so he's facing Willow's shoulder."

He was trying, but instead of stopping, she was rearing up and backing away.

"I don't think Willow likes having the walls closing in on her," Boone said, giving the horse a scratch to calm her down. He could relate to not enjoying that feeling.

"Horses are a lot like us—they're emotional animals," Jesse explained to Violet. "They also have different personalities, like we do. Willow is much more stubborn than, say, Sassy."

"She makes Sassy seem like the most easygoing horse on the planet," Violet said.

"We have to pay attention to her feelings and to our own, as well," Jesse said. "We can't let our anger or frustration take over when we're training her. She'll lose respect for us."

This was beginning to feel suspiciously like a social work lesson. Boone got Willow calmed down and led her over to where they were standing.

"It's kind of like the people in our lives. Lose your cool, lose your friends," Boone said.

Jesse grinned. "Exactly."

Violet sighed. "Oh my gosh, now you're both counseling me?"

"He needs the lesson just as much—if not more—than you," Jesse replied with a chuckle. "You two are both too good at covering up your real feelings. You use humor and sarcasm to avoid the tough stuff. But you still feel it. And when it finally comes to the surface, it usually isn't very pretty."

Boone couldn't argue with that. "So what's the answer, Mr. Social Worker?"

"It would help you both if you were more aware of your feelings. If you tackle them before they become unmanageable, you're less likely to do or say things that push people away."

Boone was a pro at pushing people away. He'd managed to do it to everyone he cared about.

Violet apparently felt the same. "But I'm so good at pushing. You always tell me to focus on my strengths."

"Just because you're good at it doesn't make it one of your strengths," Jesse corrected her.

"I'll try if you try," Boone offered. Maybe

if they did it together, they'd be more successful. The buddy system was a thing, wasn't it?

Violet bit her lip while she thought about it. "Fine. But when I do it better than you, don't cry."

"Oh, I am going to be so in touch with my feelings, I'll be crying only when it's appropriate. Like when I'm watching movies where the dog dies at the end or one of those videos of soldiers returning home and surprising their family members."

"What's up with those videos?" Violet asked. "Are they trying to wreck all of us? Did you see the one where the guy comes home and the dog is so happy to see him, it actually starts crying? The dog hugged him for, like, ten minutes."

"How about the one where the guy surprises his sister on her wedding day? That one got me choked up," Jesse chimed in.

Violet disagreed. "That one wasn't really that sad."

"That's because you don't have a brother. If you did, you would have gotten super emotional."

"One of my friends back in Nashville has a brother, and she hates him."

Boone shook his head. This child could win an argument about anything. Poor Ruby.

Just as he thought her name, she appeared outside the arena. The sundress she wore fluttered in the late-summer breeze. She was a petite thing and pretty enough that men could write songs about her.

He handed Jesse the lead rope and went over to say hi.

"How'd it go today?" she asked. Her lips were glossy, and he liked it when she wore her hair down so it fell past her shoulders. It looked soft to the touch, and he imagined it would smell sweet if he dipped his head near the crook of her neck and inhaled.

"I think Violet and I got more out of it than Willow did, but that's not necessarily a bad thing."

Her smile reached those sparkling eyes. "You mean I'm getting some free therapy out of this?"

"Heck yeah, but don't tell Violet."

"Don't tell Violet what?" the surly teenager asked.

Boone turned to the side, inviting her into their conversation. "How bad you smell. I know you're sensitive about these things."

"Be careful. If I start getting in touch with my feelings, mean words like that could hurt them."

"Did you ask him yet?" Ruby asked Violet.

"Oh my gosh, Mom. No. And thanks for bringing it up right in front of him."

Boone furrowed his brow. "Why are you always so tough on your mom? You know it's not a big deal to ask me something."

"It's nothing," Violet said, kicking up some of the dirt. "I just thought maybe you'd help me prepare for my next horse show instead of Jesse. The next one I'm signed up for is bigger than the last one, and I probably need to practice more than once a week."

The feelings her request sent bursting forth were difficult to avoid. He was both touched and scared out of his mind. "I don't know what to say. You sure you want my help and not someone else's?"

Violet's eyes cast down. "If you don't want to, it's fine. I can skip it or see if Faith will do it."

"Hey." He set his hand on her shoulder and waited for her to look up. "If you want me to help train you, I would be honored."

"You don't have to do that much, really. A couple of extra lessons should be enough. And then you could come to the show, if you wanted. Help me with Sassy's tack."

"I can handle all that."

"Since you're being so amenable…" Ruby said, reaching into her purse and pulling out a few folded sheets of paper. "Holly emailed me these questions to ask you for the interview. I figured it would probably be simplest if you just write your answers down, and I'll give it back to her. Super easy."

Boone had been looking forward to spending some time with Ruby, answering her questions, and now she was trying to get out of it? "No way. You write down the answers, not me. And it's your interview, not Holly's. If I wanted to answer Holly's questions, I would have let Holly interview me."

Ruby's face fell. "Oh, come on. This is ridiculous. I don't know what questions to ask. Look at these." She tried to hand the papers to him again. "They're harmless. You don't have to give away any personal information."

"Then I guess there won't be an interview."

"Holly will never forgive me." Ruby seemed to think about it for a couple seconds. "When can you meet to be interviewed?"

"How about tomorrow?" Boone suggested. "We aren't working with Willow, so my morning is wide-open." Jesse was the one who said having a purpose helped fight the depression. Spending some time with Ruby was a good reason to get out of bed.

"Fine. I'll be here at ten," Ruby said. Boone could have sworn he saw her fighting a smile. Maybe she wasn't so upset about doing this interview. "Let's go, Violet. I have to see a patient at the office after lunch." She turned back to Boone and said, "Until tomorrow."

"Tomorrow."

AS HE STEPPED into his trailer, Boone realized there was no way he could have Ruby in here without doing some deep cleaning. He hadn't picked up after himself very well over the past couple of weeks.

He had a stack of dirty dishes and trash that needed to be tossed. Clothes needed to be washed and put away. Everything needed a good wipe-down. More purpose. That was a good thing. Supposedly.

He picked up a T-shirt that had been on the ground and gave it a sniff. The stench almost knocked him out.

"Boone, are you in there?" Dean shouted from outside.

Boone contemplated whether he should acknowledge the question or not. If he got dragged into the studio today, he'd never get this place in tip-top shape.

Dean rapped on the door. "Boone, I know you're in there."

Boone pushed open the door. "Do you have a cleaning lady I could borrow for a couple of hours? I also need someone to wash some clothes."

"I'll help you figure that out. I've got a surprise for you. Come on."

Something about this surprise made Boone's shoulders tense. "Tell me what it is or I'm not coming."

"Just come on," Dean said, grabbing Boone's forearm and tugging him out of the Airstream.

"This had better be good." Boone tossed the smelly shirt he'd been holding back inside.

"I can't tell you how much I appreciate you working with Sawyer and offering some advice. You really helped him get over that last hurdle."

Boone didn't feel like he had done that much. Sawyer was talented; he simply needed a push in the right direction.

As they rounded the side of the farmhouse, a black Navigator came into view. "You got me a car? Finally!"

"Oh, no." Dean stopped, causing Boone to bump into him. "That's not the surprise. It brought the surprise. Come on."

Boone had a sinking feeling. Two people stood on the porch. One was an older man and the other was a young blonde woman. As soon as the woman spotted Boone, she covered her mouth with her hands like she had just been told she'd won a hundred million dollars. Was she crying?

Boone didn't follow Dean up the steps.

"Boone Williams, meet Piper Starling, your biggest fan and Grace Note's other double-platinum-selling recording artist. Piper, meet the guy who's going to teach you how to write your own songs."

He had to be kidding.

CHAPTER FOURTEEN

RUBY SMOOSHED HER lips together to make sure her lipstick was evenly applied. Leaning forward, she took a closer look in the mirror. She frowned. This was what women did when they were going on a date, not meeting someone to ask them stupid questions for an even more ridiculous newspaper article that she didn't want to write in the first place.

She grabbed a tissue and wiped the lipstick off. This was not a date. Ruby didn't date. She definitely didn't date men like Boone Williams. Who dated men like Boone? Rich and famous women. Country music stars, supermodels, Hollywood actresses. Midwives from small towns with sassy teenage daughters did not.

"Can I go to the lake with some friends? Whoa…" Violet leaned against the doorjamb. "Did you do something to your hair? And are you wearing mascara? Oh my gosh, you are! You're wearing mascara *and* eye shadow."

Ruby pulled a couple more tissues from the

box and tried to rub off the eye shadow, too. This was humiliating.

"Stop!" Violet grabbed her arm. "It looks good. Don't mess it up. I'm just surprised to see you with makeup on. You only get fancied up for special occasions. Is interviewing Boone a special occasion?"

"No. That's why I should take it off." Ruby needed facial cleanser. She was not going to get all this gunk off without some soap.

"Mom, seriously. Don't. I think you should leave it."

Ruby checked her reflection in the mirror again. Maybe it wasn't too much. "Are you sure I don't look like a clown?"

"You look really pretty, Mom."

"Really?" Ruby couldn't remember the last time Violet had paid her a compliment. She usually had a snarky comment about something she wore or how she did her hair. According to Violet, her mother was a complete embarrassment.

"Really. You need a little color on your lips, though."

Ruby reapplied the lipstick and faced Violet for final inspection. "How's that?"

"Perfect. Boone's going to freak out."

That sounded like a bad thing. Ruby turned on the water. She needed to wash this off. "Are you tricking me into making a fool out of myself in front of him?"

Violet reached around her to shut the water off. "No, I mean he's going to freak out because you're so pretty. He's going to think you look beautiful."

"It's dumb to try to look good for a guy. The only person you need to look good for is yourself."

"Oh my gosh, Mom. This does not need to be an empowerment lesson. I'm not judging you. Plus, it doesn't even matter. He already thinks you look good."

"What? Did he say that to you?"

Violet rolled her eyes as she adjusted one of the straps on Ruby's dress. "If he'd said that, I would have died. I'd literally be dead right now instead of standing in this bathroom with you."

"Then why would you say that?"

"Because he stares at you. Sometimes he gets this weird look on his face when he's doing it." Violet mimicked some moony face Ruby had never seen Boone make.

She laughed and shook her head. "You are such a bad liar."

"I am not." Violet fluffed Ruby's hair and moved some of it over her shoulder on one side. "I am a great liar. But I'm not lying about this."

"I'll probably be back in an hour. I'm going

to ask him the questions Holly sent me, write down his answers and leave."

"Whatever. Can I go to the lake with Stacy and Peyton?"

"Stacy the smoker? I don't know about that."

"She isn't a smoker. She wanted to try it, not do it all the time. I promise we won't do anything illegal. I'll be on my best behavior, I swear."

"I don't know. You just admitted you're a great liar."

"Mom! Please. I am not lying. Trust me this one time. If I screw up, you can take the horse show away from me. You know how important that is. Please."

That *was* important to her. It wasn't the kind of thing Violet would usually put on the chopping block. "Fine. But there are eyes and ears all over this town. If something gets back to me, no horse show."

"Thank you! You are the best mom ever." Violet kissed her on the cheek and skipped out of the room.

Funny how she was only the best mom ever when she was giving Violet exactly what she wanted. Violet had better not mess this up. Ruby did not want to be the bad guy who had to take away the horse show.

She gave herself a final once-over. Maybe

she did look good. Not that it mattered. Violet
had to be seeing things if she thought Boone
was ogling her. Boone was not dating material,
anyway. He was too handsome, too rich, too
famous, too good with Violet, too everything.

That was what she was going to keep telling herself.

IT WAS TEN O'CLOCK on the dot when she pulled
into the parking lot of Helping Hooves. There
was a black SUV parked in front of the main
house, and Dean and Faith stood on the porch.

"Hey, Ruby!" Faith called out as Ruby got
out of the car.

"Hi, guys. I'm here to meet with Boone.
Holly asked me to do this interview for the *Gazette*. Just what I needed—another job, right?"

"He's in the studio now. Was he expecting
you this morning?" Dean asked, coming down
the stairs to meet her.

Ruby's stomach dropped. She had placed so
much importance on this stupid interview, and
it really did mean nothing to Boone. "We set it
up yesterday. But if he has work to do, we can
reschedule for another time. It's not a big deal."

"He's collaborating with Piper Starling on her
new album. He didn't know he'd be doing that
until she showed up yesterday as a surprise,"

Dean explained. "You want me to walk you back there and we'll see how they're doing?"

Piper Starling was the it girl right now. She had skyrocketed into stardom through country music, but she was popular with fans of other music genres, as well. Not only was she a talented young thing, she was gorgeous.

"Are you sure? I can come back."

Dean wouldn't hear of it. "If he set something up with you, I sure don't want to take the heat for sending you away. Let's go see what they're up to."

Ruby followed him to the studio and heard some raised voices coming from inside before Dean even opened the door.

"That's all well and good, Heath, but I don't take orders from you. You aren't my agent or my record producer. You definitely aren't *my* father." Boone had his back to the door. Ruby inferred from his tone that he was not in the pleasant mood she had been hoping for.

"I'm not trying to tell you what to do. I'm simply making a few suggestions because I know my daughter."

"Dad, please," a woman said.

"You might know her better than anyone on this planet, but that doesn't mean you're going to hover over me like a gosh darn helicopter!" Boone shouted.

"Hey," Dean cut in. "Everything all right in here? What's going on?"

Boone turned around, his face red with anger. He seemed ready to let Dean have it until he noticed Ruby standing behind him.

"Is it ten o'clock already?"

Ruby didn't know if he was asking her or Dean. Suddenly there were three pairs of eyes on her, and she was too overwhelmed to speak.

"Boone is trying to set some pretty unreasonable ground rules here, Dean," the other man said. "I thought we had an understanding that I oversee everything in my daughter's career. If she's going to be collaborating, I need to be involved."

"I'm done here for the day. I have to talk to Ruby." Boone pushed past Dean. "I told you this was a bad idea. If you think I'm going to sit here while her dad puts his two cents in every five seconds, you're wrong."

He guided Ruby out of the studio. She almost tripped on her way down the last step, but Boone caught her.

"You okay?" he asked, steadying her on her feet.

Ruby didn't think she was. She had no idea what she had walked in on back there, only that it had been horribly uncomfortable. "Are you?"

"I am now that you rescued me."

"What was that all about?"

Boone shook his head. "That is not a question I feel like answering today. I hope you brought some better ones." He began to walk away. Ruby tried to keep up with his long, angry strides.

"Are you sure you don't want to reschedule? You seem to have a busier day than you thought you were going to have."

"Yeah, tell me about it. Dean decided this was a great time to have Piper come to town. He's been trying to get me to collaborate with her for months. I don't know why he thought I was ready for this kind of thing."

"I can come back another time." Ruby hiked her purse strap, which was falling off her shoulder, and started to back away.

Boone took her hand and pulled her close. Their bodies collided, and Ruby was suddenly on fire. His eyes were the color of the sky after it rained, a bluish gray she could have stared at forever.

"If you leave, they'll pull me back in there. Stay. Please."

Ruby worried she was trembling. No one had ever had this effect on her. He made her feel out of control and protected at the same time. His body was strong and she wanted to melt against it, but she also wanted to run, stop herself from being swept away by the emotion he pulled out of her with a simple plea to stay.

"Only if you're sure," she managed to squeak out.

"I'm sure." His voice was low and gravelly. Now she was definitely trembling in his arms. "I want you to stay."

He released her and stepped back. She followed him to his trailer, taking deep breaths to calm her beating heart.

The Airstream was homier than she'd expected. There was a kitchenette and a couch that acted as a family room. There was probably a bed somewhere, as well. A curtain hung in the doorway between the kitchen and what she assumed was the bedroom.

Ruby stood by the door, unsure of where to sit. "This shouldn't take that long. I have only a couple of questions."

"What if my answers are very detailed?" he asked with a wink. How could he go from angry to charming so quickly? He picked up a guitar case from the small table in the kitchen area. "Do you want to sit here or on the couch?"

The couch meant they would have to sit next to one another, whereas the table put some needed distance between them. She chose the kitchen.

"Have you been playing?" she asked, nodding at the guitar case.

Boone set it down on the floor. "No. Pulled it out of the storage bin, but still haven't done anything with it yet."

"Now that Piper Starling is here, that could change, huh?"

He rubbed his jaw with the back of his fingers. "Who knows? Not if her daddy thinks he's going to tell me what's happening. I don't follow someone else's rules real well when it comes to my music."

"Your music, your process."

"That's right. Although my process hasn't been creating much music lately."

"Maybe Piper will be your muse," Ruby suggested, feeling a tad jealous of the fact that she probably could be.

Boone laughed. "We'll see. I've had a pretty blonde muse before, and all I have to show for it is a messy divorce and another reason to drink."

Sara Gilmore was his ex-wife and—based on Ruby's recent Google search on all things Boone Williams—quite a music star in her own right. She was gorgeous and talented like Piper. Ruby felt like a nobody next to them.

"Maybe we should start with the real questions." Ruby pulled out a notebook and the sheet of questions. She found a pen in her purse and clicked it open. "All right, let's start with what brought you to Grass Lake."

"Dean."

Ruby waited for him to expound, but he only stared back at her with his hands folded on the tabletop.

"Like Dean drove you here, or you came here to work with him?"

Boone smiled. "He didn't drive me. My agent did. Didn't we talk about this?"

"That was all off the record. This is official."

His smile widened, and Ruby felt her own lips curl up. "I'm here because Dean promised me a retreat," he replied. "Nashville was stressful. We thought the stress might have been what was interfering with my ability to write some new music."

Ruby wrote that down. "So you're here to write some new music and get away from stress. How is Grass Lake different than Nashville?"

Boone's forehead creased. "I don't know. It's smaller. People have mistaken me for a kidnapper. That's never happened in Nashville."

Ruby burst out laughing. Mary Ellen would die if she knew he was poking fun. "You don't want me to write that down, do you?"

"No, please don't print that I was accused of kidnapping. That would not help me out at all."

"Attempted kidnapping," she corrected him. "My daughter was wise enough not to get in the car with a stranger."

"True." Boone scratched the back of his neck. "How about we say Grass Lake is quieter and more peaceful."

"Really?"

"I don't know, but that sounds like what someone who's from around here would expect me to say."

Ruby jotted that down because he was right. That was exactly the thing this town would want to hear.

"What brought you to Grass Lake?" Boone asked as she wrote.

"Me?" Her pen stopped moving. "I thought I was the one asking the questions."

"Don't you know that you have to loosen up the interviewee by telling me a little about yourself? It'll make me less self-conscious."

Ruby wasn't so sure about that but decided to play along. "Violet."

"So Violet drove you here, or you came here for her?"

His laughter was infectious. When they both controlled their giggles, she gave him the truth. "She was having some trouble in Nashville. Acting out in school and fighting everyone, not just me. I was ready to bolt to Seattle and move closer to my sister, but Holly suggested we come here. She didn't want Levi to have me arrested for breaking our custody agreement, and she swears by the small-town community support."

"Good for Holly. Can you imagine how moody Violet would be if she lived where it rained all the time?"

"Hey, I haven't given up on Seattle," Ruby said. Leaving without the possibility of being arrested was the new plan.

"You still want to move across the country? What about Violet's dad?"

Ruby didn't know what to do with his disapproving tone. "I think I should go back to asking the questions. What have you enjoyed most about visiting our small town?"

Boone's gaze fell to his hands. "Some of the people."

"Some?"

His eyes lifted, and they made her breathing hitch. "I haven't met that many, since I'm stuck out here on the farm, but the ones who show up now and again have been pretty special."

Ruby wasn't sure what to write down. Her hand wouldn't move, anyway. She cleared her throat. "Do you want to elaborate on that a little? Jesse is pretty awesome. You could say something nice about him in particular."

"Jesse is a good guy. I'm not sure I want to mention him, given his profession. That would lead to a whole lot of speculation. Know what I mean?"

Ruby nodded. Of course. He didn't need the press to write that he was hanging out with a social worker. They would assume he was getting therapy here. Maybe he was, but that was no one's business.

"Maybe Faith?"

"I was thinking more like this cool kid who's helping me train one of the horses, and her mom, who looks really beautiful today. Did you do something different with your hair?"

Ruby's face surely flamed red. She combed her fingers through her hair. "Not really. I don't wear it down a lot. Maybe that's what you're noticing."

"I like it."

She swallowed hard. She couldn't deal with his compliments or the way he was looking at her. Violet's voice in her head was whispering, *Told you so.*

"I have no clue what you want me to write for this one. You've enjoyed meeting some of the people, especially some of the ones you've met through Helping Hooves? That could be a nice plug for Faith."

"See? You're better at this reporter stuff than you thought you'd be."

Ruby finished the rest of the questions Holly had sent her, carefully writing down his answers and checking with him to make sure she didn't say anything that would bother him later.

"Okay, last one." Ruby read straight off the paper. "'Since you are single now and obviously attracted to—'" She stopped and folded over the piece of paper so he couldn't see the full question. Ruby was going to kill Holly. Thank God she hadn't handed over these questions to Boone yesterday like she had planned.

"What?"

Holly probably thought she was hilarious. This was her way of getting back at them for his refusal to meet with her and his demand to have Ruby do the interview. She lifted the paper and finished reading the question.

Since you are single now and obviously attracted to my best friend, Ruby, what can she expect when you finally take her in your arms and kiss her?

Ruby crumpled up the sheet of questions and held it tightly in her fist. "Nothing. We're actually done. There are no more questions."

"Are you sure?"

Oh, Ruby was sure. There were no more questions for him but a million more she was asking herself. What would she do if he kissed her? Did she want him to kiss her? She was beginning to think she did. That was bad. Wasn't it?

CHAPTER FIFTEEN

"VIOLET, COME AND stand on the other side of her so she has a little more pressure to turn where we want her to." Boone waited beside Willow. It had been three days since he had walked out of his brainstorming session with Piper and he had spent them horse training instead. It seemed like a much better use of his time.

Jesse wanted to see if Boone and Violet could work together to get the stubborn horse around the arena without having to use the walls to make her feel trapped.

Willow had done pretty well this session. The training was beginning to pay off. They hadn't mounted her yet, which was the next step. Having someone on her back while they led her around would most likely be a challenge for her.

"Good girl." Violet stroked Willow's neck as she took the corner and stopped when Boone wanted her to. "You are such a good girl."

"Yes, she is." Boone gave the horse some love, as well.

Dean entered the arena just as Jesse came over to talk about how they felt about what they had accomplished today. Boone knew why he was there. He must have finally convinced Heath to back off.

"What about you, Boone?" Jesse asked. "How does it feel when you think about where we started and where we are now?"

"I feel darn proud of myself. I wasn't sure she was going to comply without us using a whip or something more punitive. I'm glad we stuck with nurturing her rather than bullying her to do what we wanted."

"Kindness counts," Jesse said. "We can all win when we give people what they need instead of only focusing on what we want."

"Another social work lesson? I thought we were volunteers today, not patients."

"This isn't a mental hospital, Vi. You are never a patient," Boone reminded her. At least, that was the way he liked to think about it.

"You know what I mean. My mom isn't paying for this, is she? I told her this wasn't therapy."

Jesse put a reassuring hand on her shoulder. "This is not therapy, but you know me. I can't stop being a social worker just because it's not social work time."

Dean paced alongside the fence by the gate. He gestured to Boone to come over. Boone would rather have had a therapy session than talk to Dean about his failed collaboration with Piper. That was saying something.

"Which one of you is going to help me take her to the tack room?" Jesse asked.

"I think Dean wants me for something," Boone said.

"Oh, sure," Violet complained. "I bet you told him to show up right at the end of training so you could get out of the work. So typical, old man."

"I would rather go to the tack room, I swear. In fact, I would rather go shovel manure in the paddock."

"We could work something out, if you're really interested," Jesse offered.

"Boone!" Dean's patience had worn thin.

"Sorry, looks like the boss is calling." He jogged over to Dean, reminding himself what Jesse was trying to teach him today. "What's up?"

"I think we need to sit down and figure out the best way to approach this opportunity to work with Piper."

Boone bit his tongue. His first impulse was to tell him he was happy walking away from this so-called opportunity and that Heath Starling could take a leap into Grass Lake. But Boone needed to remember he was here to get his career back on track. As much fun as he was having with the horses, his career was music.

"I'm not sure what you want from me. I haven't been able to write a song for myself, so why do you think I'll be able to write a song for her and me to sing?"

"I thought maybe if we took some of the pressure off, you could figure it out. This song isn't just yours. She wants to learn how to write songs. Maybe some of her creative spirit will rub off on you and *bam*, you'll have twenty songs pouring out of you."

Unlikely. "I won't sit in a room with her and her dad. You want to know why that girl can't write her own music? Her father is suffocating her. He's going to snuff that light right out if he's not careful."

"Let's not worry about Heath Starling now. I will deal with Heath. I need you to tell me you're willing to sit with Piper and try to write a song. She can come here and you guys can have the studio to yourselves, or if you want to hang out in the house, we can do that, too. Whatever you want."

What Boone wanted and what Dean needed were two very different things. Jesse's lesson of the day echoed in his brain. *"We can all win when we give people what they need instead of only focusing on what we want."* Boone should at least see if Jesse was right.

"Fine. I'll meet with her as long as her daddy stays away."

"Thank you," Dean said like Boone had just offered him the sun and the stars.

Boone hoped Dean wouldn't be disappointed. Meeting with Piper and writing a song with her were not the same thing.

"I knew you'd be reasonable about this, so I got you something." Dean led Boone out of the arena. A shiny red pickup truck sat in the parking lot.

"This had better not belong to someone else you want me to work with."

"Nope, this is the truck you can use while you're here. I trust you aren't going to use it to run away and you won't break any laws that will force the wonderful state of Tennessee to revoke your license once and for all."

Boone let that comment go because he was too happy about having a set of wheels. He had nowhere to go, but the fact that he could go somewhere if he wanted to was enough.

Dean handed him the keys. "I'll see if we can work something out for you and Piper to get together a few hours a day the rest of this week and next."

Hopefully it wouldn't be a complete disaster. Boone went to the tack room to help with Willow. Jesse had been right about needing purpose to get through each day. Violet and Jesse were cleaning the filly up and checking for any problems.

"Oh, look who shows up when we're almost finished." Violet didn't look up from the horse.

"Hey, I'm feeling a little attacked. I wonder if there's something bothering you that we need to talk about. I want you to be as in touch with your feelings as I am."

"Don't mock the assignment," Jesse warned.

"I'm serious," Boone said. "We were getting along fine, and then she got snippy."

"I am totally in touch with my feelings. I'm not really mad. I'm kind of jealous, I guess. Dean shows up and you ditch us. I get it, but it bugs me."

That was way more honest than he expected Violet to be. "I didn't realize you felt that way. I'm sorry you feel like that."

"It's not your fault. It's not like anyone is paying you to do this."

"You're right, no one is paying me. Dean brought me here to write music for his record company. Recording music is my job. I do

this—work with you two—because I want to.
I hope you understand what that means."

"That I shouldn't expect you to have time
for us. You have a job to do and a life to live."

Boone glanced at Jesse for some support.
Again, her response wasn't what he'd expected.
Was that what this poor kid thought about all
the grown-ups in her life?

"Is that how you feel all the time? Like people have priorities and you fall at the bottom
because you aren't as important as someone's
job?" Jesse asked.

"Well, you make me feel important, but
that's because it's your job to do that. My mom
pays this place so you'll be here for me. But
no one is paying Boone, so he doesn't have to
be here."

"She's not paying me right now to spend
time with you. I asked you to help me with
Willow because I thought you'd like it and I
knew I could count on you."

Violet didn't seem so sure.

"When I pointed out the difference between
this and my job, I meant for you to see that I
could do anything I want when I don't have
to work, and I choose to do this," Boone explained. "That's how much I enjoy hanging
out with you and working with Willow. That
makes this way more special than work."

"Really?"

"Absolutely, kid. I'm sorry if I made you feel any different."

"I wish my dad said that kind of stuff," Violet said to the ground.

"Your dad makes you feel like other things are more important than you?" Jesse asked, taking over again. "That has to hurt."

Violet nodded.

Boone was grateful Jesse was here to handle this. He felt completely unequipped to help her through this. It broke his heart to hear this amazing kid say she didn't think she was more important than her dad's job.

A sinking feeling came over him as he listened to Jesse and Violet talk about that wound of hers. Did Emmy feel that way about him? Did she think he didn't care about her as much as he cared about his career? How many times had he sent her that message? Too many. How many times had he made her feel like drinking was more important than she was? Way too many.

He was a terrible father. It was no wonder she didn't answer his calls.

"I'm going to put Willow out and give you guys some privacy," Boone said, unlatching the leads from the hooks. He needed the fresh air more than anything. The panic and the pain were overwhelming.

He put Willow in the paddock with the other horses. She seemed happy to be with her new friends. Horses were like people. They were social beings. They needed to feel wanted.

Boone pulled out his phone and sent a text to Emmy. It simply said that he loved her. He needed her to know even if she deleted it. She would see it and it would mean something that he'd sent it to her for no reason in the middle of a random day. At least, he hoped it would.

He watched the horses play and occasionally glanced down at his phone to see if Emmy had replied. She hadn't, but he could see that she'd read it. That was going to have to be enough for now.

"Sorry for getting all emo in there." Violet stood next to him, staring straight ahead at the horses. "That was embarrassing."

"Don't apologize for having feelings, kid."

"My mom's on her way. I was thinking maybe we could all have dinner tonight if you aren't busy. We like to go to this place called Pizza Sam. You could meet us there around six," she suggested.

How could he possibly say no?

"I could do that. You probably owe me for agreeing to be your trainer for the next show."

"Probably," Violet agreed as she tried to hide her smile.

"Six o'clock at Pizza Sam. I'll be there because Dean got me a truck." He turned and pointed at his loaner.

"Nice. I feel like there's a song in this pickup's future."

Boone ruffled her hair. She really was something. "I'll get right on that. Maybe it can be the star of the duet between me and Piper Starling."

"You're singing with Piper Starling? What is it? A father-daughter ballad?"

"Hey, I'm not old enough to be her dad." That was a low blow. Piper was somewhere in her midtwenties, and he wasn't turning forty until the end of the year.

"Whatever you say, old man."

Ruby drove up and rolled her window down. He hadn't seen her since their interview. She had her hair pulled back today and no makeup on. She didn't need that stuff to look pretty, though. She was a natural beauty.

"How'd it go today?"

"Fine," Violet said, running around to the other side to get in. "Can we go to Pizza Sam tonight with Boone? He's treating."

He should have called that one.

Ruby turned toward Violet. "Don't assume he's always going to pay. That's rude."

"I think I can afford a pizza for the three of us."

Ruby's gaze met his. "You don't have to do that. If she asked you to come out for pizza, she shouldn't ask you to pay."

"Are you offering to take me out?"

Her eyes went wide like he had scared her. "Not like a date."

"No, not a date," he said in agreement. "We wouldn't be on a date. Violet's going to be there. You're bringing me along for dinner. Like…" He couldn't think of the right word.

"Like a family," Violet said. "We'll see you at six. And if I can't afford to go to college because my mom had to buy dinner, it will be all your fault."

"Violet," Ruby scolded. She turned back toward Boone. "Don't listen to her."

"I'll see you at six." For a family dinner. Why did that scare him more than a date?

CHAPTER SIXTEEN

"Can I go over to Peyton's house?" Violet had actually spent the afternoon in the family room. On her phone, but not locked away in her room. That was huge.

"What about dinner?"

"I'll text Boone and ask him to pick me up, since I'll be out by Helping Hooves."

"You'll text Boone? For real? Do you know what Mrs. Davis would say if she heard you could text Boone Williams?"

"I forget he's famous," Violet said with a laugh. "I don't know why, I even searched 'How famous is Boone Williams' on the internet. There's a lady in Texas who has an entire room in her house dedicated to him. She has pictures of him all over her walls and a hat he supposedly wore at a concert that she bought on eBay for, like, a million dollars or something, and a bandanna that she wiped on him when he was shaking hands with people in the front row so it would have his sweat on it. People are psycho."

"He's pretty famous. And you're going to ask him to pick you up from your friend's house like he's an Uber driver?"

"It's fine. He'll do it. He probably needs directions to the restaurant, anyway."

"I'll pick you up." Ruby was not going to let Violet take advantage of the man's kindness. She couldn't believe he would come out to dinner with them in the first place. He had Piper Starling in town. They could drive into Franklin and have a five-star meal. Pizza Sam was good, but not *that* good.

"Oh my gosh, Mom. It's fine. I texted him and he said fine."

"You texted him?" Ruby got up to see for herself, but Violet pressed her phone to her chest.

"Mom, privacy. He said it was a good idea. Can you please take me to Peyton's now?"

He was probably being nice. Ruby didn't have his number to check, though. Her thirteen-year-old had the contact information of one of the biggest names in country music and she had nothing.

She drove Violet where she wanted to go and stopped by Holly's on the way back. Ruby had left her a nasty message after the interview with Boone and refused to answer her calls since then. It didn't help that her best friend's first response was to laugh hysterically.

Ruby rang the doorbell and was greeted by Holly's husband, Jon. He welcomed her in and shouted for his wife.

"She was getting worried you were never going to forgive her," he said as he shut the door.

"I seriously considered it."

"Oh, come on," Holly said, coming down the stairs. "I thought you would review the questions before you read them to him. It was supposed to make you laugh, not send you into a tizzy."

Ruby held out her handwritten notes. "You can type these up and make them into something interesting."

Holly opened her arms for a hug. "Forgive me?"

"You're so lucky I didn't read him the whole question." She hugged her friend and put the whole incident behind them.

They went to sit in the kitchen while Holly reviewed the answers. She did a lot of nodding while she read, made a surprised face once, then set the papers down. "Good job. It would have been nice if you dug a little deeper, but my guess is he was a tad reluctant to give much away."

"He said meeting me and Violet was one of the best parts. He said I was beautiful." The words came flying out of her mouth like a breath she'd been holding too long.

Holly's big eyes bulged. "Are you kidding me right now?"

"And Violet has his number in her phone and he's meeting us for dinner tonight. Not only that, but he's picking Violet up from a friend's house and bringing her to dinner like he's her dad or something. This is getting really weird."

"I...I don't even know what to say." Holly sat back in her chair with her mouth agape.

"Right? I don't know what to say, either. And thanks to your little joke, all I can think about is how I would literally pass out if he kissed me."

"He's going to kiss you. Boone Williams is going to kiss you. And are you kidding me about Violet having his number? When did we enter the twilight zone?"

Ruby wished she knew. This entire thing was surreal. The first time they'd met, she hadn't even known who he was. The second time they'd met, he was a complete jerk. Now he was coming to a family dinner and she wanted to kiss him.

"Okay, we have to figure this out," Holly said, getting up and pacing around the kitchen.

"You need to invite him back to the house. Violet will go up to her room because she always goes to her room. You'll be alone. You'll offer him some wine. You'll drink, you'll talk and then…he'll kiss you."

"I can't offer Boone wine. Haven't you read the tabloids lately? He's a recovering alcoholic." Another huge red flag telling her she should stay far away.

"Okay, skip the wine. Offer him some dessert."

This was crazy. Ruby was not going to invite Boone back to her house. He was not going to kiss her.

"He's a famous singer. I am nobody. He'll be gone soon, and ideally Violet and I will be gone in a year. This is pointless."

Holly sat back down and grabbed Ruby's hands in hers. "You deserve to be kissed by someone gorgeous and famous. It doesn't mean you have to marry him. Enjoy the moment. You used to be the girl who knew how to live in the moment better than anyone."

"And look where that got me. I can't be that person. My decisions affect more than just me. I'm not sure Violet should get attached. There's no way he's going to be in her life when we move to Seattle."

"What if you stayed? Made a life here? You like it here, don't you?"

"Levi lets Violet down every time we let him get close. The best thing I can do for her is get away. Put some distance between them so she can move on and not be stuck in this limbo, wondering whether he'll show up."

Holly's boys ran through the kitchen, giggling and screaming. Trevor was in the lead with Zander at his heels. Henry trailed behind them with drool covering his chin and a giant smile on his face.

"Careful, you guys," their mom warned. She turned back to Ruby. "I don't envy the position you're in. I really don't. But I still think you should let Boone Williams kiss you if that's what he wants to do."

The boys came through again, this time being chased by their father, who was doing his best impression of a monster. The boys kept looking over their shoulders and squealing.

Holly would never understand what it was like for Ruby. She had an incredible husband. Jon loved his boys as much as he loved their mom. He was present and engaged. He helped with baths and bedtimes. Holly was luckier than she knew.

"Kiss your husband tonight," Ruby said. "He deserves it."

WHEN RUBY GOT to Pizza Sam, Boone was already there. He had on a baseball hat and had been seated in the back corner, away from everyone else. Ruby's heart began to beat faster and harder. If he did kiss her, she'd never survive.

Boone stood up as she approached the table. "Where's Violet?" he asked.

"What do you mean? She told me she was coming with you."

The confused expression on Boone's face told her that was not the case. "Why would she come with me?"

Ruby took out her phone and texted her daughter. "I dropped her off at a friend's house near the farm. She said she texted you about picking her up and you said you would."

"I never got a text from Violet. She doesn't even have my phone number."

She really was a great liar. All the worst-case scenarios began to run through Ruby's brain. "She'd better still be at Peyton's."

Ruby's phone chimed with a text from Violet with a picture attached of her eating spaghetti with her friend.

SURPRISE! Enjoy your date with Boone. You both need to have some fun.

She'd done this on purpose? Ruby replied that she did not think this plan of hers was the least bit funny. All she got back was a smiley face.

The humiliation Ruby was experiencing was beyond any she had felt in her life. "Well, apparently my dear daughter decided to set us up on a surprise date."

"A surprise date?"

Ruby put down her phone and picked up one of the water glasses on the table, emptying it in a couple of large gulps. Maybe it would cool her off before she had a complete meltdown.

"We should go. I should probably pick her up and ground her for the rest of her life or something."

Boone covered her hand with his. "Or…we could have dinner and plot our revenge."

Ruby immediately relaxed. If he wasn't mortified by their current predicament, perhaps she didn't need to be, either. They perused the menu and compared favorite toppings, settling on a veggie lover's pizza.

The waitress came over to take their order and eyed Boone for a second before asking, "Maybe I'm crazy, but did you know you look exactly like Boone Williams?"

Boone smiled up at her. "I get that from time to time."

"I mean, you *really* look like him. You could work as one of those impersonators. People would have a hard time believing you weren't really him."

"That's a good idea. I wonder how much money I could make doing that."

"I think you could do pretty well. People would hire you on the spot. That's how strong the resemblance is."

"Something to consider," Boone said, clearly wishing she would move on.

Ruby bit the inside of her cheek to keep from laughing. When the waitress finally left, Ruby's shoulders shook. "Where do Boone Williams impersonators work? County fairs? Birthday parties? Company picnics?" she wondered aloud.

"I can't imagine."

"I don't know whether I'd like it if wherever I went, people knew who I was."

"It's part of the job. But you might be surprised to know that some people have no idea who I am." He gave her a pointed look.

"In my defense, I had heard of you. I didn't recognize you."

"Fair enough."

It became pretty obvious that most of the other people in the restaurant did not have any trouble recognizing him. A young couple a few tables away had their phones out and were not-so-nonchalantly taking pictures. The girl's flash went off each time.

Boone leaned over the table. "Once those hit social media, we might be in trouble."

"Do you want to take the pizza to go? We could hide out at my house," Ruby offered. "There's no one there to alert the media."

The waitress was conferring with a family at the table closest to the door. They all glanced in Boone's direction and seemed to determine he was no impersonator.

"Do you know if there's a back door to this place?" Boone asked Ruby.

"Right through there is a game room. There are video games all along the wall. In the left corner, there's a door that goes out to the parking lot."

Boone dropped his voice to a whisper. "I'll pretend to go to the bathroom and sneak out. You ask the waitress to wrap up our pizza, and I'll meet you at your house."

The whole room was beginning to buzz. Everyone knew who was seated in the corner. It was now or never. A woman with hair bigger than Texas got up and shook off her friend who begged her not to bother "him."

"Go now," Ruby said. He didn't hesitate.

Boone took off down the hall, and Ruby stood up, blocking the woman's pursuit.

"Is that Boone Williams?"

"Is who Boone Williams?" Ruby asked, stepping to her left when the woman stepped right.

"It is, isn't it? Can I get a picture? I'm a huge fan."

"Of who?"

The woman didn't find her as funny as Ruby found herself. "Can you get out of my way? What are you, his bodyguard?"

Ruby let her past, figuring Boone should be safely in his car by now. She waved the waitress down and changed their order to takeout. As she waited, the thrill of the getaway wore off and the realization that Ruby had invited Boone to have dinner *at her house* set in.

What was she thinking?

CHAPTER SEVENTEEN

BOONE WAITED FOR Ruby and their pizza in her driveway. He wasn't sure if he should be glad their plans got changed or not. He had been so nervous about the family dinner that pizza with Ruby seemed like no big deal. Pizza with Ruby alone in her house felt like a bigger deal.

A knock on the passenger window made him jump. Ruby's neighbor waved and apologized. He didn't want to, but he rolled down the window.

"Ruby's not home. I saw her leave a little while ago when I was putting the garbage at the curb."

Boone nodded slowly. "I know. She'll be back in a minute."

"So I just have to ask, are you two really friends? How did that happen?"

Boone wanted to tell her it was none of her business, but Ruby lived next to this woman. She probably wouldn't appreciate him being nasty to her neighbor. "We met. We became friends. And, yeah, that's pretty much it."

She was unsurprisingly unsatisfied with that answer. She kept the most fake smile on her face, though. "Have you known each other long?"

"Have you?"

Taken aback, she answered, "We've been neighbors for a few months. Our kids are so far apart in age that we don't really run in the same social circles. She's not exactly attending playgroup!"

"Right. Well, it was great catching up with you. It's kind of chilly. Have a good night." He raised the window back up and gave her a little wave goodbye.

She stood there stunned for a moment and finally headed back to her house. Poor Ruby. That woman was the epitome of a nosy neighbor.

A few minutes later, Ruby pulled in next to him. She put a smile on his face every time he saw her lately. Today was no exception. He climbed out of his truck and offered to carry in the pizza for her. It smelled delicious.

"I had a nice chat with that neighbor of yours."

Ruby unlocked the front door. "Oh, no. Mary Ellen? Why do I feel like that didn't make your night complete?"

"You should know she's desperate to find out how this friendship started."

"What did you tell her?" She pushed open the door and flipped on the light.

"We met. We became friends."

"That's it?"

Boone followed her into the kitchen. "It drove her nuts that I wouldn't tell her what she wanted to know. Is it really so strange that you and I would get along? According to her, people with kids the same age tend to run in the same circles. We have kids almost the same age."

She pulled out two plates and set the table. "I think it's the fact that you've performed in front of millions of people all over the world and I deliver babies in rural Tennessee."

"So it's the fact that you have a noble profession and I'm nothing but a monkey on a stage?" Boone opened the pizza box and placed it in the center of the table.

Her laugh made his heart bang in his chest. "Right, that's it."

"Napkins?" he asked.

Ruby found some on the counter. She snapped her fingers. "I forgot our drinks."

"Water's fine." Although a glass of something stronger would sure help these nerves. He had other feelings messing with his head—feelings Jesse would tell him to identify and manage. Admitting feelings like the ones he was having could be awfully dangerous.

The kitchen was small but tidy. Boone got the impression that Ruby either loved to clean or hated to cook. Considering the refrigerator was almost empty when she opened it to get the water pitcher, he assumed the latter was true. She filled some glasses and sat down across from him. The smell of green peppers and mushrooms made his mouth water.

"Mary Ellen is probably waiting for you to come back out. Having you here once made her head spin. But twice? It will likely explode if she doesn't get to the bottom of the relationship."

"There are so many things I want to do with that information." Boone could give Mary Ellen several reasons to freak out. Part of him wanted to take Ruby outside and kiss her silly. The other part knew if he did that, he'd want to do it again and again.

If there was one thing Boone knew better than anything else, it was how easily he could become addicted to something, and Ruby had the potential to become more lethal than all the drugs in the world.

Friends. They could be friends. That was safe and made him feel happy when he considered it.

"Please don't do anything. She's really not

that bad. I think I'm self-conscious. She's so perfect and I am so far from perfect."

"What are you talking about?"

"There are people in this world who some-how manage to make life look effortless. I am not one of those people, and Mary Ellen is. That's probably the real reason she can't wrap her head around someone like you wanting anything to do with me."

Boone wanted to laugh. Ruby managed life a whole lot better than he did.

"I don't blame her, really," she continued. "When Violet and I moved in, I probably scared more than just Mary Ellen with my madness. The truck I had rented was on its last leg, and I don't think it had any shocks."

"Bumpy ride, huh?"

"Yeah, that's an understatement. I'm kind of surprised it didn't break down on the way here. On top of that, I was a terrible planner. I had things wrapped in my bath towels and old magazines because I hadn't thought about anything other than getting boxes. Thanks to those bumps and my shoddy packing, a few things were damaged, and a few curse words might have been shouted loud enough for the neighbors to hear."

Boone remembered what a fired-up Ruby

was like. "Jesse would be disappointed in you for not handling your frustration better."

"Oh, that's not the only thing that would have disappointed him. My parenting skills were less than stellar that day, as well. I think Violet set a record for eye rolls, and our shouting matches were epic, as she would say."

"There are few things more stressful than moving. I'm sure your neighbors understood that."

"Yeah." Ruby's gaze dropped to her plate as she played with a piece of crust. He was reminded of her remark about moving to Seattle. He hadn't been sure what bothered him more, that she wanted to take Violet far away from her dad or that she wanted to move far away, period.

They ate in awkward silence for a couple of minutes. Boone wanted to kick himself for not knowing what to say to snap her out of this. Luckily Ruby pulled herself out of her head on her own.

"How long do you plan to stay in Grass Lake?"

He raised his eyebrows. "I don't know. I guess either until I record something for Dean or Grace Note decides to drop me from the label because I can't write anything."

"So it could be a month? Six months? A

year?" Ruby's curiosity was curious. Was she asking because she wanted him to leave or stay longer?

"I doubt Dean is going to give me a year or six months. The label needs artists who make records. They've been more patient with me than I probably deserve. I give them my excuses and try to convince Dean I'm more important to him than I really am. But I would say I've got less than a month to prove to him that I'm still an asset."

That was the sad reality. Boone was on the verge of being a washed-up has-been. He hated thinking he was replaceable, but there it was. The public had a short attention span. He was fortunate that anyone still cared about him.

"Less than a month," Ruby repeated. She got up and put her plate next to the sink. She stood with her back to him. "Violet will be sad when you go. She almost likes you better than Jesse, and that's saying something."

The pizza in his stomach suddenly felt like a lead weight. Boone had become more attached to Violet than he'd ever imagined he would be. And based on what she admitted today after the training session, she must have felt the same. It really wasn't surprising that she had tried to set Ruby and Boone up. The kid was obviously looking for someone to step up as her dad.

Boone wasn't her dad. Couldn't be her dad. He was already failing miserably at being Emmy's dad. There was no way he wanted to ruin someone else's life.

But he was an addict, and addicts wanted what they shouldn't have. He wanted not only to be part of Violet's life but to be in Ruby's, too. He came up behind her and put his hands on her hips.

"I like her, too. I care about you both. I shouldn't. I'm not good for either one of you, but I can't stop these feelings."

Ruby leaned against him. Her eyes were closed as she let her head fall back on his shoulder. "We're all wrong for each other," she said.

Boone ghosted his lips down the side of her neck and planted the softest kiss where it met her shoulder. Her mouth fell open and she shifted to face him. Her eyes glowed in the soft light of the kitchen. She felt so right in his arms, he couldn't convince himself to stop making this mistake.

"So wrong, but you're so beautiful I can't help myself," he whispered before capturing her mouth with his own. He wanted this. He wanted her. It was selfish, something he was so good at being.

Ruby's hands traveled up his chest and over his shoulders, linking behind his neck. She wasn't pushing him away or asking him to stop. She pulled him closer, kissed him back deeper.

Kissing Ruby was like putting a Band-Aid over a cut that needed stitches. It couldn't fix what ailed him, and it was going to hurt like heck when she ripped it off. He pulled back enough to catch his breath. Resting his forehead against hers, he wished the room would stop spinning.

She brought her hands to his face, grounding him and bringing him back to earth. When he dared to open his eyes, hers were there, staring back with a kindness that stole his heart. She kissed the corner of his mouth, a sweet little peck like she was testing his ability to be gentle.

"I wish I was stronger." Her voice trembled. "You're a dream I can't resist but a risk I can't take."

Her words broke his heart. If he were a better man, he'd give her the world. Right now, he'd have to settle for giving her the space she deserved. Even though his body felt like it was made of rubber, he stepped back and took her hands from his face.

"I should go. Thank you for dinner. Sorry for…" There were no words to describe what had just happened between them.

"You have nothing to be sorry about," she assured him.

As much as he wanted to kiss her again, Boone mustered up the courage to do the right thing and walk away.

BOONE MANAGED TO make it back to the farm without stopping at a liquor store. When he got in the trailer, he nearly tripped over his guitar case.

The Gibson guitar that had been specially made for Boone hadn't seen the light of day in so long, it might be nothing but dust by now. An ache in his chest made him set the case on the table and unlatch the buckles.

His hands tingled with anxiety. They wanted to wrap around the neck, slide down the strings, glide along the curves of the body. They shook as he lifted the guitar out of the case. He took it back to the bedroom and switched on the bedside lamp.

She was a pretty guitar. Not that she didn't have her scars. There were some dings in her body from being on tour after tour. The back of the neck was worn from use. He used to play her all the time. Back when music filled Boone's soul instead of draining it.

He strummed the strings. She was a little out of tune. It had been a while. But after a few adjustments, she sounded like the pro she was.

She reminded Boone of Ruby. She was a little bruised and battered but still beautiful. She needed someone to care about her, to hold her and bring her to life. Ruby had been so alive when they'd kissed. So had Boone.

Kissing Ruby wasn't something he was going to forget anytime soon. She made him feel things he had tried so hard to block out. Being numb had become his normal. It was the way he survived each day.

Numb. Comfortably numb.

Ruby's affection for progressive rock was rubbing off on him. Boone wasn't the greatest guitarist of all time—he was no David Gilmour—but if he could hear a song in his head, he could make his hands play a rough version of it.

He pulled up a song by Pink Floyd on his phone and listened to it with closed eyes, letting it all sink in. It was one of those songs people knew no matter what kind of music they liked.

The words tugged at something deep inside.

When the song ended, Boone picked up his guitar. He strummed a couple of chords. And then he let the music have its way with him. He sang about the pain, he sang about taking a shot to forget the pain, he sang about floating away and he sang about being comfortably numb even though he was anything but.

As the words came, so did the emotion. For the first time in a long time, Boone didn't hold back or fight it from coming to the surface. He welcomed it with open arms as the tears ran down his face and dripped down his chin, landing on his jeans.

He would be numb no more.

CHAPTER EIGHTEEN

RUBY STOOD IN her kitchen, unable to move, unable to process what had happened. Boone had kissed her. It wasn't a sweep-you-off-your-feet kind of kiss. It wasn't naive or shared between two people ready to put their hearts on the line. It was full of all the messy things that were sure to make it a mistake. They were both afraid and unwilling to open up too wide because they both knew where that would lead.

It was the most honest kiss she'd ever shared with someone. All wrong, but so right. Two people giving in just enough that they didn't completely break.

When her legs remembered how to move, she snatched her keys off the table in the hall and went to pick up Violet.

There was a grin on Violet's face as she got in the car. She thought she was smart, but she was too young really to understand.

"Did you have fun tonight?" she asked, obviously pleased with herself.

"We need to talk."

"Oh my gosh, Mom. I know I shouldn't lie. I was trying to do something nice for you guys. You both like each other, but you're too chicken to ask out someone famous like Boone. And he's a guy and guys are clueless. Tell me you didn't have fun."

Ruby wasn't sure how to explain this to a thirteen-year-old. "I know you've gotten close to Boone at the farm. I know he's been there for you. And believe me, I appreciate that. I think he's been wonderful to you."

Violet immediately jumped to the wrong conclusion. "You blew it. Didn't you? I swear, if you were mean to him or said something—"

"Vi," Ruby interrupted. "We had a perfectly fine time. What I want you to understand is that grown-up relationships aren't easy. And as much as Boone and I might like each other, we aren't ready to go on dates together, especially surprise dates."

"What's the big deal? I know he likes you. You like him. Don't even lie and tell me you don't. I thought single moms were supposed to be happy when their kids liked the guy they wanted to date."

"It's not that simple, honey. Boone is going to be in Grass Lake for maybe a month. And then what? He'll go back home to Nashville and we'll be here."

"Maybe we should go back to Nashville," Violet said, taking the conversation in a direction Ruby did not want it to go. "Boone and Dad both live there. It's perfect."

"We aren't going back to Nashville. Do you remember how much trouble you were getting into there? Listen, you know how we talked about visiting Auntie Brit in Seattle?" Violet nodded. "Well, I've been thinking about moving us out there. We would be close to family and have a fresh start."

"How am I going to see Dad if we move to the West Coast? It's hard enough now."

Ruby gripped the steering wheel a little tighter. When had this conversation turned into one about Levi? She could feel her control slipping.

"It is hard. It's always going to be hard because your dad is your dad. He has different priorities than we do. I know you wish he would be more involved. I do, too. But it seems to me that you are doing a lot better the farther we get from him."

"You want to take me away from Dad?"

"No, honey. I want to take you away from the pain and disappointment. I want you to be happy."

Violet stared out the window wordlessly.

She looked about as happy as a snowman in the rain.

"The point of this conversation is, I don't want you to get your hopes up that something is going to happen between me and Boone."

She parked the car in the driveway, and Violet didn't waste a second. She pushed open the door and climbed out. "Don't worry, Mom. I get it. You ruin everything. You say you want me to be happy, but you just make me miserable."

She slammed the door behind her. That went how Ruby should have expected it to go. Didn't every conversation end with Violet telling her she was failing at this mom thing?

Ruby rested her head on the steering wheel, and the tears came even though she begged them to stop. Violet wanted something she couldn't have. Ruby understood how hard that was. She wanted things, too. Things she couldn't have because they wouldn't last. They wouldn't be what she needed in the end.

THE NEXT MORNING, Violet stayed in her room listening to music and probably texting her friends about how much she hated her mom. Ruby sat at the kitchen table with her laptop and tried to make sense of her financial situation.

Violet might think she wanted to stay in

Tennessee, but that wasn't what was best for her. Ruby was her mother, and sometimes she had to make tough decisions for the family.

"Hello?" Holly was right on schedule. Ruby was actually surprised she hadn't been at the door first thing this morning, fishing for date night details. She hadn't even heard about Violet ditching them.

"In the kitchen," Ruby called out.

Holly had Henry on her hip. "Soooo…"

"Soooo, what?"

She took a seat at the table and set Henry on her lap. "Rumor has it that Boone Williams was spotted at Pizza Sam last night with an unidentified redhead. Not a redhead and her teenage daughter, just a redhead."

"Interesting." Ruby tickled Henry's belly, and he quickly hid his face against his mother's shoulder. She wasn't sure what she should tell Holly about last night.

"I also heard from June Anderson, who heard from Betsy Clausen, that Mary Ellen claims she saw Boone Williams sitting in his truck in your driveway. He told her he was waiting for you."

"I didn't know Mary Ellen was such a gossip."

"Totally!" Holly went to playgroup every other week to get Henry out of the house. "Those moms are all about everyone else's business. Where do you think I get all my good information from?"

"I'd better be careful what I say around you."

"I am not a gossip!" she protested. "But I will tell you that Mary Ellen told Betsy that he was being very coy about your relationship. She's sure you two are…" She waggled her eyebrows.

Small towns and their rumor mills. Unbelievable. "Boone and I are not…anything. He got recognized at the restaurant. We had to leave so he could eat in peace. We came here and ate pizza, and he left. I'm sure Mary Ellen saw him leave."

"I'm sure she did. But I can't believe he only ate pizza while he was here. There had to be some conversation, maybe a kiss good-night?"

"There was some conversation." She could at least cop to that.

"No kiss?" Holly looked so disappointed.

"Can we talk about something else?"

Holly narrowed her eyes, obviously thinking about what that meant. Ruby could tell she was suspicious that there had been a kiss but that she wouldn't admit it. "What would you like to talk about?"

"I need your opinion on my life plan."

"Well, that's a little more serious than a kiss, I guess."

One of the things Ruby missed most about Levi was having someone to make plans with. In the honeymoon phase of their relationship, they had talked about what they wanted and helped each other figure out how to get there. Now Ruby usually had to figure it all out on her own. Getting Holly's advice was a godsend.

"Given my current income and regular expenses, I should have enough money to hire a lawyer before Thanksgiving. If I can get a court hearing after the holidays, Violet and I would have to spend only this school year in Grass Lake, and she could start high school in Seattle."

Levi would put up a fight in the beginning, but when it came down to it, he'd miss a court date and the judge would see that giving her full custody and the choice to leave Tennessee was the right thing to do.

"And you really think what you want is far away from here?"

"Violet set me up on a date with Boone last night. She ditched us so we could…I don't know…fall in love. She thinks that if I got together with Boone, we could move back to Nashville and she'd have Boone and her dad in her life."

"That sounds like a pretty good life for both of you."

Ruby wasn't a fan of fangirl Holly. "That's a fantasy. I need her to live in reality. Boone and I can't date. He told me last night he's not good for me or Violet. How do I argue with that?"

Henry was restless. All this grown-up talk was boring him to death. He wiggled off Holly's lap and took off running.

"Is Violet around?" Holly asked. "Maybe she could entertain him for a minute so I can talk to you about this life plan of yours."

"She's been locked in her room since last night. Come on, Henry! Do you want to see Violet?" The little boy came running back in and nodded. Ruby took his hand and helped him up the stairs. She knocked on the door, knowing she wouldn't get a response. "Vi, Holly's here with Henry. He really wants to see you. Can he come in?"

She wouldn't let Ruby in, but no one could resist a red-cheeked two-year-old with big sky blue eyes like his mom's. Violet didn't come to the door, however.

Ruby turned the knob, but it was locked. "I told you what would happen if you kept locking this door. Open up, please."

Still no answer. This was ridiculous. Henry knocked on the door with his little fist. Ruby pulled out the bobby pin holding her hair out of her face. She straightened it and stuck it in the tiny hole on the doorknob. The locked popped right open.

"You are seriously grounded," Ruby said, madder than a wet hen.

The bed was made like no one had slept in it. The music playing came from the tablet on the desk, and Violet's window was wide-open.

Ruby couldn't think or speak. Her heart beat so hard it felt like it could break her ribs. She picked Henry up and ran downstairs.

"What's the matter?" Holly took Henry from her.

"She's gone."

CHAPTER NINETEEN

WHAT AMAZED BOONE the most about some singers was that they could own a song so thoroughly on stage, but they didn't have the first clue what it took to write that song. Piper was one of those singers. The girl was so talented; she had the voice of an angel. But she didn't have any idea about writing songs.

Her lack of knowledge placed the burden to write this duet squarely on Boone's shoulders. He hadn't been able to write a song in years.

"What do you usually write first, the melody or the words?" Piper asked. The two of them had been sitting on Faith's front porch for two hours. Their brainstorming session had been fruitless thus far.

"It depends. Sometimes a riff gets stuck in my head, and sometimes I have something specific I want to say and have to figure out how to put it to music afterward."

"Well, what do we want to say? Maybe we should start there."

That was the million-dollar question. Boone

set his guitar down. Thanks to his emotional breakthrough last night, the only thing he wanted to sing about was how good that kiss had been. He didn't feel comfortable singing that kind of song with Piper.

"Maybe I'm trying to inspire you."

Piper rubbed her hands together. "That's good. Inspire me to do what?"

Write her own darn songs so he had to worry only about himself. "I don't know. To climb every mountain? Swim every sea?"

Her eyebrows pinched together. "I think some of that's already a song."

"I know." Boone leaned back in his rocker. "What do you want me to inspire you to do?"

She thought about it for a minute and came up with nothing. "Songwriting is hard."

Boone laughed. She was cute. Too young for him in a romantic sense, but cute in a little sister sort of way. "That's why you should always be good to your songwriter."

"Maybe it could be a father-daughter thing. Something every girl will want to dance to on her wedding day with her daddy."

Daddy-daughter hit a little too close to home. In the same way singing a love song seemed wrong because of his feelings for Ruby, singing to Piper as if she was his daughter felt like a betrayal to Emmy.

"I'm not old enough to be your daddy, sweetheart. Let's stick with the motivational theme."

"What if I'm in love with you, but you aren't in love with me, or vice versa? I could be crushing on you big-time and you could be telling me to find the right guy, but that he's not you."

"That might work." He picked his guitar back up and tried to find a melody that could spark some lyrics. "We need a good hook."

He played around with a couple chords. Nothing was right.

A car that Boone immediately recognized as Ruby's came barreling down the lane. She was in an awful hurry to get here. He set his guitar back down and went to the railing.

"Is she here?" Ruby shouted as soon as she got out of the car.

"Violet?"

"Yes, Violet!"

Boone smirked. He had to give the girl credit for working so hard to get the two of them together. He came down the steps and was about to make a snarky comment when he noticed the tears in Ruby's eyes and the way her bottom lip was trembling.

"What's wrong?"

She fell into his arms and tried to explain through her sobs. He made out a word or two. The most important ones were *run* and *away*.

He hugged Ruby tight, afraid to let her go. "When's the last time you saw her?"

Ruby calmed herself enough to make sense. "Last night." She pulled back. "She hates me. She thinks I ruined things with you on purpose and that I want to keep her away from her dad. Oh my gosh, what if she tried to get to Nashville on her own? What if she's on her way to Levi's?"

She ran back to her car. Boone stopped her. "Hold on. Relax. Did you call him?"

Ruby shook her head. "I didn't want to tell him what happened until I checked with her friends and here first. But she's not here. You haven't seen her?"

"That doesn't mean she's not here. If she took off last night, she could have hunkered down somewhere. Let's go look in the barn."

The stalls had already been mucked, and the horses were grazing in the pasture. Boone wasn't sure where to look that someone hadn't already been this morning until he remembered that the hay room had plenty of space to hide in.

He opened the door and checked high and low. In the back corner of the loft, he spotted a pair of boots sticking out from behind a stack of hay.

"Violet, I swear, if that's you, I am going to

strangle you," he said, waiting for her to show herself.

The legs disappeared. "It's not me. So you can go away."

Of course she was going to be difficult. "She's up here," Boone called down to Ruby. He climbed all the way up and crawled over to where Violet was hiding. "What was the plan, exactly? Move in, live off horse water and hay?"

"Go away, Boone. I'm serious."

Violet had a backpack and some major dark circles under her eyes. "Looks like you had a hard time sleeping last night." He sat next to her even though she turned away from him. "Your mom was worried sick. Goal accomplished."

"I don't care about her. She doesn't care about me, so what's the point?"

"I know for a fact that your mom cares about you a whole lot. And that you love her, too. I mean, why else would you try to hook her up with somebody as amazing as me?"

"Yeah, well, she ruined that, didn't she? She says she wants me to be happy. She doesn't even know how to do it herself. She doesn't even try."

"That's not true," Ruby shouted from the ladder. "I know how to be happy. I don't need a man to be happy, Vi."

"Oh, great. Here comes another empowerment speech. We don't need guys to be happy. Girl power. We can do whatever a boy can do. Guys will only let you down. Dad doesn't love us. Boone will never love us."

"I never said that," Ruby argued. "You know I didn't say that."

"That's what you meant."

Boone suddenly felt caught in the middle. He glanced over his shoulder. Ruby was still on the ladder. "Do you want to switch places with me?" he asked her. Ruby climbed down so he could get out of her way. He gave Violet's knee a squeeze. "I think you and your mom need to talk without me."

"I hope you know she likes you, but she loves being miserable more. She's such a hypocrite. She wants me to be happy, but she's scared to be happy herself."

"Your mom's not alone. I'm scared, too, kid. As much as I like your mom, I'm terrified of messing things up for you. For her."

"You won't mess things up if you don't want to mess them up. Jesse says we can't control how we feel, but we do get to choose how we act."

She was a wise young lady, but screwing things up had become a habit Boone was struggling to break. He hated letting Violet down.

She was another name to add to the long list. But he didn't trust himself not to hurt the both of them in the long run.

"You're not the only one who listens to Jesse. He'd also say you chose to run away because you were mad. Now you have to deal with the consequences."

Boone backed out of the hayloft and climbed down the ladder. Ruby looked so completely defeated, he had to give her a hug. She fit against him perfectly, like they were made to support each other. He kissed the top of her head. "Do you want me to find Jesse?"

"That would probably be a good idea," she whispered against his shoulder. "I'm a terrible mother."

"No, you're not." He would have given anything to take away her pain. Hers and Violet's. "I'll get Jesse."

He left them in the barn and sought out the only person who might actually help them get through this. Jesse was in the arena with Faith and another client. He didn't hesitate to come to Ruby's aid when he heard what had happened.

"Violet listens to you," Boone told Jesse. "She's trying to do the things you tell her, but there's a world of hurt inside that little girl."

Jesse nodded. "Listening is easy, emotions

can be overwhelming and changing old habits is hard."

Wasn't that the truth.

Boone watched Jesse go into the barn and said a prayer that they'd work it all out. He returned to the porch, where Piper was patiently waiting.

"Is everything okay? Did you find that woman's daughter?"

"We found her."

"Oh, thank God. Poor kid. Things must be really bad to make her want to run away."

Boone didn't want to talk about Violet with Piper. She could never understand. Piper came from an intact family with a father who was involved in her life. Too involved, if you asked Boone. Piper looked at the world with her rose-colored glasses. She didn't have a clue about the heartache and pain that lurked out there, but maybe she could sing about it.

Inspiration hit, and Boone picked up his guitar and played some chords. He hummed a tune, and the words came to him in a rush. He grabbed the pen and the blank notepad on the table between them.

Boone poured all of Violet's heartache into Piper's verses and filled his with all the frustration he felt for not being able to be the one who could help her through it. The emotion fueled his art in a way it never had before. He had all the lyrics written before Ruby, Violet and Jesse emerged from the barn.

"How did you do that?" Piper stared at him in awe. "And can you teach me how?"

"I don't know how to teach you. I suggest you go out in the world and get your heart ripped out a few times. Apparently that helps." Boone tore the pages out of his notebook and handed them to Piper. "Copy these down. We'll try to put them to music tomorrow in the studio."

He couldn't let Ruby and Violet go without knowing if they'd sorted things out. He put his guitar down and jogged over to their car. Violet had her backpack slung over her shoulder. She appeared to have packed for more than a few days.

"Heading home?"

Ruby's eyes were rimmed red, and Violet looked like she could fall asleep standing up. A nap might do them both some good. "We are," Ruby answered. "Thanks for your help."

"Anytime. Maybe I can come get Violet later and bring her back to work on some stuff with Sassy. Are we still going to the show this weekend?"

His question seemed to add to Ruby's weariness. "I don't know. I need to think about it."

Violet let out a disgusted sigh.

"Hey," Boone snapped at her. "You made the choice. You deal with the consequences."

She gave him the evil eye but didn't argue, opening the car door and tossing her backpack in first before getting in herself.

"Whatever you decide is fine," Boone told Ruby. "I just thought maybe it would be good for her to have a purpose today. Sulking in her room might not help her work through this."

Ruby rubbed her eyes. "We'll see."

"What's your phone number? I'll text you later and see what's up."

"You want my number?" she asked, a tad more surprised than he thought she should have been.

"I can't text you if I don't have your number. I promise not to call in the middle of the night or send you anything inappropriate." That earned him the slightest smile. He'd take it.

She rattled off her number, and he sent her the pizza slice emoji to make sure he got it right. She glanced down at her phone and let out the tiniest laugh. He'd take that, too.

"Now you have my number," he said. "Don't call me in the middle of the night, but feel free to send me inappropriate texts if you want."

She replied back with an emoji that definitely wasn't telling him he was number one. "Is that inappropriate enough for you?"

"Not exactly what I was referring to, but I'm sure you'll get the hang of it eventually."

"Thanks again," she said, touching his arm. "Sorry for showing up here such a wreck."

"No worries." He opened her door to keep himself from kissing her sadness away. She got in and he closed it behind her.

Not caring about them was impossible. Figuring out what to do about that was his next challenge. Violet and Jesse were right—he couldn't control his feelings, but he had a say in what he did about them.

VIOLET SLEPT THE day away. Boone heard from Ruby when she finally rose from the dead. She texted that Violet was interested in riding if he was still willing to come get her.

Violet was quiet on the drive to the farm. Her dark hair was pulled up in quite a messy ponytail, and her cheek had pillow marks on it from sleeping so hard.

"So I spent the day playing my guitar and put on a one-man show for myself. I'm pretty impressive," he said, breaking the silence.

Boone hadn't been able to come up with something else new, but he'd revisited lots of his songs that he hadn't sung in years. He'd performed all his greatest hits and some that only the people who bought his albums ever heard.

"You sang your songs to yourself?" Violet asked.

He had sung to himself, and that was just fine. The music was his friend right now, and he didn't want anyone else to get in the way.

"All the cool kids are doing it."

"Right." Violet acted uninterested.

"You inspired me. You've been showing me up with this being-in-touch-with-our-feelings challenge Jesse gave us."

"A lot of good that's done me."

"It will all work out. You've got the right people helping you. Your mom. Jesse."

They were the same people helping Boone. He knew what Violet was thinking; it was similar to what ran through his head every day. What if there was no helping someone like him? He truly believed Violet had a shot at coming out of all this all right. Boone's damage was more extensive.

Violet was a victim of a bad situation. Boone was the victim and the perpetrator. The more he learned about why Violet was the way she was, the more he wanted to encourage her to tell her dad to get lost. It was an uncomfortable position to be in, considering how badly he didn't want Emmy to give up on him.

"Don't talk to me about my mom. If she tries to make me move to Seattle, I'll ask the judge to let me live with my dad."

Emmy was like Violet in so many ways except for the fact that she had lost hope her dad was going to get it together. Boone envied Levi. He had screwed up so much, and somehow it was Ruby who took the heat.

"You'd break your mom's heart."

"What about my heart? What if moving to Seattle breaks *my* heart?"

Boone didn't have an answer to that. The thought of Violet and Ruby on the other side of the country kind of broke his heart, too.

CHAPTER TWENTY

RUBY STARED AT her computer screen. She had written and deleted the first paragraph of her monthly advice column three times. What kind of advice could a single mother with a kid who hated her so much she ran away give to anyone? Mary Ellen should have been writing this column, not Ruby.

Her phone rang, giving her an excuse to take a break. It was Levi, and he didn't waste any time getting into it as soon as she answered.

"Why did I get phone calls and texts from Violet in the middle of the night about running away? And why is she asking me to come and get her before you force her to live in Seattle?"

Never mind that he was only getting around to asking these questions *hours* after those calls and texts had been sent.

"She was very emotional last night. I already had a session with her social worker, and we talked about how running away is not the answer when she's mad."

"Are you telling her you two might move to Seattle?"

Ruby wasn't ready to show her hand just yet, but apparently Violet had spilled the beans. "I have been thinking about visiting Brittney, and who knows? We might like it out there."

"You can't move out of the state per the custody agreement, Ruby. Don't think I won't take you to court if you try to take my kid away."

"Maybe I plan to take *you* to court so I *can* take your kid away. It's not like you want her, anyway. When was the last time you had her over for her weekend visit? When was the last time you even saw her in person?"

"Don't start with me. I have been really busy. Weekends are the worst for me. I have to ride to pay my child support. Do you want me to quit my job and stop giving you money?"

Threatening not to pay his child support was one of Levi's favorite tactics. She couldn't understand why he wanted to get under Ruby's skin more than he wanted to take care of Violet.

He had no idea that Violet would trade all the money in the world for some of his time. She'd have been happy with the same amount of time that he spent on a bull's back.

"It's been a really emotional day," Ruby said, "and I don't want to fight with you."

"That's what you always say. But you push my buttons anyway."

"I push *your* buttons? You're worse than a toddler with a remote control! All you do is push *my* buttons!"

Ruby squeezed the bridge of her nose. Fighting with him was always exhausting, and when she was tired, she tended to get mean.

"I called to find out what's wrong with Violet, not get into a war with you."

"What do you want me to say, Levi? Your daughter is doing everything she can think of to get your attention. She wants a dad so badly, she tried setting me up with Boone Williams the other night."

He barked out a laugh. "She wanted to set you up with Boone Williams? The country music star? What did she do, email his fan club or something?"

His disbelief rubbed Ruby the wrong way. "As a matter of fact, Boone Williams, the country music star, is in town writing a new album for his record company. He's staying on the same property where Violet takes riding lessons and meets with the social worker."

"You've got to be kidding me. And Violet asked him to take her mom out on a date? Did the guy laugh or run away as fast as he could?"

Ruby's face heated, and she tightened her

grip on the phone. He needed to be put in his place. "We're actually quite friendly. He came to cheer Violet on at the horse show you missed and plans to be at the next one. Violet set us up on a dinner date, and we had a really nice time. He came back here and we...oh, you don't want to hear about all this."

She didn't care what kind of assumptions he made. Levi could think whatever he wanted.

"I don't believe you," he said, but the growl in his tone told her he feared it was the truth.

"Well, like I said, you can see for yourself if you come to the next horse show. But I know you have a life and it might be too hard to fit your daughter in."

"Whatever, Ruby. I'm going to call Violet to make sure she doesn't want me to come get her."

"She might not answer you right away, since she's at the horse farm with Boone. He's helping her get ready for the show. He's really great with her," Ruby said to add salt to the wound.

"I'll see you in court if you try to take her out of Tennessee." He hung up.

Ruby had hoped for a smug sense of satisfaction, but that feeling didn't come. Instead, guilt and regret showed up. She wasn't doing herself any favors making Levi mad. If a judge asked Violet which parent she wanted to live with at the moment, it would most likely not be Ruby. Levi could petition for custody just to spite her.

Why had she brought Boone into the mix? She was trying to make Levi jealous. Not just of a possible romance but also of his relationship with Violet. Using him like that made her sick, especially after everything that had happened in the past twenty-four hours.

A few hours later, the front door opened and Violet called out, announcing she was home. Boone stood in the foyer when Ruby came out of the kitchen.

"I'll see you later, kid. Good job today," he said to Violet before she took off for the solitude of her room.

"Did it seem to do any good?" Ruby asked him. Hopefully the ride and some fresh air had a positive effect.

"She's super grouchy today. I'm not even sure coming home to a new puppy would have improved her mood."

"Thanks for trying. I don't know what anyone can do to help her."

"We could fall madly in love, get married and live happily ever after. I think that might cheer her up."

He meant it to be funny. Ruby knew this, but it still did something to her to hear him say those words. It was like being kissed all over again. He had this way of drawing her in when she knew she should put up her walls.

She tried humor to keep the distance intact. "I'm sure that would do the trick. Too bad that's impossible. I'm a little out of your league."

"That you are," he said instead of giving it back to her. He reached out and cupped her cheek, setting her skin on fire. "What I wouldn't give to be what you needed."

Booned. She was so completely Booned, she didn't know what else to do other than lean into his touch. He had awakened feelings inside her that she thought were in permanent hibernation. If she could just get out of her head for a minute, she'd let go and kiss him one more time.

He dropped his hand and stepped back. His eyes were stormy blue, like he was waging his own war inside his head. "I'll see you around."

She couldn't manage to push any words to the surface, so she nodded and let him out. He'd see her around, but not for much longer. One month. He'd likely be gone in less than that, and this would be nothing but a memory.

Violet trudged down the stairs in a clean shirt and her favorite black leggings, which she wore so often they had a hole in both knees. "What's for dinner?"

"Leftover pizza," Ruby answered, but there were more important things to talk about. "Did your dad call you when you were at the farm?"

Violet frowned as she hit the landing. "No. Why?"

"He called to find out why you wanted him to pick you up last night."

"Oh, he finally got my texts and messages, huh?" She walked toward the kitchen.

Ruby almost wished Levi had come to get her last night. At least Violet would have felt cared for and important enough for him to drop everything.

"This is why I think going to live by Auntie Brit could be really good for us. We wouldn't have to sit around wondering if your dad is going to show up. We would know we were on our own. We would be choosing that."

Violet opened the refrigerator and pulled out the leftovers. "What if I don't want to be on our own?"

"I know you don't, but we are."

Violet didn't say anything. She put the pizza slices on some plates and stuck them in the microwave. Another gourmet dinner at the Wynns'.

"Say something," Ruby said. She realized

the slap of reality wasn't easy to take. But Levi could say whatever he wanted; he didn't have it in him to be there when Violet needed him. They had been on their own for a very long time and that was never going to change.

The microwave beeped and Violet retrieved their dinner, setting both plates on the table. She slid into her seat and took a napkin from the holder.

Ruby sat across from her, waiting to hear that she understood. In Seattle, Violet would have her aunt and uncle nearby, cousins to hang out with. It was a good plan.

Violet blew on her slice of pizza and set it back down. She put both elbows on the table and looked her mother right in the eye.

"I've decided that I want to go live with Dad."

CHAPTER TWENTY-ONE

ONCE BOONE HAD the lyrics of his new song cleaned up, the music came easier than it ever did. He had a song for Piper, one that would convince Dean he wasn't wrong for not giving up on him.

Wyatt thought it was incredible. He wanted to get some tracks laid immediately. For the past week, they'd worked on the arrangement without Piper, since she didn't play an instrument. Two days with some musicians, and they had the beginnings of something with real potential.

"Tomorrow we'll do vocals," Wyatt said as they shut things down for the night. "Maybe you and Piper can sing some of it together. I think it will help her to have you here."

Tomorrow was Sunday and Boone had plans. "I'm working with Jesse in the morning, but my afternoon is free."

"I'll set it up with Piper. She's been waiting for us to finish."

Piper had no idea what waiting was. Boone

had been waiting for this breakthrough for years. He'd finally found his voice again. His career might be resuscitated after all.

JESSE WAS WAITING for him by the smaller paddock behind the barn that Sunday morning after what seemed like the whole town, except for Boone, had gone to church. They had decided to meet for a bit before Ruby brought Violet over to work with Willow. It was their first official counseling session. Boone had pretended long enough that talking to Jesse wasn't therapy. It was the first therapy that seemed to be working.

"What do you say we ride instead of work today?" Jesse asked.

"Sounds good to me. No reason to act like I'm not here to talk."

They saddled up Willow and Sassy for a ride around the property. It was time to test the filly and see how she did with someone on her back. Boone believed all their hard work would pay off and she'd do great.

Grass Lake was surrounded by rolling hills the same color as Ruby's eyes. There was so much green, Boone sometimes forgot to feel blue. Willow showed no signs of trouble as they headed out.

"How's the song coming?" Jesse asked once they hit the trail.

"Good. I got one song written. I hope the rest will be that easy."

"And it felt good? I know you were worried about what emotions were going to come out of you in the process."

Terrified was more like it. "It didn't hurt. I actually channeled a little bit of Violet, so it wasn't my pain."

"Your relationship with Violet is an interesting one."

Boone waited for Jesse to ask a question, but he just left it at that. "What's that supposed to mean?"

"Nothing. I just wonder what it is about her that you relate to. Is it that she's about the same age as Emmy, or is it that something about her life reminds you of yours?"

Boone had to think about it. There were a lot of reasons he felt connected to Violet. She was funny and didn't treat him like anyone else he knew. She was like Emmy, but not. Emmy was blonde and blue-eyed. She loved being a girl and wearing dresses. At least, she had when she was younger.

"I don't know. I feel bad for her. She's hurting, and it's hard to see someone in that much pain and not want to do something about it."

"So you relate to her pain?"

"That, and my daughter won't talk to me. She hasn't answered any of my calls or replied to one text or voice mail. Violet lets me be there for her. She talks to me. She wants to know what I think about things. I would give anything for Emmy to do that."

"She fills that space that Emmy refuses to occupy in your life right now."

That was it. "Is that bad?"

Jesse adjusted his hat. "Do you think it's bad?"

"I don't think I'm doing Violet any harm. Except maybe giving her false hope that I'm going to fall in love with her mom."

Not that he couldn't fall in love with Ruby. He knew he shouldn't, so he wouldn't. For once, he was going to do what was right instead of what felt good.

"That's tough but not surprising. Violet feels connected to you. Wanting to find a way to make the connection more real, more concrete, is pretty normal. It's like the kid from a broken home who wants his dad to marry his favorite teacher."

"I never had a teacher I wanted to bring home. I never got the sweet ones. The school always put me with the strict disciplinarians."

"I wonder why," Jesse said with a laugh.

"I guess I've always been a little opinionated and quick-tempered."

Jesse just smiled and held in the sarcastic comment Boone was sure he wanted to make.

"You came here to make an album, and you're on your way to doing that. What happens afterward?"

"Get back in it. Tour, make public appearances, get on the radio, make videos."

"What about Emmy?"

What about Emmy? Boone wasn't thinking about his personal life, only his professional one. "I don't know. At what point do I give her what she's asking for?"

"What is she asking for?"

"She doesn't ask for anything. She doesn't want anything to do with me. She wants me to leave her alone."

"You know that for sure?"

"Well, no. But that's the message she's sending by not responding to any of my attempts to connect."

"It sounds like you want to walk away. Focus on your career and let her live her life."

Boone took a moment to mull that over. There was something very tempting about that plan. A man could take only so much rejection. Every unanswered call and text broke Boone a little bit more.

He also knew that no father was better than a bad father. Many times in his life, Boone had wished his own hadn't been around. His only memories of his dad were of an angry and unhappy man. Chase Williams had been critical and impossible to please. He had torn Boone down every chance he got. When he died, Boone had actually been relieved rather than in mourning.

Boone wasn't his father. He also wasn't the same man he had been a year ago, but he still wasn't the father Emmy deserved.

"I'd probably be doing her a favor."

"Do you really believe that? After all the work you've put in to get sober, to work through your issues, you don't think you deserve a chance to be in her life?"

"I can't be in her life if she won't let me," Boone argued.

"That's true," Jesse said. "I guess you need to decide what you want to do about that. How you're going to solve that problem. You have a lot of options. One of them is to let her go." He had Sassy speed up to a trot and moved ahead of Boone and Willow. "I'll be interested to hear if you think of some others."

The other option was to spend the rest of his life sending texts to someone who read them and probably deleted them. Soon he wouldn't even have Violet to make him feel like he was a decent replacement dad. Seattle was too far away for them to have any meaningful relationship in the future.

Boone's agitation distracted him as he rode. Something in the long grass alongside the trail spooked the typically anxious horse, and Willow jumped and changed direction so quick, Boone lost his balance. He was thrown to the ground and landed hard on his right shoulder.

Jesse doubled back to make sure he was all right. He was alive, but the searing pain shooting down his arm made Boone grit his teeth. His shoulder was definitely dislocated. Jesse chased down the scared horse and then helped get Boone on Sassy.

The ride back to the barn felt significantly longer than the ride out. Every bump in the trail made Boone want to cry out in pain.

Ruby and Violet pulled into the parking lot as Jesse was helping Boone into his car. They both came over with worried faces.

"What happened?"

"Tried riding Willow and she got spooked. Tossed me off and my shoulder's in bad shape."

"Why don't we take you to the hospital so Jesse doesn't have to leave work?" Ruby offered.

Jesse appreciated the help, so Boone got out of his car and into Ruby's. Violet had a million questions. She was concerned and a little mad that they had tried riding Willow without her there.

"I thought we were going to try riding her in the arena, where we could control things a little better."

The kid was right—that would have been smarter. The pain in his shoulder made Boone wish they had done that instead. "She was doing fine until I lost my focus."

"What were you thinking about? Willow is fragile right now. She needs you to guide her, not for you to be distracted by writing the next number-one song with Piper Starling."

"Hey," Ruby snapped. "Lay off him a bit, okay? You can give him a hard time later. Right now he needs to get that arm looked at."

Boone was grateful for her intervention. Little did Violet know he'd been thinking about how depressed he was that she and Ruby couldn't be a permanent part of his life.

A half-dozen people sat in the ER waiting room, keeping themselves busy in a variety of ways. Boone thought maybe he could use his celebrity to get him to the front of the line, but it was actually Ruby's connections that got him into a room fast.

"I'm sorry you have to waste the day here

with me," Boone said. Ruby had enough on her plate. She didn't need to be babysitting him.

"It's fine," Ruby assured him.

"Promise you'll never try something new with Willow without me, and I'll forgive you," Violet said from her spot by the door.

"Violet." Ruby's tone was a warning. There seemed to be something going on between them. He guessed they were still trying to get over the whole running away incident.

"What? We were supposed to be helping Jesse together."

Violet felt left out. Boone and Jesse should have thought of that before they saddled Willow up. "I promise that our work with Willow will always include you."

"Okay, you're forgiven."

If only Boone could gain everyone's forgiveness that easily. Violet hadn't experienced his failure to follow through on promises, though. She didn't know that sometimes he said he wouldn't do something and then did it anyway. The other people in his life knew better than to trust him.

Ruby squeezed his good hand. "Everything is going to be okay. They're going to pop that back in and give you something to take away the pain."

Boone closed his eyes. Her kindness was

overwhelming, but she didn't realize that medicine couldn't take away the things that truly pained him.

BY THE TIME they made it back to the farm with Boone's arm in a sling, it was late afternoon. No broken bones, but he had some nasty bruises. He had thought the dislocated shoulder hurt until the doctor had to pop it back in place. He now knew the meaning of the word *excruciating*.

"That doctor had to be kidding me—twelve weeks until I can go back to normal?"

Ruby came over to his side of the car to help him out. Boone shooed her away. He didn't need to be babied. He was fine.

"You should listen to the doctor. You don't want to do anything that makes that thing pop back out."

That was for sure. No way Boone wanted to go through putting that sucker back in again. He'd be cautious for a little while. Probably not twelve weeks.

"How are you going to play guitar with your arm in a sling?" Violet asked.

"I'll figure it out. I don't need to wear it all the time. It definitely won't interfere with my singing. Which I'm supposed to be doing right now. Thanks again for everything," he said, looking directly at Ruby.

"Glad you're all right. Call me if you need anything."

"I've got your number."

Her smile almost kept him from wanting to do anything else but stare at her for the rest of the day. "Yes, you do. Use it if you need it. Inappropriate texts are still a no-no."

"You ruin all the fun," he teased, returning that smile.

"I'm standing right here," Violet announced. "Can you two stop being so weird?"

Ruby and Violet went home, and Boone headed straight for the studio. He expected Piper to be in there recording her vocals. What he wasn't expecting was that someone else would be with her.

Standing next to Piper, Sawyer was putting his heart and soul into Boone's part. The part Boone had written. The part Boone had spent hours getting just right. He wasn't just singing it—he was singing it brilliantly.

Dean and Wyatt didn't even notice Boone come in. They were grinning from ear to ear, watching the two of them sing Boone's song.

"What's going on? A man can't be a little late after getting thrown off a horse?"

Dean turned and greeted Boone with arms

wide-open. "Oh, man. Look at you. Is it broken?"

"Why is he singing my song?"

Dean glanced back at the two youngsters giving it everything they had. Their chemistry was off the charts. It made Boone furious, and the angrier he got, the more his shoulder throbbed.

"Piper wanted to hear what it sounded like with someone singing your part," Dean explained. "You weren't here and Sawyer was hanging out, so we had him come in and mess around with it."

"This is my song."

"Yeah, of course it is." Dean had on that fake smile that Boone wanted to punch off. If he had a right arm that could punch, he might have done it.

"I'm here now." Boone glared at Dean, who wasn't getting the message. He shifted his focus to Sawyer, then back to Dean, waiting for him to put a stop to this.

"Oh. Yeah. Wyatt, stop the music playback."

"Just let them finish," Wyatt said. "I want to hear him sing the end again."

"How many times has he sung my song?" Boone could feel his blood pressure rising.

"We'll get you in there. Are you sure you're

up for it? Did they give you some pain medication?"

Boone had refused anything stronger than the over-the-counter stuff. He had a fear of pain meds. Too many people got hooked on those, and one addiction was enough.

"I'm fine," he growled back. He wasn't going to be fine for much longer if he had to continue listening to Sawyer sing his song. Thankfully it was almost over.

They finished, and Piper smiled up at Sawyer like he had handed her a platinum record. Dean hit the intercom to let them know how *amazing* they were. Boone adjusted the strap of his sling and winced at the pain shooting down his arm.

"Boone's back!" Piper squealed, finally aware of someone other than the twentysomething song-stealer standing beside her. "Did you hear that? How amazing is this song?"

Her enthusiasm was annoying. "I want to record my part in the booth alone," Boone told Wyatt.

"Okay. We tried her part solo, but it didn't go as well, so I don't have her track to play back for you."

"I don't need it."

"Come on out, Piper," Wyatt told her.

Everyone had a million questions about

Boone's shoulder and accident. Questions he didn't feel like answering right this minute. He wanted to record *his* song. He slipped into the booth and with some difficulty put on the headset with one hand.

"Let's work," he said. His chest was tight and his shoulder ached. He did a couple of vocal warm-ups while Wyatt pulled up the music playback.

The music started and Boone reminded himself to breathe. He sang the song, trying to push his anger aside and focus on what he was saying. Wyatt cut the playback.

"Let's try that again. You sound like you're mad. I'm not sure that's the emotion we're going for here."

No, mad was not the emotion he was going for. It was the one he was feeling. He needed to calm down, needed to think about something other than how Sawyer had come in here and sung his song like he owned it, like it had been written for him. Boone took a deep breath.

"Okay, from the top," he said into the mic.

Wyatt started the music. Boone tried again, and Wyatt let him get through the whole thing before offering his criticism.

"It sounds like you're shouting at her. Do you want to hear the track with Piper and Sawyer's overdub?"

"No, I don't want to hear Sawyer's overdub. I know how to sing the song, Wyatt. I wrote it, remember?"

Wyatt threw his hands up, his eyes widening. Dean hit the intercom.

"You're wound up. Maybe we should do this tomorrow. You've been through a lot today."

"No! I want to do it today. Get everyone out of here." He pointed at Sawyer and Piper. "I don't need an audience."

Dean frowned but asked them to leave. He probably said a whole lot of other things, but Boone couldn't hear him. He surely apologized for Boone's bad behavior. Well, maybe they should have thought about how he'd feel when they tried to steal his song.

With Piper and Sawyer gone, Boone went back to work. He ran through it ten more times. None of them were very satisfying.

"Let's call it a day. You're getting tired and sloppy," Wyatt said. "I can try to comp some of this together and see what we've got."

"No, I can get it. Let's just do the second verse a few more times. I'll get it."

Wyatt didn't look too excited but knew better than to argue. He cued up the part Boone wanted and they tried again. Boone couldn't get the words to come out the way he heard them in his head. It didn't help that his memory of Sawyer's version distracted him.

Three more goes and Wyatt called it quits. He pointed out that Boone seemed completely drained and it wasn't going to get better, only worse. Experience told Boone that Wyatt was right; pride made him want to do it again.

"I'll have Piper come in and sing it on her own, and I'll mix the two together. You can listen to it tomorrow," Wyatt said.

Reluctantly Boone pulled the headphones off and exited the booth. Dean had a sympathetic look on his face. It was worse than the fake smile.

"Get some rest. If you need anything, let me know. That shoulder will be feeling better in the morning."

Boone said nothing. He wasn't going to need anything. The damage had already been done. He couldn't sing his own song because Dean had ruined it by letting someone else have it first.

Back in the trailer, Boone tried lying down, but his shoulder wouldn't allow him to get comfortable. His head ached right along with the rest of his body. He tried to get his mind off the song and his pain. It drifted back to his conversation with Jesse that morning.

What other things could he do to get Emmy

to forgive him? Was there really anything that could work? He picked up his phone and called her. He had no idea what he was going to say. If she didn't answer, he wouldn't even leave a message.

"Emmy's phone," someone said after the second ring.

"Hello?"

"Hello. Who is this?" It was a boy. Why did a boy have Emmy's phone?

"This is Emmy Lou's dad. Who the heck is this?"

"Oh, sorry, Mr. Williams. Hang on."

Boone could hear the conversation going on the other side. The boy told Emmy her dad was on the phone, and she let him have it for answering. She told him to hang up and he refused. Maybe this boy wasn't as bad as Boone thought. The boy begged Emmy to take the phone and just say hello. When she refused, he suggested she tell Boone she couldn't talk right now. There was silence for a few seconds, and Boone worried Emmy was going to hang up.

Then her voice came over the line. "Please stop calling me. I don't want to know about how great your life is right now or how hard you're working to be a good dad. A good dad doesn't have to call his kid to find out what's happening. He doesn't have to ask how she's doing because he already knows."

"Em—"

"For the record, I'm great. I'm doing great without you. I've been doing great without you. I don't need you. Leave. Me. Alone."

She hung up and Boone sat frozen, the phone still pressed to his ear. How could he have thought resetting his shoulder was the worst pain he could feel? Hearing Emmy's plea was more excruciating than anything he'd ever experienced and ever would.

Feeling was for the birds.

CHAPTER TWENTY-TWO

"THERE'S LITERALLY NOTHING to eat in this house," Violet complained. She shut the refrigerator and went to the pantry. "I'm starving."

Ruby hadn't made it to the store. She hadn't been able to do much since Violet had dropped the bomb about wanting to live with her dad. Even as the days passed, she felt immobilized by the idea that her daughter would rather live with the man who had done nothing for her in the three years since the divorce and very little in the ten years before that.

"I need to go to Valu-Save."

"Let's go. I'll pick out what I want."

Ruby checked the clock. It was after six. Probably a decent time to go to the store. Surely all the good moms were home feeding their children wholesome meals complete with something from all five food groups. Plus, it was a Sunday night. They'd be able to get in and out relatively quickly.

Ruby grabbed her keys and suggested Violet bring a sweatshirt. That seemed like something a good mom would say. Violet rolled her eyes and headed out the door sans sweatshirt.

At the store, Violet didn't want to push the cart. She was too old for that. Too old to ride in the cart, too old to push it, too old to be tucked in at night, too old to give her mom a hug or kiss in public, too old to care that she was breaking her mom's heart by asking to leave.

Ruby roamed the aisles without much of a plan. They needed the basics—bread, milk, eggs.

"I'm going to go grab some of those snack cakes I like. I'll be right back," Violet said as Ruby compared the yogurt prices. Why were there so many choices, and why were some so much more expensive? Was there really such a thing as gourmet yogurt?

No yogurt. Violet didn't eat it, anyway. Ruby always ended up eating two cups a day to use it all before it went bad. She pushed ahead, skipping the baking aisle. Everyone knew Ruby didn't bake except when desperate to get Violet's attention.

She turned down the next aisle and spotted Boone immediately. His arm was still in its sling and a grocery basket filled with bottles was at his feet. He was taking another bottle of wine off the shelf.

Something came over her, and she barreled

down the aisle and hit his basket with her cart, ramming them both into him. Not the smartest thing to do with glass bottles around, but she would happily smash every bottle in the store if it meant Boone couldn't drink from any of them.

"Ow! What the—" His anger was quickly extinguished when he realized who he was talking to. His expression went from enraged to ashamed in a flash.

"Walk with me." She wasn't asking, and he knew it.

He left the basket where it was but didn't put down the wine in his hand. They walked out of the aisle and back to baking. Violet chose that moment to reappear. Ruby took the bottle from him and set it in her cart.

"Hey, old man. Come to buy some dinner like us?" She dumped an armload of junk food into their cart.

"Something like that," he mumbled. He didn't sound at all like himself.

"How's the arm? You don't look so good." Genuine concern was etched across Violet's face.

Boone was so out of it, he looked down at his sling like it was the first time he'd seen it. "Um, it hurts."

Violet didn't seem to notice anything was

off. Ruby was grateful for that but worried sick. Obviously he was in physical pain, but something major must have happened to push Boone to take two falls today, one off a horse and one off the wagon.

"How are you going to carry your groceries with one arm?" Violet asked. "Do you want me to get you one of those little baskets or a cart?"

Boone glanced over at Ruby. His shame weighed him down like a suit of armor.

"That's nice of you, Vi. Go grab him one of those baskets. We'll help him do some shopping." There was no way Ruby was letting him finish this trip alone or with anything alcoholic.

When Violet was out of earshot, Ruby turned to Boone. "Why didn't you call me?"

Boone didn't answer.

"Come over for dinner. I don't think you should be by yourself."

He shook his head. "Don't do that. Don't care about me, Ruby."

"Too late. We can call Jesse from my house. Whatever it is, we'll get through it without any booze. I'm here for you."

She put a hand on his good shoulder. He looked away and swallowed hard. His jaw was tight, and he pressed his fingers to his closed eyes. Ruby hadn't meant to make him cry in the middle of Valu-Save.

Wrapping her arm around him, she tucked herself under his arm and against his chest. He let his arm fall around her and kissed the top of her head.

"Thank you," he choked out.

Ruby gave him a gentle squeeze. His pain broke her heart, even if she didn't know where it was coming from. She let him go before Violet came back and got the wrong idea.

Boone sniffed loudly and wiped his face, pulling himself somewhat together. Violet returned with a basket. She had put a bottle of pain reliever in it.

"I'll carry your basket. You tell me what to put in it," she said. Her willingness to help put a lump in Ruby's throat. She was such a good kid underneath all her teenagerness.

"He doesn't need much. He's coming over for dinner," Ruby said, knowing he wouldn't decline if Violet was expecting him.

The three of them finished shopping and went to check out. Ruby had forgotten about the wine until they were unloading the cart at the cash register. Boone stared at it with a mixture of desire and regret. Ruby handed it to the cashier.

"We don't need this." And what Boone needed and didn't need was much more important than what he wanted right now.

Ruby suggested Violet ride with Boone. It was her guarantee that he'd come straight over without any stops at any other stores.

When they got home, Violet helped carry in all the groceries until she got a phone call from a friend. Upstairs she went, leaving Boone and Ruby alone.

"Should we call Jesse now or eat dinner first?" Ruby had no idea what she was doing. She could handle delivering a breach baby or consoling the parents of a stillborn, but talking an alcoholic off the ledge was unfamiliar territory.

Boone sat at the kitchen table. He scrubbed his face with his hand. "I don't know. I should go. I shouldn't be here."

"No, you shouldn't be alone. You shouldn't be standing in the grocery store with a basket full of enough alcohol to kill yourself."

He groaned and let his head fall back. "Had the liquor stores been open today, I might have been able to buy a lethal dose. A couple of bottles of wine wouldn't have done me in."

"Boone, what happened?"

"Let's eat first. We'll call Jesse later."

"Do you want to talk about it with me?" she offered as she unpacked the groceries. She wasn't sure if she wanted him to say yes or no.

"I can't go there right now," he admitted.

"Tell me about you. Have you two worked out your differences yet? I got the feeling that you were a little frustrated with her today."

"I'm not sure that hearing about me and Violet is going to cheer you up any."

"Why not?"

Ruby opened the pantry, grateful he couldn't see her face. She was sure it showed her misery. "Violet wants to live with her dad."

"What?"

"That's what she told me the day she came home from riding with you." She chanced a glance his way. His brow was furrowed. "I don't know what to do. She thinks we can talk to Levi about it after the horse show."

"You aren't going to let her go, are you?"

She lowered her voice, worried Violet might overhear. "I think I'm more afraid he's going to tell her no, and then I'll be left to pick up the pieces."

"You think he'll say no?"

Ruby didn't think. She knew. Levi had never contested the original custody agreement. He had no problem with Ruby being the residential parent. He was given his visitation and rarely followed through. There was no chance he was going to take on a thirteen-year-old full-time.

"Is dinner ready yet?" Violet shouted from the stairs.

The groceries weren't even all unpacked. Did she think they would unpack themselves? "Come help," Ruby called out. She moved closer to Boone. "It hurts that she wants to go, though. I can't stop thinking about it."

"It's not because of you. It's because of him. You know that, right?"

Ruby didn't know, but Violet shuffled in, looking none too happy about having to help. She'd have to wait until dinner was over and Violet returned to her room to continue this conversation.

Boone shifted in his seat and grimaced. He gave his shoulder a gentle rub. Ruby might not know how to solve all his problems, but she knew a thing or two about pain relief. She made an ice pack and poured him a glass of lemonade. Placing a couple of ibuprofen in front of him, she handed him the glass.

"Ice will help with the swelling. The pills will hopefully take the edge off." She could tell he wanted to say they wouldn't do the job as well as the wine she'd stopped him from buying, but he swallowed the pills anyway.

Violet voted for a taco dinner. Boone said he thought he could manage that one-handed.

As long as he didn't have to cut anything, he was safe.

"Are you still going to come to the horse show?" Violet asked Boone while Ruby cooked.

"Why wouldn't I? I'm not the one who has to ride."

"Just making sure. Sometimes people have to change their plans when things like this happen."

Violet thought that because of Levi's never-ending list of excuses. He always made it sound completely normal for him to back out of everything. It made Ruby sad that her daughter would always have trust issues, would always assume that people would let her down.

"I heard your dad might be there," Boone said, and Violet shot Ruby a look. Was she not supposed to mention it?

"He's going to try. His weekends are usually crazy, and when he doesn't have a rodeo or competition, he likes to chill out, since he doesn't get to do that very often."

"Can I ask you something?" Boone said to Violet. Ruby's shoulders stiffened. She didn't want him to ask her about moving in with her dad.

"I guess," Violet said, equally wary.

"What does your dad do or say that makes you willing to give him another chance?"

"I'm not sure this is a conversation we should be having," Ruby said, glaring at Boone.

"I'm not asking to make a point," he clarified. "I'm asking because I have a daughter and she says she's done with me. I'm wondering what Violet's dad does that keeps her willing to put up with the stuff he does—or maybe I should say *doesn't* do."

The reasons for his trip to Valu-Save were becoming clear.

"What did you do or not do to make your daughter say she's done?" Violet asked.

"That might be a little personal, Vi," Ruby warned. These two sure walked a fine line with each other.

"I'm trying to understand," Violet said. "I think Boone is nice. Why would his daughter not want anything to do with him?"

"Some things are private, honey."

"It's okay, Ruby," Boone said. "Maybe she should know."

"So, what did you do?" Violet asked again.

"I have a problem with alcohol. A bad one. I used to drink a lot every day, and when I was drunk, I did dumb things like try to drive a car and get in fights with people."

"You drove drunk?" Violet was flabbergasted. "Did you do it with your daughter in the car?"

"No, of course not. I usually wasn't around my family. My job took me away a lot, but when I was home, I was either fighting with her mom or drinking until I passed out."

"Wow. I can't picture you like that." Violet sat down across from him. "But you don't drink now."

"Haven't for a few months. I had to go to this place that helped me stop. Then I had to come here so I could figure out what to do instead of drinking when I was feeling bad."

"That's why you talk to Jesse."

Boone nodded. Violet needed a minute to process what he had shared. Then she asked, "What did she say to you that makes you think she's done?"

He scratched at the back of his neck and grimaced. "She said she doesn't want to talk to me and that I should leave her alone."

"I tell my mom that every day."

That was true. But Ruby could tell, based on Boone's reaction to his conversation with Emmy, that she wasn't simply being a touchy teen. His daughter's words had cut much deeper.

"I don't think she meant to leave her alone for a couple of hours. I think she meant for good. It's the first time she's talked to me in months, and she told me she's better off without me."

Violet propped her chin on her hand. She seemed to be trying to put herself in Boone's daughter's shoes. "Did you ever say sorry?"

"Did I say sorry for what?"

"For everything you did. You were a pretty bad dad. Really bad."

Ruby couldn't believe how blunt Violet was with him and how Boone didn't even flinch at her assessment. When had they gotten this comfortable with each other?

"I was a terrible dad. But I don't want to be anymore."

"Tell her that and say you're sorry. But you'd better mean it and *never* drink again."

The tips of Boone's ears turned red. He had almost failed tonight. He would have gotten drunk enough to do something stupid if Ruby hadn't caught him in time.

"I'm trying."

"I saw Mom give the lady at the grocery store that bottle. It reminded me of a lighter I didn't need but thought I wanted." Violet got up from the table. "Try harder."

CHAPTER TWENTY-THREE

VIOLET WAS WISE beyond her years. Boone had never met anyone like her. Or like her mother, who had literally saved his life tonight. He wasn't sure how he had gotten lucky enough to have these two in his life. Someone up above must have been looking out for him.

After processing everything with his thirteen-year-old therapist and eating dinner, they played some friendly card games until Violet lost two in a row.

"You two are cheating. You can't team up against me so Mom can win every time."

"Seriously?" Ruby said with a laugh. "You lost. No one cheated."

"I cheated, but I was trying to beat your mom, not you," Boone admitted.

Violet snatched the cards from his hand and pulled the pile together to shuffle. "See? I knew it."

"Cheaters always know who's cheating," Boone said to Ruby.

"I don't cheat," Violet said as she dealt a new game.

"Well, you don't cheat well. That's for sure," Boone teased.

Violet rolled her eyes and huffed. "I'm going to beat you so bad this game."

And she did.

"No fair." Boone tossed his cards down. "I totally cheated and you still beat me."

Violet and Ruby both laughed, and it was like medicine for his soul. They had no idea how much they were changing this day for him. But when things were good, when he was surrounded by people, it made the bad times and the loneliness that always came later that much more unbearable.

Boone needed to call Jesse. He needed to talk through some of the things that Violet got him thinking about and his fear of never having a family again. Because that possibility was beginning to sink in. As he sat in Ruby's kitchen playing cards, he realized what Emmy's rejection meant. It was the end of his family.

"I'm going to excuse myself and go make a phone call. You ladies feel free to play without me for a couple hands."

Ruby winked, and Violet carried on sarcastically about how it wouldn't be the same without him.

In the quiet, dimly lit family room, Boone sat down on the overstuffed couch. A framed picture of Violet as a toddler sat on an end table. She had hair the same color as her mother's. He wondered why she would ever dye such a beautiful color black.

He pulled up Jesse's number on his phone.

"Boone?"

"Any chance you've got some time to talk to an alcoholic who almost bought the entire wine selection at Valu-Save tonight?"

Jesse didn't hesitate. "When do you want me to come over?"

"ARE YOU SURE you want to go back to the farm? We have a spare bedroom," Ruby offered for a second time during their goodbye.

"I should go. Jesse's meeting me in half an hour."

"Jesse could come here," she suggested.

"Ruby," he said in a desperate sigh.

Violet had gone upstairs, and the temptation to kiss Ruby all night long instead of going back to the farm was strong. She must have been feeling the same way. She took his hand in both of hers and lifted it to her lips. She pressed a gentle kiss on his knuckles.

"I'm worried about you. I'd feel better if you

stayed here and let me take care of you and your hurt shoulder."

"It feels better, thanks to you," he tried to reassure her.

"If you leave, I'm going to be up all night worrying. If you stay, I'll know you're safe. I'll be able to get some sleep."

Her concern was touching, and he hated the thought of her up all night worrying about him. Staying here was tempting. Relying on her care was, too, but Boone needed to prove to himself that he could do this on his own. Ruby wouldn't always be there to save the day.

"I promise I won't do anything stupid. I'll keep Jesse there until I'm sure I'm okay."

She rested their hands against her chest. He could feel her heart beating. Did she have any idea what she did to his heart?

"I'm sorry it hurt so much to hear Emmy say those things to you. You know I understand better than anyone what it's like to be pushed away."

Her empathy was appreciated but misplaced. She was missing the bigger picture, the reason why he was trying not to fall for her. "But you and I are not the same."

"I know," she said, dropping his hand. "I'm not saying I understand everything you're going through, but I do know what it's like to love your kid and not always feel like she loves you back."

She didn't see what to Boone was so clear. They both might have felt rejected, but only one of them deserved it.

"No, I mean I'm not like you. In my family, I'm Levi. I have no idea why you even open your door to me."

"What are you talking about?"

"If you were my ex-wife, you would hate me and have every reason to do so. I've spent so much time convincing myself Sara's the bad guy in our relationship, I never thought about what I have really put her through. You and Violet have forced me to see the other side. Sara has been battling with me like you've been doing with Levi."

"You and Levi aren't the same."

"Aren't we? I've let my daughter down more times than I can count. I've put my career and my problems in front of her since she was born. I'm worse than Levi. At least he's apologized for not being around."

"More like given Violet thin excuses, Boone."

"I've never apologized. I blamed Sara. I blamed my drinking problem. I blamed everyone and everything except myself. I'm the bad guy."

Ruby's eyes welled with tears. "You're not a bad guy."

He cupped her cheek and wiped her tears with his thumb. "Thank you for thinking that."

Maybe someday he wouldn't be. It was time to change. To be the person he should be.

Boone stopped before opening the front door. "I hope you know that your amazingly honest and thoughtful daughter didn't get that way on her own. You taught her to be that way, Ruby. You should be proud."

JESSE WAS WAITING for him outside the Airstream. The concern on his face was greater now than when Boone had been thrown off the horse. Jesse knew all about addicts. He knew there was reason to be concerned.

They went inside and talked about what triggered today's episode. Boone told him everything from the issues with the song to the call to Emmy. He even shared Violet's insights.

"Making amends. Step nine. Are you sure you're ready for that?" Jesse asked. "There are quite a few steps to tackle first."

"I think I need a refresher on all twelve." Boone had only halfheartedly participated in AA—in any treatment, really. He had wrongly believed that the only thing he needed to do was not drink. He hadn't realized there was so much more to being sober.

"Making amends requires showing a lot of humility," Jesse said. "It's very much out of your comfort zone. But I think you can do it."

Being humble was one of Boone's biggest weaknesses and therefore the one he should tackle first. He had to do something.

Even after everything that had happened today, Boone said, "I think so, too."

Jesse had Boone make a verbal commitment to pick up the phone first the next time he was tempted and call Jesse. That was an easy promise to make. Boone never wanted to forget the shame he'd felt when Ruby spotted him with the bottle in his hand.

It was almost midnight when Jesse left. Boone felt like some of the weight he had been carrying had lifted. Funny that people called an addiction a monkey on someone's back, because Boone thought he could handle a monkey. He was lugging around a gorilla most days.

His guitar sat on his bed and called to him. Maybe music could put to rest the heavy thoughts filling his head. His shoulder had begun to ache again, but not enough to stop him from taking off the sling so he could pick up that old Gibson.

The farm was usually so full of life during the day. There were always people around. Faith had an army of volunteers who helped keep the place running. Clients came and went. The horses whinnied and nickered. But at night, it was so serene. The whole place went into a sleepy silence.

Boone strummed the guitar. The sound filled the empty space around him. If there ever was a night he needed the music, this was it. He didn't have a plan or a song on his mind. He let the music decide.

While he played, he thought about Emmy. He thought about how she must have felt when she needed him and he wasn't there. He pictured her on her bed, crying herself to sleep when she missed him. He thought about how much it must have bugged her to hear him talk about going to Violet's horse show when he hadn't attended one of hers in over a year.

He played and he thought until the words came. That night, Boone wrote a song. One about knowing it might be too late to say sorry but saying it anyway. He would be sorry for the rest of his days. It was also a song about making a promise. A promise to do better. To prove his *sorry* wasn't only a word. Words were nothing without actions.

That night, Boone wrote a song. A song he only wanted one person to hear, and he'd make sure she did.

CHAPTER TWENTY-FOUR

THE FOLLOWING SATURDAY was the horse show. Ruby's nerves had nothing to do with how Violet would handle the competition. She was more worried that Levi wouldn't show up. If he did, by some miracle, make it, then she had to worry about what he'd say when Violet asked him if she could live with him.

Everything seemed headed in a disastrous direction. How would she ever steer them back on course?

"Dad says he's going to meet us by the practice ring," Violet said as she typed something into her phone.

Wary of Levi's promises, Ruby asked her, "Did he say that today or before?"

"Just now. He said he's already there. The venue was closer to him than he thought."

Ruby was rendered speechless. Levi was not only coming but was already there? That never happened. He was perpetually late. It was his most reliable trait after being unreliable.

She tried to focus on the road and Helping

Hooves's truck and trailer ahead of them. It wasn't easy to ignore the creeping sense of dread, however.

"We should probably wait to talk to Dad about your living situation until after the show," Ruby suggested. She was in heartbreak preparation mode. She needed all the time she could get. "I don't want to start a big discussion right before you get on a horse."

"Whatever," Violet said, still staring at her phone.

"And I want you to remember that no matter what we decide today, Dad and I love you and only want what's best for you."

"I know, Mom."

"And there are a lot of things we have to work out before anything would be final."

"I *know*, Mom. Do you see any of my bags in the car? It's not like I thought I was going home with Dad after the show."

Ruby took a deep breath. She needed all her patience to get through today.

Once they made it to the exhibition center, Ruby prayed she wouldn't throw up. This show was much bigger than the last one. There were so many people, she wondered how they'd even find Levi if he really was here.

"I don't think I realized it was going to be this big," Boone said, echoing the thought in her head. "I have a feeling it won't be so easy for me to go undetected here."

She always forgot how his celebrity played a part in everything he did. It was very likely a high percentage of people here knew who Boone Williams was.

Jesse was unable to come to the show this time, so Faith had sent her brother along to help manage the horse. Boone's bad shoulder made it impossible for him to have full control of a thousand-plus-pound animal.

"Do you want me to go check her in while Sawyer and Violet get Sassy set up?" Ruby asked.

"Sounds like a good plan." Boone put on his sunglasses. He wore them like a shield. "I guess I'll stick to being more of a spectator today."

"You can hang out with Levi," Ruby said, dropping the bomb. "He's already here, supposedly."

"Oh, wow." He sounded worried. "I guess you'll be having that talk after all. Are you okay?"

"I'm terrified. But the show must go on."

He grabbed her hand. "It'll be okay. Whatever happens, I'm here for you. I know you'll figure this out."

His support and belief in her gave her the

boost she needed. She gave his hand a squeeze and let go so she could check Violet and Sassy in.

The registration area was packed with people. Some teams had several riders and horses competing in multiple levels. Helping Hooves had Violet. She was a one-girl team.

The coach in front of her in line had a list of at least ten riders. His black cowboy hat and boots reeked of money. His dark hair fell over his collar, and he had light stubble on his face. He looked more like a fashion model for some high-end Western clothing line than a riding coach.

Ruby glanced around at some of the other people in line. They all seemed to have a roster of riders. She tapped the man in front of her on the shoulder.

"Excuse me. Am I in the right line? I have only an individual rider."

He answered, "This is where you stand to check in teams." He dropped his list, and Ruby bent to pick it up for him. As she was handing it back, she noticed one of the names, and her heart clenched.

Emmy Lou Williams.

Ruby didn't hear a word the man said as he pointed out where she should check in her individual rider. Boone's daughter was here.

What if he ran into her? What if she said something to him that sent him into another tailspin? What if his ex-wife was here, too? She had to be here. She was like Ruby. She was the one who went to everything. Boone was Levi. No one expected him to show, yet here he was.

Only, Boone didn't know he was at his daughter's show. Ruby asked the man if she could see his list one more time. His eyebrows knit together. Maybe he wondered if she was scouting the competition. He let her see, watching her carefully.

Emmy wasn't in Violet's class. She had much more experience. With so many people here, there was a good chance their paths wouldn't even cross. Unless Boone wanted them to. She had to tell him. Prepare him like she'd prepared Violet.

"ALL CHECKED IN?" Sawyer asked when she found them by Sassy's assigned stall. Sawyer was a light in a dark room. He always had a smile on his face. His boyish good looks and abundance of charm made him impossible not to like.

"Where's Boone?" She was anxious to tell him what she'd learned at registration.

"He went to get our water bucket out of the trailer."

Violet seemed quite content, brushing and talking to Sassy. Ruby needed to get to Boone.

"Can you keep an eye on Violet? I'm going to go help Boone."

Sawyer gave her a curious look but didn't question her. Ruby made her way through the crowd, trying to remember where exactly they had parked. She spotted Sawyer's truck and nearly knocked someone over in her attempt to reach it.

Boone had his arm around a young woman in front of the truck. Was she too late? They seemed friendly, the opposite of what Ruby expected from this particular father-daughter reunion. She noticed a man with his phone out taking their picture. He gave them the thumbs-up, and the woman thanked Boone profusely.

Fan, not family.

"It was nice meeting y'all," Boone said as they took off. The woman excitedly checked the pictures her friend had taken.

"You've already been spotted, huh?"

"I told her I'd only pose for a picture if she promised not to post it to social media until after the show. She seemed trustworthy enough."

"Emmy's here." The words just tumbled out.

Ruby didn't mean to spring it on him with no warning.

"What?" He stepped toward her like he had been too far away to hear her correctly.

"When I was checking Violet in, I was behind a coach who had a list. I saw her name on it. She's here. She's competing today."

Boone paled. "Emmy's here."

Ruby nodded. She could scarcely imagine the thoughts running through his head. It had been almost a week since his accident. He had barely had enough time to get over the last interaction with his daughter, and now this.

He picked up Sassy's water bucket and started walking without waiting for Ruby. She caught up to him and slipped her arm through his.

"Whatever happens, I'm here for you." She wanted to be as reassuring as he was to her when they first got here, but she wasn't so sure everything would be okay.

Boone apparently wasn't feeling too confident, either. He wasn't ready to discuss how this would all play out.

"We need to get Sassy out and about," he said. "Get her used to this place so she doesn't get anxious when the competition starts."

Sawyer and Violet had Sassy ready to go when they returned. Violet was excited about showing off her horse to her dad.

"Do you want me to take Sassy for a walk around?" Sawyer asked Boone. "I'm not as famous as you are just yet. I don't think anyone will be stopping me for autographs."

Boone's eyes were searching the crowd. There was no telling where Emmy and her horse were. There were four barns on the property, and two of them were being used for the show. Emmy and her horse could easily have a stall in the other one.

"Yeah, that would be good. I already had one photo op in the parking lot. Hopefully once things get going around here, no one will notice me."

Ruby wondered if he wanted Emmy to know that he was here or not. "I'll stay with Boone. I'm a pretty good bodyguard. You and Violet take Sassy to get acclimated."

"If we find Dad, we'll bring him back with us. Okay?" Violet asked.

Ruby had almost forgotten about her own issues. Levi was here somewhere, as well. This day was getting better and better.

"Sure." She couldn't tell Violet no.

"Well, this day is not going the way I expected," Boone said once Sawyer and Violet were gone.

A nervous giggle bubbled out of Ruby. "Tell me about it." She took his hand. "Do you want to go look for her? I can come with you or I can stay here. Whatever you want to do."

He brought her hand to his chest and placed it over his racing heart. "I think I might be having an anxiety attack."

Beads of sweat appeared on his forehead, and his eye twitched. She encouraged him to take some deep breaths. As if she was helping him through labor, she talked him through the panic and breathed with him to keep him from going too fast.

"What's the worst thing that can happen?" she asked.

"She could freak out when she sees me and lose the competition and blame me for the rest of her life. There could be some terrible scene that gets recorded on all the cell phones in this place and finds its way to all the national media outlets. Sara could file to have all my rights taken away, and I'll never see my daughter ever again."

He was much too good at coming up with worst-case scenarios. "Boone, none of that's going to happen."

"It could." His breathing became labored again.

She modeled slow, deep breaths and waited for him to calm his body, at least. "No one is going to make a scene. If you're worried about seeing her before her competition, then let's not go looking until we know she's been in the ring."

"Maybe I should leave," he said. Ruby's face must have given away her opinion on that idea. "I wouldn't go anywhere but back to the farm."

"What if she's glad you're here? What if your being here makes things better? You let that lady take your picture. When this is all over, she's going to post that she saw you at this show. How would Emmy feel if she found out you had been here but didn't make an attempt to see her?"

He grimaced. There was no escaping this. "I shouldn't have taken that picture."

"Let's watch her ride, and then you can say hello. If she doesn't want to talk, that's fine. At least she'll know you were here and that you watched her. That will have to mean something. I know it would to Violet."

"Will you come with me?"

When he looked at her with those desperate blue eyes, he could have been asking for the moon. There was no way she could turn him down.

CHAPTER TWENTY-FIVE

BOONE ADJUSTED HIS hat and squinted at the agenda he had been handed on his way out of the coaches' meeting. He'd felt guilty about leaving Ruby alone before Violet and Sawyer came back, but Sawyer must have lost track of time, so Boone had decided to attend in his place. The sun was shining bright, which seemed ironic given the darkness that threatened to send him back over the edge.

The more he thought about his options, the more he realized he was damned if he did, damned if he didn't. No matter how he handled this turn of events, it was unlikely to end well. Sara and Emmy weren't going to be happy to see him but would be mad if they heard he had been there and not shown his face.

"Are you who I think you are?" a man in a bright yellow shirt asked as they exited the meeting area.

"I don't know. Who do you think I am?"

"You're Boone Williams, aren't you?"

At the mention of his name, another man

dressed head-to-toe in black stopped and turned back to take a look. His eyes widened for a second and then he took off.

Boone decided to go with the truth and hope for the best. "I am. You are?"

"Oliver Townsend. But I'm nobody. Are you really a coach for a team around here?"

Boone lowered his voice, hoping Oliver would, too. "I'm here with an individual rider. I'm doing a favor for a friend."

"Like a Make-A-Wish thing or something? How incredibly cool of you."

"Not exactly. Like I said, just helping out a friend. It was nice to meet you, Oliver."

"Can I get a picture? And could you sign this show program? My wife is a huge fan. Are you going to be around all day? What class is your rider in?"

He wanted to get back to Ruby and Violet, but this gentleman dressed brighter than the sun seemed to want to hold him up all day.

He tried to find his patience. "I'm here to enjoy the show, not make a big scene, if you know what I mean."

"Right," Oliver said, catching his drift.

"But if you have a pen and you're willing to help me, I'll sign your program for your wife."

Oliver lit up. "Great! I've got a pen right here. I thought maybe I'd need to take notes."

He rambled on a few seconds more while digging his pen out of his pocket.

Boone managed to sign the program even with his arm in a sling and headed back to the barn on high alert. There were plenty of chances for him to run into Emmy or, worse, Sara.

At least he wasn't the only famous person here. Sara was sure to attract some attention. She had a highly anticipated album coming out in November. People were champing at the bit to get their hands on it, since she hadn't recorded anything since their marriage fell apart.

There were also enough people around that they might miss each other. Boone wasn't sure which to hope for, but first he had to deal with another problem.

Levi Wynn had a rather unassuming presence. He had a bull rider physique—compact but strong. Boone should have expected him to be small; it helped riders when their center of gravity was lower on the bull's back. Boone had loved the rodeo as a kid, but he didn't feel like much of a Levi fan.

Violet came running up as soon as she spotted him. "Hey, come meet my dad."

She tugged him by his good arm and wore the biggest smile he'd ever seen. Having her dad here obviously meant the world to her.

Ruby, on the other hand, looked like she was waiting for the firing squad to show up.

"Dad, meet Boone Williams. You know who he is, right?"

"I've heard of him." He extended his right hand before noticing Boone couldn't shake properly with his arm in a sling. "It really is you. Part of me thought Ruby was pulling my leg."

"Ruby's as honest as they come," Boone replied, flashing her a smile.

"Well, I'm sure you can imagine how hard it is to believe someone like you would be hanging around my two girls."

The hair on the back of Boone's neck stood on end. First of all, Ruby wasn't his girl. She didn't belong to anyone. Second, there was absolutely no reason someone like Boone wouldn't hang out with someone like Ruby. She was a kind, compassionate, smart, beautiful woman. Why wouldn't he spend time with her?

He was about to mention that when Ruby chimed in, "We should probably go to the practice ring. Don't you think so, Boone?"

The high school–aged riders competed first at the show. Emmy's group was scheduled two groups before Violet's. "I was thinking maybe we could go watch the JV and varsity classes ride and then do some practice before it's Violet's turn."

Ruby smiled and nodded. Of course she understood why without him having to say. "I think that's a great idea."

Maybe with her by his side, he would survive what was about to come. He certainly intended to do whatever he could to get her through her own family reunion.

"I think Violet should take advantage of as much practice time as she can get. If you don't want to take her, I can," Levi said, throwing a nice wrench in the plans.

"It's not a matter of him wanting to take her," Ruby snapped. "He's suggesting we watch some of the more experienced kids, and then she can practice."

"Mom," Violet said with a look of warning in her eye.

Boone tried to smooth things over. "If you want to take her to practice, Sawyer can go with you guys. My daughter is in the competition, and I'd like to see her ride."

All of Violet's defensiveness disappeared and was replaced by her unending curiosity. She rattled off a million questions without a breath in between to give Boone a chance to answer any of them.

"Emmy's here? Did you know she was going

to be here? When does she go? Are you going to say something to her? Can I meet her?"

"Violet, I'm not sure you should meet her today," Ruby said.

"Why not? Maybe if I tell her what her dad's like now, she'll get it. I would do that, Boone. I could tell her that you're kind of cool."

"Oh, wow. Thanks for that glowing reference."

"You know what I mean." Violet stuck out her tongue, making him laugh.

"I don't know what you mean. Why would you need to talk to Boone Williams's daughter? What is going on here?" Levi asked, understandably confused by their conversation.

"It's sort of private, Dad."

Sort of private was a bit of an understatement. The last thing Boone needed was to share his personal tribulations with a guy who used to be in love with the woman Boone wished he could be in love with. Or the father of the kid Boone had bonded with because her dad was such a deadbeat.

"Ruby, can I talk to you for a minute?" Levi pulled Ruby outside the barn.

Sawyer hand-fed Sassy some hay. "Well, this whole thing just got super awkward. It's too bad Jesse couldn't come today. He's a little better at this stuff than I am. But whatever you need me to do, I'll do."

Boone wished Jesse had been able to come, as well. He was still feeling a tad resentful that Sawyer sang his song better than he did, but the guy was so nice about everything that he made Boone feel like a real jerk for holding a grudge.

His phone chimed with a text.

What are you doing here?

Boone searched the barn for Sara. She knew he was there, but where was she? They were definitely not in the same building. Word must have gotten out that he was on the grounds.

His phone chimed again.

Please don't ruin this for her.

He dialed her number. He couldn't explain this over text. She picked up right away.

"Why are you here?"

"I didn't know you were here. I'm helping out a friend whose daughter is riding in another class."

"Of course," Sara said with a sigh. "How silly of me to think you would be here for your daughter."

He was the bad guy for possibly showing up to see Emmy and the bad guy for being here for someone else. He couldn't win.

"I'm not really sure how I am supposed to know what Emmy's up to when she won't talk to me. But I am glad she's here, and I plan to watch her."

"Why would you do that to her? She needs to be focused on riding, not on the father she hasn't seen in months."

Boone felt the sting of her words. "Does she know I'm here?"

"No, and I'd like to keep it that way until she's finished."

"Fine." He didn't care when Emmy found out. He simply wanted to see her. "I'd like to say hello when it's over. It's been too long."

"Whose fault is that?"

It was a rhetorical question, but he answered it anyway. "Mine. All mine."

Sara was quiet for a second. She didn't have a snide comment in response to his honesty. "Well, I can't promise she'll want to talk to you. Don't be disappointed if she has little to say."

"That's fine, Sara. I get it. Whatever happens happens. I'll take what I can get."

Again, she had nothing to say to that. "Then I guess we'll see you when she's done."

She hung up without a goodbye. Ruby and Levi came back into the barn. Ruby didn't look too pleased, and neither did Levi.

"Violet, what do you want to do? You can go practice with your dad or come watch Boone's daughter. It's up to you," Ruby said. Her arms were folded across her chest.

Violet wrung her hands. She didn't want to disappoint her dad, but Boone knew she also wanted to see Emmy. They had talked about her enough that Violet had to be curious.

"I kind of want to see Boone's daughter. But I want to ride for Dad, too."

"It doesn't matter to me what you choose, honey," Ruby assured her. Boone noticed she only spoke for herself and not for Levi. "Whatever you want is fine."

Levi didn't bother to offer her the same assurances. He clearly wanted her to pick him to prove a point.

Boone decided to put in his two cents. "There's plenty of time to practice after you watch Emmy. Let's head over to the arena now, and you and your dad can warm up as soon as she's done." He started for the exit. If they really wanted to come, they would follow him.

The arena was a flurry of activity. A small crowd stood in line outside the concession stand near the entrance. People lined the fence, and a smattering of spectators sat in the white folding chairs along the curves of the ring. Boone learned the hard way that those were VIP seats. An older gentleman in a blue suit coat told him to move along when he tried to enter the roped-off area.

"I think we're supposed to go sit in the stands," Ruby said, pointing to the spot where the general public was seated. The entire Wynn family had followed him. Levi didn't seem too happy about it, but Boone didn't exactly care how he felt.

"If I'm not VIP, I don't know who is," he argued.

Ruby leaned in close. She smelled like berries, and it was distracting. "This is not about being a celebrity. This is about watching your daughter," she reminded him.

Being humble was not easy. They walked over to the stands while Boone scanned the crowd for Sara. He finally found her seated in one of the chairs in the VIP section on the opposite side of the arena. Part of him wanted to know how she got seated there when he didn't. The other part knew it was probably better that they couldn't sit by one another even if they wanted to.

Emmy's class came out one at a time. There were twelve competitors, and Emmy had drawn the first spot. She entered the ring on a gorgeous black pony that reminded Boone of Renegade.

The announcer introduced her to the crowd, and those who were paying attention clapped. Boone climbed the bleachers and found a spot where they could all fit. Ruby sat next to him, and Violet sat between her parents.

"She's different than I pictured her," Violet said. "I didn't think she'd be blonde."

Emmy had the same coloring as her mother. She was a mini-Sara except that her eyes were the same shape and color as Boone's.

"She's beautiful," Ruby said. She placed her hand on his leg and gave him a reassuring pat. "Breathe."

He appreciated the reminder.

Emmy performed well. He wanted her to be happy with how she did. She was one of the younger competitors in this age group, and he was proud of her for showing such calm under pressure.

He clapped a little longer than everyone else when she was finished and couldn't help but smile. It had been a long time since he'd watched her do the thing she loved. He never wanted to miss another competition.

"She did a great job," Ruby said.

Violet shared her assessment, as well. "She

was awesome. Did you see that lead change
when they were loping the figure eight? Perfect."

The anxiety began to build again. It was
time to go down and say hello. Emmy was either going to tell him to get lost or ignore him
altogether.

"Should we say hi?" Ruby asked. "We could
all tell her how great she did."

Her support meant more than she would ever
know. Without her, he wasn't sure he'd have
the courage to leave the stands. He felt para-
lyzed by the fear of his impending rejection.

Sara was standing beside the horse when
Boone approached them. Emmy noticed him
first.

"Dad?"

Boone wasn't sure what had happened to his
voice, but he couldn't make his mouth work.
He wanted to take her in his arms like he used
to when she was little, spin her around until
she giggled so hard it hurt.

Ruby threaded her fingers through his and
gave his hand a squeeze. That snapped him
out of his stupor.

"Hey, sweetheart. You did amazing out there."

Sara stared at Ruby and Boone's interlocked
hands. "Who's your friend?"

"Ah, this is Ruby. Ruby's daughter is competing in the Future group." He introduced

Violet to his ex and daughter. He didn't bother to mention Levi.

"You did really awesome," Violet said. "Your dad brags about what a good rider you are all the time. I thought he was exaggerating like he does about how famous he is, but he was pretty right on about you."

"Thanks," Emmy said, dismounting from her horse. She gave her mother a questioning look. "Did you tell him to come here?"

Sara shook her head.

"I didn't know you were competing today," Boone explained. "I'm sure glad you were, though. It was nice to see you ride."

Emmy seemed unsure how to respond. With Ruby and Violet there, she apparently didn't want to make a scene.

"Well, it was good to see you, Boone." Sara's manners were greatly improved thanks to the presence of strangers. "We have to head back to the barn."

He got the sense that she didn't want him to come with them. There was no way he'd get a chance to speak to Emmy alone, so this was it. He'd have to say what he'd been feeling in front of everyone. "It was really good to see you, Em. I remember what you said on the phone the other day, but I want you to know that I'm sorry for the way things have been and the things I've done, and even more sorry for the things I didn't do that I should have."

"What do you want me to say, Dad? Sorry doesn't change what happened."

"You don't have to say anything. I just want you to know that I love you and I'm going to show you by doing better."

Emmy didn't reply. She led her pony past them and out of the arena. Boone felt sick. The tension in his shoulders was painful. It was humiliating to be dismissed by his child in front of other people. Having her reject him privately had been bad enough.

He needed to go. Tears pricked at the corners of his eyes, and the last thing he needed was to cry in front of everyone. He bolted outside in search of a place to hide. He ducked behind an equipment shed. Crouching down, he pressed his fingers against his eyes to stop the tears from coming.

"Boone." Violet's voice was quiet and full of unnecessary sympathy.

He stood back up and blinked away those darn tears, trying to keep himself from looking even more like a fool. "Don't worry about me, Vi. Go practice with your dad before your group is up."

"I need to tell you something, and then I will."

He sniffed loudly and tried to pull himself together. "Don't feel sorry for me. I deserve everything I get from her."

"Just don't give up, okay?" She tugged on her ponytail. "It matters that you keep trying. The worst thing you could do is give up. That would only prove you never cared. This is a test."

Boone wrestled with the guilt of making his daughter question his love for her. "I hope you're right."

"I'm right. I know exactly how Emmy feels. She's just way braver than I am." She glanced back. Ruby and Levi were a safe distance away. They could see them but not hear what Violet was saying. "I'm too scared to put my dad to the test." She lowered her voice to a whisper. "I think he might fail."

CHAPTER TWENTY-SIX

RUBY'S HEART WAS BREAKING.

"What is the deal with this guy? And why do you let Violet have anything to do with him? Because he's famous?" Levi put his hands on his hips and scowled in Boone's direction.

"We don't care that he's famous. I can't explain it." Boone and Violet had a bond that defied logic. They were both hurting for opposite reasons. He suffered because of his failures as a father, and Violet struggled with the pain of her father failing her.

Yet somehow they found a way to heal one another. Violet accepted Boone and his failures, allowing him the chance to prove he could be a good person, and Boone made Violet feel like she was worthy of his time and attention.

It made Ruby love the two of them more than she thought possible.

The realization almost caused her to fall over. It hit her like a ton of bricks. She was in love with Boone. There was no doubt about it.

"Well, that one magazine is right. Celebrities are just like us. They have ex-wives who treat them like crud. Guess money and fame don't protect you from that."

Levi made her blood boil. "Why do you do that? Why do you always make it out like you're the victim? You know why Violet is attached to Boone? He reminds her of you."

"Of me? Why, because his ex-wife turned the kid against him like you're trying to turn Violet against me?"

Ruby put both hands on her head. He was beyond frustrating. "I'm not trying to turn her against you. And Boone hasn't been there for his daughter, but he's at least trying to change and take responsibility for his mistakes."

"You want to move her across the country so that I never see her again. What do you call that?"

"I call it trying to protect her from constant disappointment."

Levi's face changed. The angry lines in his forehead faded. The corners of his lips dipped down. "Is that what I do, constantly disappoint her?"

Ruby blew out a breath. "I think the real question is, do you want to, and if not, what are you going to do differently?"

Violet gave Boone a hug, and the two of them emerged from his hiding spot. Ruby wanted to wrap her arms around him, as well. She wanted him to know he wasn't alone.

Levi and Violet decided to get Sassy to the practice ring while Boone and Ruby took a walk, promising to meet them over there.

Ruby didn't miss the way people were beginning to stare a little longer, whisper when they passed by. As soon as Boone had approached Sara and Emmy, he had outed himself to anyone who had paid attention. Boone had told Ruby more than once that he and Sara were constantly in the tabloids when they were going through their divorce. This little reunion wouldn't go unnoticed.

"I thought it could have gone worse," she said when they finally found some privacy along the practice ring fence.

"That was because you and Violet were standing there. Sara has an image to uphold. She'd never make a scene in public."

"Well, I think Emmy was surprised to see you, and not in a bad way. It meant something that you were there, even if she's still guarded."

"That's what Violet said." He winced and gave his shoulder a rub. "She told me not to give up. And she's really nervous about asking Levi if she can live with him."

"She told you that?"

"She's scared to test him. She doesn't think he's going to choose her."

Ruby knew that was true, but it still hurt to hear it. "I'm not sure he even realizes how much is riding on how he handles this."

Boone turned and slipped his good arm around her waist. His touch sent the butterflies fluttering. "No matter what, she's got you. And she knows that without a doubt. You're a good mom, Ruby. Stop thinking different."

She wasn't sure what came over her, but Ruby lifted up on her tiptoes and kissed him. Right there in the middle of everyone. She didn't care if people were gaping or taking pictures with their phones. She needed to show Boone how she felt, and this was the best way she knew how.

Kissing Boone was like floating high above the ground in a hot-air balloon. There was reasonable fear that was quickly eased by the beauty of the ride. Everyone and everything else seemed so far away, making them untouchable.

"What was that for?" he asked when she came back to earth.

"For being real."

VIOLET'S CLASS WAS much bigger than the one she had competed against at the last event.

Ruby sat between Levi and Boone, too distracted by what was going to happen after the ride to concentrate on the action in the arena.

"She's perfect so far," Boone said. He put his arm around her and gave her shoulder a reassuring squeeze. "Violet's got Sassy doing everything she's supposed to do."

Another, younger rider wasn't so lucky. The pony he rode started backing up when everyone else was stopped. The boy tried to get it under control, but the horse began to gallop around the other competitors. Another horse took that to mean it was playtime and began to chase after him. Ruby's heart raced right along with them. She watched Violet holding her reins for dear life. Somehow she managed to keep Sassy still.

Levi also breathed a sigh of relief. "She would have been so mad if that guy threw her off her game. Violet is not someone you want to mess with."

Boone chuckled. "No, she is not."

They went down to meet her when it was over. Violet unclipped her helmet and took it off.

"Did you see me hold her still when that horse ran off? She wanted to go, but I kept telling her she was a good girl, and she stayed put."

"You did awesome, Vi," Ruby said as Sawyer helped her dismount.

"What did you think, Dad?"

All eyes turned on Levi. He pushed back his cowboy hat and narrowed his eyes. His long pause made everyone anxious.

Finally he spoke. "I think I just saw the future rodeo queen. You did awesome, like your mom said."

Violet's face broke into the proudest smile, and her chest puffed out a bit. It was everything she had hoped to hear.

"What do you think, old man? Am I going to be as good as Emmy someday?"

Ruby loved it that even after getting her dad's approval, she still wanted Boone's. "I think you'll be tough competition for her real soon."

The awards ceremony proved that to be true. Violet ended up scoring high enough to put her in the top five in her class, and Emmy won a second-place ribbon. Boone looked like a proud papa during both announcements. He sent Emmy a text congratulating her, and she actually sent back a thank-you. Ruby watched Boone take a screenshot of it, like he was afraid it wasn't real and needed proof.

Levi stuck around until they had Sassy all loaded up and ready to go back home. This was the part of the day that Ruby had been dreading. The whole day had been a roller-coaster ride. Things were so good right now, the last thing she wanted was for it to all come crashing down. Violet hadn't said anything yet, and maybe she was thinking the same thing.

"I'm real proud of you, Vi. You should come with me to the Rhea County Fair Rodeo next weekend. Maybe I can make you proud," Levi said as he walked them to their car.

"Can I?" Violet asked Ruby. It wasn't like her to look for Ruby's approval.

"I don't see why not."

"Cool," Levi said. "Maybe I'll come get you a couple of days earlier and we can just hang."

Ruby cringed. She hated when he made this kind of plan. The *maybe*s and the *we should*s always turned into *not this time* or *I can't* in the end.

"Well, Mom and I have been talking, and we wanted to ask you something." Violet took a second to get her thoughts together. "We were wondering…well, *I've* been wondering how you would feel about me coming to live with you…maybe…you know, for a little bit."

This was it. Ruby braced herself for whatever came next. She hoped he'd let her down easy. Maybe he'd use the current custody agreement as an excuse. Or maybe he'd tell her he'd like to start being more consistent about visits first. Ruby watched Levi's face for some sign of how he was going to handle this. What she wasn't expecting was what she got.

"I think that's a great idea," he said.

Ruby imagined she looked like one of those cartoon characters whose eyes popped way out of its head while its jaw dropped down to the ground. He wasn't supposed to say yes.

"You think it's a great idea?" She needed to clarify in case she had only dreamed those were the words that came out of his mouth.

"It's a better idea than moving to Seattle," he replied.

"School starts after Labor Day. I already registered her in Grass Lake. There's a lot to think about. Don't you think you should think about it?"

"We can talk about everything when I come get her for her visit. How about that?"

That was a terrible idea. The whole thing was a terrible idea. Violet couldn't leave Ruby alone and go live with Levi. The man had no idea how to be a 24/7 parent. He barely managed being a once-a-month parent.

"Okay," Violet answered. She hugged her dad around the neck, and he lifted her up off the ground. She laughed like a carefree child, something she hadn't been her entire life. He set her down and kissed her on top of the head.

"See you later this week, Ruby." He opened his arms for a hug as if they were suddenly friends. She didn't have a good reason not to share the embrace. Before he let go, he whispered in her ear, "How's that for not being a disappointment?"

CHAPTER TWENTY-SEVEN

THE HOUR'S DRIVE felt longer on the way back to the farm than on the way there. Sawyer whistled along with every song on the radio while the day replayed in Boone's head. From finding out Emmy was there, to meeting Levi, to talking to Emmy, to getting Violet's take on everything, to that kiss Ruby gave him. It had been one heck of a day.

"So when are you going start recording your new album? I know Dean's excited you got that song for you and Piper written, but he wants an entire record."

"Oh, I know Dean wants a lot of things. He'll get something. I've been writing some new stuff." He had written the song for Emmy and two others since that night. His shoulder made sleeping rough, but that gave him plenty of extra hours to write.

"Well, if they're anything like that song you wrote for you and Piper, you're sure to have the comeback album of the year."

Boone didn't want to get ahead of himself,

but these songs *were* pretty amazing. They were different than his old stuff. More thoughtful and real. He had to admit he was excited to see how they all turned out.

What didn't feel right was making his return with Piper Starling at his side. The more he thought about it, the more he wanted to make a real statement with his first single. It had to be just him and it had to be his apology to his daughter, to his fans, to the world.

"What if the song I wrote for Piper and me wasn't sung by Piper and me?" Boone asked Sawyer.

"Who would you sell it to?"

"What if I gave it to you?"

"Me?" Sawyer nearly ran the truck and trailer off the road.

Boone braced himself with his good arm and held his breath until they were back under control. "Goodness, man. Try not to kill the guy who is about to make you famous beyond your wildest dreams."

Doing a duet with Piper could catapult Sawyer right up the charts. A song with her meant performances on talk shows and at award shows. The two of them would blow it out of the water.

"Why would you give me that song?"

Boone hated to admit it. "You sang it better than I could. Once I listened to you two, I haven't been able to put myself back in it. Every time I hear it in my head, I hear your voice, not mine."

Sawyer's mouth hung open. "I don't even know what to say. That's…that's the most incredible thing anyone has ever said to me. Thank you."

"Don't thank me too much. I still own the song and, with you singing it, should make some good money in return. I do have one other thing I want to give you that's a tad more altruistic. It's not a song, though. It's some advice."

"Lay it on me."

There were many lessons Boone wished he hadn't had to learn the hard way. He felt like he should pass on some of his hard-earned wisdom. "First, stay humble and always be gracious. Nobody out there owes you a thing. It doesn't matter if you have a hundred number-one records or not. Tomorrow you could be sitting in the general public stands instead of VIP."

Sawyer nodded and smiled.

"Second, choose the people around you carefully. Again, no one owes you anything, but they are all going to want something from you. You're lucky you found Dean straight out of the gate. He's one of the good ones. But there are a lot of not-so-good people out there in every part of the industry. Trust your gut. If something seems off about someone, something is probably off."

"I'm a pretty good judge of character," Sawyer said.

"You need to be an excellent judge of character." There had been too many people over the years who didn't have Boone's best interests at heart. "All right, my last bit of advice is the most important." This was the hardest lesson Boone had had to learn. "Be kind to those who love you. Don't let this business get in the way of your family. Be present. Don't get wrapped up in all the attention and fame. Remember who's really important to you and don't let them go."

Those were words Boone intended to live by.

BACK ON THE FARM, Boone texted Ruby to find out how it had gone with Levi. He prayed Violet wasn't too upset with her dad for saying no to her relocation idea.

Ruby's reply was worrisome.

He said YES.

This was followed by three rows of crying emojis. Levi said yes? Why in the world would he get Violet's hopes up like that? Boone was ready to drive to Nashville and let Levi know exactly what it was like to crush someone.

His shoulder protested, so he got in his truck and headed to Ruby's instead. Given her mood and her panache for last-minute dinner plans, he figured it was a safe bet to bring over a bucket of fried chicken with all the fixings.

"Boone!" Unfortunately Mary whatever-her-name-was Nosy Neighbor appeared out of nowhere when he got out of the truck. "Look at you. Aren't you the sweetest?" She checked her watch. It was almost eight. "Bringing dinner over at this hour?"

He could hear the judgment in her tone and didn't like it one bit.

"Violet had a horse show today. We've had a full day. No time to cook. I'm sure you know what that's like." He had to keep reminding himself to be nice.

"You three are like one happy family lately. I still can't get over it. You and Ruby. Friends."

Be nice. Be nice. BE NICE.

"Have a good night, Mary Sue." He made a break for the door but was cut off as he rounded the truck.

"It's Mary Ellen," she corrected him.

"Have a good night, Mary Ellen."

He tried to pass her, but she stepped in his way. "Are you two friends or more than friends?

I ask only because people in a small town have a tendency to talk, if you know what I mean. And I would hate for rumors to be spread about Ruby that weren't true. If I had the facts from the man himself, well, then I could make sure to squash any false information that comes my way."

An angry heat crept up Boone's neck. He'd known his share of people like Mary Ellen. She truly believed the garbage coming out of her mouth.

"Ruby is the most amazing woman I have ever met in my entire life. She's a single mother who brings life into the world. She has endless amounts of patience and understanding. Never gossips. Is beautiful and smart. I love her sense of humor and her laugh. Basically I would be an idiot not to be madly in love with her."

As soon as he said it, he knew it was true. He was in love with Ruby. He loved her and Violet. As hard as he had tried not to let it happen for their sake, he had fallen for them.

"And I'm a lot of things, but an idiot is *not* one of them," he admitted. The shock on Mary Ellen's face was priceless. She was much easier to get around when she was frozen. Boone rang the doorbell.

Violet opened the door. "Are you kidding me? You are my savior!" She took the food and left him on the front porch. He glanced back at Mary Ellen, who was still standing where he'd left her.

He stepped inside and closed the door. Ruby came down the stairs and stopped short when she saw him. Her hair was up in a messy bun, and she had changed into sweatpants and a T-shirt.

She tugged on the hem of her shirt, unnecessarily self-conscious. He didn't care about her clothes. He loved her no matter what she wore.

"What are you doing here?"

He smiled up at her. "I brought food, but the teenager confiscated it, and I'm not sure there will be anything left when we find her."

"You didn't have to do that."

"I know I didn't have to. I wanted to. I was worried about you."

She plodded down the rest of the steps. Up close, he could see her eyes were bloodshot from crying. He wished he could fix all of her problems, but the one Levi had created today most of all.

"What can I do?"

"You're doing it. Thanks for bringing dinner. No wonder she doesn't want to live here anymore. I barely feed her." Her voice broke and her eyes got watery.

"Hey, now." He pulled her close with one

arm. "Don't do that. I told you this wasn't about you—it's about him. She needs him to prove he cares."

"It still hurts."

"I know it does. But let's not get ahead of ourselves. A lot of things can change between now and when they think she's going to move in with him full-time."

She lifted her head from his shoulder and wiped her face. "You're right. I need to pull it together."

They found Violet in the kitchen with greasy fingers, chowing down on some corn on the cob. "I ate two biscuits. There were four, so you both still get to have one."

"My goodness, child. I saw your mother buy you food at the concession stand for lunch. Don't act like you haven't eaten all day."

"That was, like, a million hours ago."

Ruby handed Boone a plate, and they all sat and shared the meal like a family. Boone passed Violet a napkin. Ruby got everyone a glass of milk. Violet reviewed the highlights of her day.

After dinner, they all helped clean up and settled in the family room to watch a movie. Violet chose some horror flick that she swore she'd seen in the theater and wasn't that scary. Her definition of not scary must have been very different than her mother's. Ruby watched the entire thing through her fingers and screamed every time something jumped out at someone on screen.

"Why is she going in there? She's obviously going to die if she goes in there. Don't go in there! Stop. Oh my gosh, she is so stupid. I can't watch." Ruby scooted closer to Boone and hid her face against his arm.

"She's not going to die. She's the main character. Main characters don't die until the very end, or they're the only ones who survive," Violet said from where she lay on the floor atop all the throw pillows from the couch.

"I thought you saw this already. Don't you know what happens to her?" Boone asked.

"I don't remember, but I think she makes it to the end."

Ruby peeked out from behind his arm just as the ghost in the story killed the character Violet had just assured them would live. Ruby wailed in fright and practically climbed into Boone's lap.

"If you did that on purpose to make me look, I will never forgive you, Violet."

Violet rolled with laughter. "I swear, I forgot that part," she said through her snorts.

Ruby carefully removed herself from Boone's

body. Not that he minded holding her that close. He liked it when she leaned on him.

Boone and Violet finished watching the movie while Ruby held a pillow in front of her face and listened to the rest of it. Turned out that the character they thought had died was really alive at the end.

"See, I was right!" Violet stood and held her arms up in victory. "I knew she made it."

"That was the worst movie I have ever half watched." Ruby threw the pillow at Violet.

Boone loved them. He loved the way they laughed together and the funny things they said to give each other a hard time. He loved the way Violet said "Oh my gosh, Mom." And the way Ruby called her Vi for short. He loved their smiles and the way they loved one another. He loved everything about them.

"Time for bed. You've had a long day," Ruby said to Violet.

"Fine. I'm tired, anyway." She thanked Boone for dinner and gave her mother a kiss on the cheek. He could tell that wasn't something she usually did by the way Ruby touched the spot when Violet was gone.

"I should head out, too."

"Thank you for coming over and…making me feel normal."

"I owed you." She had done the same thing

for him the other night. When they were together, things just fit.

His phone chimed with a text. He thought
maybe it was Dean, but it wasn't. His heart
must have skipped a beat or two.

"What is it?" Ruby asked.

It was Emmy.

The black horse at Tressman's was named
Shadow. He was my favorite.

CHAPTER TWENTY-EIGHT

THE NEXT MORNING, Violet and a few other girls had plans to go swimming at the lake. With only a couple more weeks left in the summer, the kids were trying to squeeze in all the fun they could in the time they had left. Ruby was happy to see Violet building friendships with the girls but sad that all that would be lost if she went back to Nashville to live with her dad. This was true if she moved her to Seattle as well, but that was different. Wasn't it? In that scenario, the benefits outweighed the costs. Ruby believed that much.

"Did you pack some sunscreen?"

"Yes."

"The one with the higher SPF? You're a red-head under all that hair dye, and your skin needs more protection than the other girls might need."

"I know, Mom. I brought the right one." Her phone buzzed. "They're here. Bye!" And she was gone.

Gone. She could soon be gone for good. The thought made Ruby want to cry again.

Boone would tell her not to worry until worrying was all there was left to do. She was worried about him, though. They had enjoyed another fun night together, and then he'd gotten a text from someone and couldn't get out of there fast enough.

It would be so much easier if she wasn't in love with him. But she was. He had weaseled his way into her heart, and there was no telling what damage he was going to do in there.

Ruby went to clean up the breakfast plates as Holly came charging through her front door.

"Are you kidding me?"

"Is that a real question or did something happen?"

Holly was dressed for the gym in yoga pants, a tank top and a matching sports bra, but it was more likely she was headed to the office.

"I was putting the finishing touches on our Boone Williams interview and thought it would be nice to get a picture of him, but given his dislike of anything related to news about him, I figured he'd be difficult about it. So I decided I would find an old stock photo or press release."

This didn't seem like something to freak out about. "Okay. And you couldn't find one that worked, and now you want me to ask him if we can take a photograph of him for the paper? Is that it?"

"No, that is not it." Holly held out her phone and showed Ruby the screen. "I found this instead. It's all over the place."

Ruby took the phone and stared at the image of her kissing Boone at the exhibition center yesterday. The headline read Boone Williams Makes Out with Mystery Woman. There was also another picture of them walking hand in hand. Ruby's face was clear as day. The article went on to report that Boone and ex-wife Sara Gilmore were there to watch their daughter compete in a horse show, but Boone ran off as soon as it was over to make out with this mystery woman.

"He did not run off to make out with me right after the competition. That is not what happened."

Holly took her phone back. "It sure looks like that's what happened. Is that not you and him making out?"

"I kissed him," Ruby conceded. "But he didn't *run off* to go *make out*. They make it sound so scandalous. A lot of things happened after we watched his daughter ride."

"I don't care what the article says. You kissed Boone Williams and didn't tell me!"

Ruby apologized and tried to explain the situation even though she had no idea what was going on anymore. It dawned on her that perhaps his hasty getaway last night had something to do with the picture on the internet.

"I wish I had a crystal ball so I could know how everything is going to turn out. Between Violet wanting to live with her dad, who suddenly thinks that's a great idea, and Boone doing everything in his power to make me fall in love with him while telling me we can't fall in love, I'm going crazy."

Holly had to sit down. She dragged Ruby into the family room and onto the couch. "Are you falling in love with Boone?"

There was no reason to lie. The picture said it without words. "Let's just say I am beyond being Booned. It isn't the way he looks at me. This isn't about his eyes or his smile. I love his compassion and quick wit. I love his playfulness and his laughter. He's so good to Violet. He treats her like his own, and not like some guy might if he was just trying to get with me. His feelings for Violet are completely separate from his feelings for me."

"What kind of feelings do you think he has for you?"

"I don't know. I think he's torn. He keeps saying that he's no good for me."

Holly was about to hyperventilate. "Boone Williams told you that he's no good for you. Kissed you and is sweet to your daughter. I think I need to lie down." She let herself fall over on the couch. Her dark hair covered her face. "I don't think I can handle this."

"You don't think you can handle this? This is my life right now!"

Holly pushed her hair away and sat back up. She gave Ruby a hug. "I'm sorry. I can't imagine being you right now. You're on the internet! You could be in the next issue of *People* that shows up in my mailbox."

"I can't even deal with this Boone stuff right now. I've got my hands full figuring out how I am supposed to handle Violet moving in with her father."

"Do you really think that's going to happen? I have a feeling once Levi understands what that entails, he isn't going to be so in favor of that plan."

That was a possibility but not a guarantee. The reality was, there was a chance Violet could move out. "He's picking her up on Thursday for a weekend visit. I guess I should wait to see if he shows up. Then I'll decide how much worrying I need to do."

"That sounds like a smart idea." Holly

grabbed Ruby's hand and scooted closer. "Can I ask you one important question, though?"

Ruby's brow furrowed. "Sure."

"What was it like to kiss Boone? Did you see fireworks or stars? Did it make your heart race faster than the speed of light? Was it as mind-blowingly amazing as I imagine it would be?"

Ruby gave Holly's hand a pat. "It was better."

Holly fell over again with a jealous sigh. "I knew you were going to say that!"

THURSDAY AFTERNOON, RUBY checked the clock on her phone five times in the span of twenty minutes. Levi was supposed to pick Violet up at three, and it was now three thirty. She knew she'd ultimately be relieved if he didn't show, but it was the heartbreak Violet would be dealing with that would keep it from being a positive thing until later.

"Have you seen my black shirt with the pocket on the front?" Violet asked from the top of the stairs. She was keeping herself busy by packing and repacking. Ruby knew she had to be paying attention to the time, as well.

"I think I washed it, but it could still be in the basket I brought upstairs."

Violet disappeared in search of the shirt she suddenly wanted to wear during the weekend she might or might not spend with Levi. Ruby started to text him as the doorbell rang.

Disbelief held her in place. Violet came racing down the stairs. "Oh my gosh, Mom. Didn't you hear Dad ring the doorbell?" She flung the door open and jumped in her dad's arms. "I knew you'd make it."

Violet was a *very* good liar.

Levi set Violet down and stepped into the house. "There was an accident as soon as I got out of the city limits that had me dead stopped for twenty minutes. I thought I could make the time up, but I wasn't that lucky. Hope no one was worried." He gave Ruby a pointed look.

"We're glad you made it safely," Ruby said with a forced smile. It was true—she was glad he was safe—but that was pretty much all she was happy about.

"I'm still packing. I'll be down in a second," Violet said, dashing back up the stairs.

"No problem. Your mom and I have some things to talk about before we go."

Ruby had been preparing for the big talk they had agreed to have before Levi took Violet for the weekend. She'd written two pages of notes with every valid point she could think of to discourage the idea of Violet moving back to Nashville with him. Ruby led him to the kitchen.

She decided to start by seeing if he would back out on his own. "Now that you've had a few days to think about it, are you still sure you want to tell her she can come live with you?"

"I have thought about it, and I still think it's a great idea."

"Really?"

"I mean, now that you are in the middle of some hot and heavy affair with Boone Williams, wouldn't it be helpful if you didn't have Violet to worry about?"

Ruby didn't realize Levi read gossip magazines. Although apparently the rest of the world did, because the calls had been coming in all week from her sister, her mother, several old friends from Nashville, a cousin in Atlanta and two patients. All these people had called her except for Boone, whom she hadn't heard from since that day.

"I am not in the middle of anything hot and heavy, thank you very much. And neither one of us is married, so no one is having an affair."

Levi held his palms up. "I saw some pictures from last weekend that tell a very different story. I just thought maybe that's why you were looking to pawn her off on me."

Ruby's temper flared. "I am not in favor of

this move, Levi. I think it's a terrible idea. Your daughter is the one who wants this. Not me."

"You think I'm going to believe that? You're dating some famous country star and all the sudden Violet wants to come live with me. Seems like more than a coincidence."

"Boone and I are not dating. It's…complicated."

"So you make out with guys you aren't dating while hanging out at your daughter's horse show?"

How dare he accuse her of being someone who didn't take relationships seriously. When they were married, he was the one with a wandering eye. He had come to her and admitted he didn't think he could stay in a committed relationship for the rest of his life and suggested a separation. Ruby had decided to skip the separation and go straight to a divorce. There was no way a few months of being apart was going to change his desire to be faithful.

"What part of complicated do you not understand?"

"Okay. So it was Violet's idea and you hate it, but you're going to let her go?"

"I could say no if I want to." This was something Ruby had strongly considered. "Our custody agreement names me as the residential parent. But Violet is thirteen, and I want her to feel like she has some say in her life the older she gets."

Levi considered that for a moment. Once he seemed to believe her, he said, "Then let's try it."

"This isn't like going to a restaurant you've never been to before or experimenting with a new toothpaste. This is taking on the responsibility of being a full-time parent. It's not something you *try*."

"I know that." He rolled his eyes as skillfully as his daughter. "I wasn't being flippant."

She went to the counter to get her list. "I wrote down a few things I think you need to consider before you agree to do this."

Levi took the sheets of paper and laughed. "Are you serious? I'm supposed to read all this?"

"If you want your daughter to move in with you, I suggest you do."

Violet came in carrying her pillow and dragging a suitcase behind her. "I'm ready when you are. Did you guys get everything figured out?"

Levi glanced down at Ruby's list and shook his head. "We're done for now. Let's hit the road so we can get back to Nashville by dinner."

The uneasy feeling in Ruby's stomach was back. She got up and hugged Violet tight. "Be good. And I'll be there to pick you up on Sunday."

"Don't come too early. Dad and I like to sleep in later than you do."

She didn't want to let go. Ruby kissed her head. "I love you."

"Oh my gosh, Mom. I know. I'm not leaving forever. It's only one weekend."

For now. Ruby choked down the emotion threatening to surface and let her go. "Text me when you get there so I know you made it safely."

"I will."

She followed them to the door. "And call me if you need anything."

"I won't need anything. Chill." Violet handed Levi her suitcase so he could put it in the trunk of his car.

"Well, make sure you wear your retainer at night. Your orthodontist will know if you didn't."

Violet put her hands over her ears. "I *know*, Mom. Stop."

Ruby stood on the porch, watching her get in the car and buckle her seat belt. As soon as Levi started the engine, Violet changed the radio station and glanced out the window at Ruby, who waved goodbye as the tears began to well in her eyes. She hoped they stayed in until they had driven away.

Levi put the car in Reverse, and Violet made the sign for *I love you* with her fingers. Ruby mouthed, "I love you more," as the tears rolled down her cheeks.

CHAPTER TWENTY-NINE

"THESE ARE ONLY DEMOS. Don't judge the quality," Boone said, fiddling with the playback. It was Saturday and he knew Jesse had other things to do, but Boone really wanted him to hear these songs.

"I'm not here to judge anything," Jesse said from his spot on the studio couch. "You said you can explain yourself better through your music, so I wanted to listen to some of it."

That was true. It was a lot easier to sing his feelings than talk them out. Plus, he was awful proud of what he had accomplished this week. He had spent every day in the studio working on the three songs he'd written and was singing himself.

"All right. Here we go." Boone pressed Play and listened to the first notes of the song he'd written for Emmy.

Boone and Emmy had texted every night this week. She didn't always have a lot to say, but she responded to his messages and occasionally sent one his way first.

It meant everything.

Jesse tapped his foot and bobbed his head to the music. "I like this one."

"It's my favorite of the three." Of course, Emmy was the only one who really needed to love it.

They listened to everything Boone had recorded. Jesse gave him a round of applause when the last one ended.

"One week, three songs. That's impressive. Dean must be happy."

"He's optimistic that I might actually release an album before he dies, so yeah, he's happy."

"The music is a safe place again. Why do you think that is?"

Boone filled him in on the things that had happened. He told him everything, including his realization that he was in love with Ruby.

"I guess I should admit that I saw the photos of you two at the horse show," Jesse said. "In case you're wondering why I'm not acting shocked by this."

Boone had seen them, too. His publicist had contacted him earlier in the week to make him aware of the pictures that were all over social media and the rumors that were flying around.

He had directed her to respond with no comment to anyone who came asking questions.

He wanted to keep Ruby out of the public eye from now on if he could.

"I was careless. And she kissed me, so I wasn't exactly expecting it. I should have been more careful with her, though. I knew we had eyes on us."

"Have you talked to her about the pictures?"

Boone was embarrassed to admit he hadn't. Sara had called him about it, since all the articles had to mention that she'd attended the same show. Like he was trying to make her jealous or something. She didn't really care who he kissed, but she was concerned about what Emmy would think. So was he. What Emmy thought was constantly on his mind.

"I've been avoiding Ruby."

"How come?"

"I'm sorry that she has to deal with this kind of stuff because of me. I'm afraid she'll hate me for it."

Jesse's brow furrowed. "You said she kissed you. Do you think she could go from having feelings that make her want to do that to hating you so easily?"

"I don't want her to hate me, but I don't want her to be in love with me, either."

"But you're in love with her?"

"Yes, that's where things get complicated." Boone rested his elbows on his knees and leaned forward. "I'm definitely in love with her. She makes me happy, but something changed the moment I got that text from Emmy. There I was, standing in the middle of Ruby's family room, feeling guilty, like I was doing something I shouldn't when my daughter needed me."

"What were you doing that was wrong?" Jesse questioned.

"I don't know. Being with Ruby and Violet is like being home. They make me smile and feel so darn glad to be alive. When Emmy texted me—I was ecstatic, don't get me wrong—but I realized we have a lot of work to do to repair the damage I've done."

"So you felt guilty about this great relationship you're building with Ruby and Violet when your relationship with your daughter is still in disarray."

"Exactly." And those photos splashed all over the internet weren't helping. "I'm worried she's going to feel like I'm replacing her and her mom with Ruby and Violet. Sara and I didn't work out for a bunch of reasons. Most of them had to do with me and my drinking problems, but some of them were simply about us not being right for each other. But Emmy Lou is my daughter, will always be my daughter. I don't ever want her to feel like she has to compete with someone else for my attention or love."

Jesse rubbed his jaw. "Interesting."

Boone waited for him to say more. "That's it? All you got is *interesting*?"

"I can tell you've really thought about this. And that's good. You're thinking about how your actions affect others. You're not making decisions based on what you want or what makes you feel good. I'm proud of you."

Boone leaned back in his chair, feeling better about himself than he had in a long time. He'd never imagined Jesse's opinion would matter as much as it apparently did now. "Okay, so I'm finally not a completely self-centered jerk. But what do I do?"

"I'm not here to tell you what to do, Boone. You've got to make these decisions on your own. If I tell you to do something and it goes badly, who are you going to blame?"

"You. That's why I want you to tell me what to do."

Jesse laughed. "Exactly. I won't be your crutch, man. You are accountable for your life, and I am accountable for mine. That's the way the world works."

"I don't want to hurt people anymore, but this is the first situation I've been in where I feel like whatever I do, someone I care about could get hurt."

He'd spent too many hours thinking about this. If Emmy was willing to open the door, he wanted to do everything he could to make sure she let him back in. That would be hard to manage from Grass Lake.

"What do you think you need to do?"

"Go back to Nashville. Work on reestablishing my visitation. Spend time with my daughter. Make amends with my ex-wife even though I don't really want to."

Sara had done some things during the divorce that still made Boone so angry. He might have started the war, but she didn't always fight fair.

"And if you go back to Nashville, you're worried about Ruby."

Ruby. Her name took him right back to his happy place. All he wanted was her head on his shoulder, their fingers entwined, her lips on his. He missed the smell of her hair and loved the idea that someday he might wake up with her at his side.

"If I leave, I leave her. She's already dealing with Violet and her stupid plan to go live with her dad."

"Let's not judge Violet's plans. Violet gets to make her choices. And mistakes."

"That's what moving in with her dad would be. A big mistake. I know because it would be a mistake for Emmy to come live with me. I'm not ready to be in charge of her full-time. Our relationship isn't strong enough to survive the ups and downs that come with living with a teenager."

"I appreciate your concern for Violet and Ruby. But if people had told you when you were thirteen there was no way you could become a world-famous singer because there was no way *they* could become a world-famous singer, would you have believed them? Should you have believed them?"

Jesse always made it impossible to win an argument with him. Boone gave up trying. "I don't want Ruby to be alone."

"Now, that makes sense. You don't want Violet to leave because you feel like you need to leave."

"Bingo. So what do I do?" He hoped Jesse would just tell him what he thought, but Jesse wasn't giving it up.

"Let me ask you this—why don't you think Ruby could handle it? Is there a reason she wouldn't survive if you and Violet moved to Nashville?"

Boone didn't need Jesse to straight-up tell

him what to do. He always asked the right questions to lead Boone to the correct conclusion.

AFTER HIS SESSION with Jesse, Boone knew he needed to do the right thing. He started by letting Dean know his plan, and then he hopped in his truck to see Ruby.

As he headed out, he spotted her car driving in. Her little red sedan was kicking up dust along the dirt path to the Helping Hooves parking lot.

He shifted into Reverse and went right back to where he came from. Leave it to Ruby to know when he needed her. She got out of her car. Her hair was pulled up in a ponytail, and she had on a blue sundress that showed off her legs in ways he wasn't sure he could handle today.

"Were you going somewhere?"

"To see you," he told her as he approached her.

Her smile told him she was flattered. "I've missed you. And I've been missing Violet. I figured I needed to stop missing one of you, and I took a shot that you were the one who wouldn't yell at me for showing up on your doorstep."

His chest tightened, and his throat felt like it was closing up. Hurting Ruby could be the death of him. Boone reached for her hand, selfishly needing to touch her to make himself feel better.

"I would never yell at you for coming to find me."

"That's good to know."

He brushed back the wisps of hair that framed her face and tucked them behind her ear. Her green eyes gazed up at him like he was someone worthy of her kind of love. It made him reconsider every decision he'd made in the past couple of hours. Being loved by Ruby was more tempting than all the liquor in the world.

"I'm in love with you," he confessed. "I know I told you I wasn't going to do that— fall in love with you—but you made it impossible not to."

She reached up and touched his face. Her hand was soft against his skin. He would long for her touch for eternity. "You love me." She said it like she couldn't believe it.

She slid her hand around his neck, and he knew she was waiting for him to bend down and bring his lips to hers. And there was absolutely nothing he wanted to do more than just that.

But what Boone wanted wasn't as important

as what Ruby needed. What Emmy needed. What Boone needed.

He grabbed her wrists and stepped out of her grasp. Confusion flitted across her face. "But I need to talk to you about something. That's why I was coming over."

She swallowed hard. "Okay," she said, her voice trembling ever so slightly.

"I love you. I love Violet. You are both so special to me."

Ruby's chest rose and fell with heavy breaths. He could tell she wasn't sure if she should be happy or not. Something was telling her this wasn't going to end the way she hoped. He was sorry that was true.

"The other day when I was at your house, Emmy texted me."

"That's great news. You're still in touch?"

Boone nodded. The tightness in his throat was going to make this next part harder than it already was. He tried to clear it. "I've decided to head back to Nashville. I'm going to finish recording my album up there and focus on repairing my relationship with Emmy in person, not over the phone."

"You're leaving?"

He nodded again.

"When?"

"Tomorrow morning, if I can get someone to come get me."

"Tomorrow," she said with a gasp. "And you can't do this… You can't be with me while you're doing that."

He had no voice. All he could do was nod.

Her bottom lip started to quiver, but she quickly bit down on it. "Great. I'm sure Violet's going to be really impressed with how fast you could ditch us and run back to your real family."

Her anger was justified, but the words still cut deep. "I'm not ditching you," he finally choked out. "I'm trying to do what's best for my daughter. I know you're going to be okay. I know you don't need someone like me messing up your life."

Ruby blinked back the tears. "As Violet would say, please don't give me the empowerment speech. I'm fine. I don't care what you do. I was coming to tell you that I think I'm going to go to Seattle by myself. Maybe I need a little distance from this place and everyone in it."

"Ruby…" he said, but she waved him off.

"No, really. Don't feel bad. You got to slum it with us little people for a bit, and now it's time to go back to your real life."

"Being with you was not some social experiment. I care about you so much. I'm not doing this to hurt you—I'm doing this so I can heal my relationship with my daughter. I have to do that, Ruby."

"Of course you do. Goodbye," she whispered and ran to her car.

CHAPTER THIRTY

THERE WAS AN old Elvis song called "Can't Help Falling in Love" that summed up Ruby's problem perfectly. She was a fool. A complete and utter fool for letting herself get carried away by these feelings she had for Boone.

But she couldn't help it, no matter how hard she tried. And she *had* tried.

Foolish. So very foolish. Thank goodness she hadn't made a complete idiot out of herself by admitting she loved him back. That would have been a nightmare.

Ruby pressed the doorbell outside Levi's house. She was later than she had planned, but she figured Violet wouldn't care. Nobody really cared how Ruby felt. Not her father when he left when she was a kid, not her sister when she up and moved to Seattle, not Levi when he admitted he couldn't be married, not Boone when he left to go back to his real family, and certainly not Violet, who always cared more about gaining Levi's affection than Ruby's.

Everyone always left Ruby behind. That was just the reality of her life.

Levi opened the door. "You made it. We were starting to get worried. Violet was sure you'd be here before breakfast. Late night with the famous Mr. Williams? Should I check TMZ?"

Ruby had to keep breathing. The tears were just begging to flow freely, and she was not going to give Levi the satisfaction of making her cry.

"I'm kidding, Ruby. Are you okay?" Levi actually seemed concerned.

"Is she ready? If you hand me her stuff, I'll go put it in the car."

"I'm ready," Violet came up behind her dad, pulling her suitcase and holding her pillow. "Bye, Dad." She kissed him goodbye, and Ruby had to look away. She couldn't handle seeing their affection right now. Violet never wanted Ruby to hug or kiss her. Ruby was forbidden to touch her most days.

"I guess we'll talk later this week about what's next, huh?" Levi asked. "I think it would be better to get her up here at least a week before school starts, right?"

Ruby took that to mean he was still planning to take Violet away.

"Ruby?" He snapped his fingers in front of her face. "What's going on with you?"

"We'll call you. We need to get going." She headed for the car.

Violet loaded her stuff in the car and waved goodbye to her dad once she was situated in the passenger seat. Ruby started the car, and Violet turned the radio on.

"You weren't listening to music on the way here?"

Ruby shook her head and put the car in Reverse.

"Are you okay? You look like someone died. Is Grandma okay?"

"Grandma is fine, as far as I know."

"What's the matter, then?"

There was probably no good time to tell Violet that Boone was gone. Ruby figured she might as well tell her now.

"You should know that things are going to be a little different when you go to Helping Hooves tomorrow. Boone decided to go back home. He left this morning. He's sorry he didn't get to say goodbye."

Violet didn't say a word for the next ten minutes. The silence in the car was deafening. Ruby couldn't bring herself to say anything else, though.

"He's going to come back and visit, right?

Doesn't he have to finish recording his album? He has to come back."

"He's finishing his album up here. There's no reason for him to go back to Grass Lake. His family is here in Nashville."

Violet picked up Ruby's phone that sat in the cup holder between them. "I'm going to text him that he has a really good reason to come back. That he can't just leave us." She searched through Ruby's contact list. "Where's his number?"

"I deleted it. There was no point in keeping it."

"Oh my gosh, Mom! Seriously?" She set the phone back down and folded her arms across her chest. A few minutes later she said, "I'll ask Jesse. He probably has his number."

They drove the rest of the two hours home without saying a word.

MONDAY MORNING, VIOLET was ready to go to Helping Hooves an hour before she was due for her session with Jesse. Ruby gave in and drove her over there a little early.

"Can you come back early, too? I want to talk to you and Jesse about moving to Dad's."

Ruby couldn't wait. The first time Violet invited her to a session and it was to iron out the plans to leave her. Fabulous.

"Sure. I'll see you in less than an hour."

Ruby drove to the end of the drive and parked there to wait. She had nowhere else to go. Forty-five minutes felt like an eternity. When it finally passed, Ruby dreaded getting out of the car. The parking lot was nothing but a nasty reminder of being dumped by one more person she'd bothered to love.

Violet and Jesse were hanging out near the larger of the two paddocks. Jesse greeted her with a smile. As if there was anything to smile about.

"Violet and I had a really good discussion today. I'm glad we can all talk a little bit."

"Did she tell you about her plans to move back to Nashville?"

"We talked about Nashville. Actually, Violet, why don't you tell your mom what we talked about?"

Violet turned away from the horses she had been watching and pressed her back to the fence. "I don't want to move in with Dad. I never really did. I actually thought he was going to say no. When he didn't, it felt so good to know he wanted me that I didn't say anything."

Ruby couldn't believe what she was hearing. "You don't want to live with your dad?"

"Why don't you tell your mom how you

were feeling about the other thing?" Jesse prompted Violet.

"I was kind of mad when you didn't fight Dad about it. You just said if that was what I wanted, I could go."

"You were trying to get me and Dad to fight?"

"I didn't want you to fight. I mean I wanted you to say no. I wanted you to make me stay so I didn't have to admit to Dad that I don't want to go."

Ruby considered pinching herself to make sure she hadn't fallen asleep behind the wheel and was actually still at the end of the drive.

She grounded herself by touching the fence in front of her. She couldn't do that from her car, so this had to be real. "Violet, that's not the right way to handle—"

"Maybe you could start with how that makes you feel," Jesse interrupted.

"That makes me feel pretty mad and frustrated because she's always changing the rules on me. I thought that she wanted to be more independent, so I tried to let her make choices without interfering. Now she's mad at me for not interfering?"

"What I'm hearing is, it makes you feel like you can't win. Right?" Jesse asked.

"That's right."

"We talked about how you might have felt like that." He shifted his focus back to Violet. "Not being honest about your feelings really messed things up, didn't it?"

"I'm sorry I didn't tell you the truth, Mom. I feel bad that I made you think I didn't want to be here with you."

It was a day of many firsts. Violet usually wasn't much of an apologizer.

"Apology accepted. Thank you, Violet."

Jesse smiled his approval of their good work. "Violet and I talked a lot about how her behavior affects others. And how it affects your feelings. And that brought up another issue. Violet's been worried about you."

"Worried about me?"

"Are you sad or mad that Boone left?" Violet asked.

Jesse's words about the dangers of not being honest about their feelings made her take pause. "I'm both. How are you feeling?" she asked Violet.

"At first I was really mad. Then I was sad. But after talking to Jesse, I think I'm proud of Boone."

"Why are you proud of him?" Ruby couldn't understand where that came from, because she felt a lot of things, and proud was not one of them.

"He's doing the right thing. He's trying to be a good dad to his daughter. He didn't think he could be, so I'm proud of him for really believing in himself for once. Plus, it had to be hard for him because I know he cares about us, too."

He said he cared, but Ruby didn't believe that once he said he had to leave. She was so wrapped up in how his choice impacted her that she hadn't thought about what it had taken for him to make it.

"I wish he could have stayed, though," Ruby admitted. "That probably makes me a bad person."

Jesse cocked his head. "Why does that make you a bad person?"

"Because I wanted him to choose me even though I knew choosing me meant he couldn't choose his daughter. Of course he should have chosen his daughter."

"You love him, Ruby. You wanted him to choose you. Just like you wanted Violet to choose you. I'm guessing there are other people in your life you wish would have chosen you."

He was freakishly accurate in his assessment. "Well, the good news is, Violet doesn't want to move to Nashville."

"I didn't say that," Violet interjected.

"What do you mean, you didn't say that? You said you want to live with me."

"I do want to live with you. But I don't want to move to Seattle."

Ruby was over Seattle. Even though she'd told Boone she was going by herself, she couldn't move so far away from Violet. Levi wasn't going to agree to letting Violet leave the state, and Brittney wasn't begging her to come, anyway. Her sister had her own family to worry about, and a relationship with Ruby had never been one of her priorities.

"We don't have to move to Seattle. Your dad seems to be willing to try harder. I think we should show him a little more patience. Maybe he'll surprise us."

"But I don't want to stay in Grass Lake, either," Violet said. "Two hours is too far to go to see Dad every other weekend. And Boone lives in Nashville. I know you have a job here, but babies are born there, too. Everything we need is in Nashville."

All of those were good points except one. "We can't force our way into Boone's life, Vi."

"Oh my gosh, Mom. He didn't want to leave us. He had to. But what if he didn't have to? What if we were closer? What if he could be there for Emmy and us? People blend families all the time. Didn't you ever watch *The Brady*

Bunch when you were a kid? Luckily we don't have to let three boys move into our house if you marry Boone."

Jesse burst out laughing. "She makes some really good points, Ruby."

She certainly did. But risking her heart like that wasn't something she was sure she could do. Could she?

CHAPTER THIRTY-ONE

CHATEAU WEST WAS neutral ground for Boone and Sara. The hotel had a private room that they could reserve and food that tasted like it was actually worthy of the prices they charged for it.

Sara had agreed to meet there for dinner with their legal representation to discuss the current custody agreement and some tweaks Boone wanted to propose.

Her lawyer was not a Boone Williams fan. Although Boone often wondered if the woman and her permanent scowl were really fans of anyone. She walked in first and was not happy that Boone and his lawyer were already seated.

"It really would have been more appropriate for you to wait outside the room until we arrived. That way we could have chosen where we were going to sit with a tad more fairness."

This woman could make the color of the sky a debate. "Would you like to sit here, Ruth?" Boone stood up. "I promise I didn't lick the silverware yet."

She didn't find him funny at all. Of course, he doubted she found anyone—or anything, for that matter—funny.

"We're fine," Sara said, taking the seat diagonal from Boone so he would have to sit across from Ruth.

"Thank you for agreeing to this meeting," he said. "I know that there's been a lot of bad blood between us, but I'm really hoping we can start over. I mean that."

"I'm here because your daughter asked me to come. She would like to resume visits, not me."

Boone couldn't let himself forget where he was and who he was with. There could be no jumping for joy. He and Emmy had talked about visits on the phone a few times, but he hadn't expected her to mention it to her mother.

"I would like to resume visits, as well. I assume you have some conditions."

"Number one being the first time you show up to a visit drunk will be the last time you have a visit."

She was hitting hard right out of the gate. "I have absolutely no plans ever to be drunk again. But I agree that condition should be in there."

Sara's eyebrows pinched together. "You agree?"

"Absolutely. I need to be held accountable. Emmy's safety and well-being are the most important things, and if I jeopardize that, I should lose my privileges to spend time with her."

She didn't seem to know how to respond to him when he wasn't being argumentative. Neither did Ruth.

"We need to think about that. And how it should be worded."

"It's your condition, Ruth. What is there to think about?" Boone's lawyer questioned.

Ruth looked over at Sara, who clearly did not have an answer. "Fine. Second condition..." Ruth and Sara took turns going through all of their concerns and stipulations. Boone didn't fight any of them. He maintained his cool and forced himself to take responsibility for the things he had done that had caused Sara to feel like she needed to set those terms.

Once he had agreed to everything, he presented his condition. "I only have one request, and it's that we do a family dinner once a month on a day when we are all in town and available."

"What?" Sara's eyes widened.

"As much as you might wish we'd never met, we are forever bound by our daughter." Boone searched within himself for some humility. "I have wronged you so many different ways that

I don't blame you for having a hard time believing that I've changed. But I don't know how I can prove to you that I have if we never see each other."

"You expect me to cook for you once a month?"

"We can go out. We can switch off hosting. It really doesn't matter to me where we eat. What matters is that we show Emmy that we can be civil. She hasn't seen that enough, and it scares me. I don't want her to be afraid to get married someday or to think it's okay to withhold forgiveness."

Boone needed her to give him this one thing. If he was ever going to right his wrongs and move forward, he needed this condition.

Sara was trying to figure out what his end game was. Her suspicion was understandable but unnecessary. Boone's intentions were pure.

"I'll agree to three months of once-a-month family dinners with a review at the end to see if more should be added or if it does more harm than good."

"Fair enough. I agree."

"Is it wrong that I want to pull out my phone and record you saying that, so when you come back saying something else, I can prove you actually did agree to my terms?"

"That was the point of having the lawyers

here, Sara. But if you want me to say it into your phone, I'll do it."

Ruth stopped taking her copious notes and pushed up her glasses with her finger. "Who are you?"

"I finally figured out what's important, Ruth. I hope you can do that someday, too."

She rolled her eyes, and Boone felt a sharp pain in his chest. Things that reminded him of Violet tended to do that. He missed her, and being reminded of her always led to thinking about Ruby.

Sara had stopped glaring and was now watching him as if she was more curious than angry. "So whatever happened to that girlfriend of yours? Thankfully you've managed to stay out of the tabloids."

Rehashing all the things he had done in the past was rough but totally allowable. Discussing Ruby was not.

"I heard your release day got pushed back. What happened?"

"Touché," Sara said, tipping her water glass in his direction. "Let's not get too personal."

"Good idea. We should practice sticking to safe topics for those family dinners." Family dinners that unfortunately wouldn't include everyone he wished were part of his family.

BOONE CALLED DEAN on his way home from
the restaurant. He wanted to make sure he was
okay with the studio he had booked to record
the rest of his album.

Dean had no issues with the space but had a
question about who else might visit during recording sessions. "Piper was wondering if she
could sit in and learn a little more from you
about writing songs. You have no idea how
disappointed she was when you dropped out
of the duet. She looks up to you, Boone."

The man could try to butter him up all day.
It wasn't going to work. Boone wasn't the man
for the job. Teaching Piper how to write songs
simply wasn't in his skill set.

"What about Sawyer?" Boone asked.

"What do you mean, what about Sawyer?"

"What if you had Sawyer teach Piper how
to write songs? He writes songs. They seem
to get along. Now that their single has hit the
airwaves, they should be spending lots of time
together promoting it. It would be the perfect
time for a little Songwriting 101." Dean didn't
hate the idea.

Boone turned down his street and noticed
two people standing beside their car outside
his gated driveway. It had been a long time
since fans stood out there waiting for him. He
used to tell them if they didn't get out of there

by the time he made it to the house, he'd call the police.

It was a wonder he had any fans left.

He was a new man now. He couldn't go around threatening people every time they annoyed him. Boone couldn't control the feelings—and annoyed was one he felt quite often—but he was working hard to manage the way he acted. Especially when he was annoyed.

"I have to call you back, Dean. Looks like I have some unexpected visitors."

The stalkers had parked their car at the curb and were clearly looking for a way over the gate. Hanging out was one thing, but trying to break in was another. He'd give them one chance to get out of there before he took more serious action.

He pulled into the driveway. Both of them shielded their eyes, and both of them had red hair. They almost reminded him of Ruby and Violet, if Violet didn't color her hair black.

He shut off his lights and rolled down his window. "Hey there. Can I help you?"

"It's about time, old man. We've been standing out here for, like, ten hours."

"Don't exaggerate. Ten minutes is more like it. I'm pretty sure one of the neighbors would have called the cops if we had been standing out here for ten hours like stalkers."

"Oh my gosh, Mom. Who would stalk an old country singer?"

"He has lots of fans, Violet. You're the one who did the internet search, remember?"

"Oh, you mean like that lady who has a shrine set up in her bedroom? She would totally stalk him. You need to get a bigger gate, Boone. That lady would definitely come prepared with a ladder to get over this little thing."

Boone covered his mouth with his hand. He couldn't believe they were really there. He also couldn't believe Violet had gone back to her natural hair color.

"What up, Red? I left town and you went reverse emo on me."

"First of all, no one says *what up* anymore. Your age is showing again, and I know how much you hate that. And second, don't call me Red. My name is Violet. One color name is enough, and I had to sit through hours of torture to get the black bleached out so they could dye it this color that I hope will match what grows in. So don't tease me about it or else I'm going back to black. Third, can you please get out of the car so we can hug you, because it's been, like, two months and we've been missing you."

Not nearly as much as he'd been missing them. Boone hopped out of his car and Violet jumped on him, wrapping her arms and legs around him like a koala bear hugged a tree.

"How's it going, kid? You staying out of trouble?"

"Working on it."

The hair was different, but Violet was the same. She detached herself and stepped aside so he could greet Ruby. She was exactly the same. Beautiful as ever and capable of breaking his heart with one look.

"Sorry to just show up like this," she said. "We thought knocking on your door was going to be easier than it was. We should have expected a little security."

"Never apologize for coming to find me." He wanted to hold her, feel her in his arms again, but she didn't leap at him the way Violet did, and he was too afraid to make the first move.

One side of her mouth lifted in a crooked smile. "Noted," she said.

"Are you going to let us in or what?" Violet asked. She randomly pressed buttons on the keypad.

"Press the wrong pass code in more than three times and the police are going to show up."

Violet put her hands in the air. "Seriously?"

"No, but it's good to know you're still gullible." Boone laughed, earning him his first eye roll since he'd left Grass Lake.

He unlocked and opened the gate and had them follow him up the drive. His house was a bit bigger than the Airstream back in Grass Lake. Violet was slightly impressed.

"How many bedrooms?"

"Seven."

"How many bathrooms?"

"Five and a half."

"How many secret passageways?"

"If I told you that, they wouldn't be secret anymore, would they?" Boone unlocked the front door and let them in. It felt so strange to have them in his house, yet so right.

"That wouldn't be spoiling the secret," Violet argued. "The secret part is, I wouldn't know where they are or where they lead."

"Fine. None. Are you happy?"

"You could be lying to keep it more secret. I may have to do some investigating later."

Ruby shook her head and apologized. "She's a little hyper tonight. Since she started school, I think having to be quiet for so many hours makes her ten times more talkative in the evening."

"It's fine. I've missed her." Boone touched her hand. "I've missed both of you."

Ruby pulled her hand away like he'd stung her. He hated that, hated the distance that existed between them even though they were merely inches apart.

"Come on back here," he said, leading them to the kitchen. "Can I get you guys something to drink?"

Violet was all over that, while Ruby politely declined.

"So how's Nashville treating you?" he asked Violet, assuming that if school had started, she was living with her dad.

"It's good. School is school, but I tried out for the school play and actually made it."

"That's awesome!" He smiled over at Ruby. He hadn't forgotten how he had once suggested she get into acting. "Has your dad found you a place to ride yet?"

"No, but Mom has. We had Faith give us some suggestions before we left. It's pretty nice. Best part is, it's only five minutes from our house."

"Your dad lives five minutes from a horse ranch? I thought he lived downtown."

"Not five minutes from my dad's place. Five minutes from our place. Me and Mom moved up here so we could be closer to the people we love. Right, Mom?" Violet raised her eyebrows until they disappeared under her bangs.

"Yes, that's right, Violet."

"Is there something else you want to say, Mom?"

"Not right now with you standing here," Ruby said through gritted teeth.

"Fine. Hey, Boone, where's one of the five-and-a-half bathrooms in this place?"

He pointed down the hall, and Violet left the two of them alone. It seemed too much to ask that Ruby would have moved back to Nashville for him. She had been so adamant about getting away to Seattle.

"So Violet still lives with you?" He walked around the kitchen island that was separating them.

"Turns out she didn't really want to live with her dad, just wanted to see if he'd say yes. When he did, she hoped I would put my foot down and make her stay with me."

"Jesse would call that trying to pass off the accountability. Have someone else make the decision so you can blame them when it all goes wrong."

"Thankfully she came clean, and we've been doing so well that I'm sometimes afraid something bad is going to happen and ruin it all."

"She seems happy. And what's with the hair?"

Ruby shrugged. "It's the new Violet. She wanted to do something different. She thought maybe getting rid of some of the black would help change her attitude." She took a step toward him, and his heart started acting up again. "How are things with Emmy?"

"Really good. These last two months have been exactly what we needed to start rebuilding that foundation. We're going to start visits back up. I just came from a meeting with Sara and our lawyers."

"I'm in love with you," Ruby blurted out. Her cheeks turned redder than her hair. "Violet and I are both working on being honest about our feelings so there are no misunderstandings. I love you and we're here… *I'm* here to say we want you in our lives. In whatever capacity you can be in them."

She was close enough to touch, and his fingers were tingling in anticipation. "I'd like that."

"Are you sure? Because I was really mean to you the last time I saw you."

"I get it." He wanted her to know he didn't need her apology.

"No, I was hurt, and I have some pretty massive trust issues. I believe everyone I care about will eventually want to leave me. But I'm working on it."

"I have some issues with being trustworthy, but I'm also working on it," he admitted.

"That's why it took so long for me to come by." Ruby took a deep breath. "I'm terrified, but I needed you to know that I felt the same way you did when you left. I fell in love with you even though I didn't want to."

"We have a lot in common. I think that's a pretty good place to start." He wanted to prove to her that he would never leave her now that she'd forgiven him.

"Violet told me I need to take this risk. That she knows you'll be worth it."

Boone's heart swelled. The kid still had a soft spot for him. That meant everything.

"I promise to be worthy of whatever you're willing to give me."

"Good. We don't live too far from here. Maybe you could come by for dinner sometime?"

"I could do that, but I need to do something first."

A tiny crease appeared above her nose. Boone reached to smooth it out. Her skin was soft. He brushed the back of his hand against her cheek. She leaned in like a purring cat, craving more. Cupping her face with both hands, he kissed her slowly and purposefully. He wanted her to feel it from head to toe. He needed her to know exactly how he felt so there were no misunderstandings.

His lips trailed down her neck and back up to her ear. "I love you, too," he said clearly.

"Finally!" Violet shouted from the hall. "I mean, please don't kiss when I'm around because gross, but feel free to be in love any other time."

"Don't kiss like this?" Boone placed another kiss on Ruby's lips.

Violet shook her head. "Cut it out."

"How about this?" He took Ruby's hand and kissed the top of it.

"Don't be weird," Violet warned.

"Is this weird?" He grabbed Ruby up in his arms. He dipped her dramatically and kissed her the same way.

"I'm going looking for secret passages so I can find where you keep all your money! You'll be broke when I'm done with you. I hope all that kissing was worth it!"

Boone smiled against Ruby's lips. It was.

CHAPTER THIRTY-TWO

"IT'S A GIRL!" Ruby announced, placing the newborn in her mother's waiting arms. "She looks good. Strong set of lungs."

As the baby wailed, the new dad looked a little worried. "A girl? Are you sure?"

There weren't a lot of ways for her to be wrong. "I'm sure."

"I don't know what to do with a girl," he said, panicked. "I have five brothers. We don't have girls in our family."

Ruby took off her gloves and placed a reassuring hand on his shoulder. "She will be the sweetest thing you've ever known. I have a girl and I can tell you they are a blessing. So helpful and kind. Not messy and loud like boys."

Ruby's phone chimed with a text for what felt like the hundredth time. She left the new parents to bond with their new baby while she checked her messages. She had twenty new texts. All of them were from Violet. Most of them were MOM in all caps followed by a line

of nothing but exclamation points. The last two
were her favorites.

WHERE ARE YOU???????????????

If you don't get here soon I'm moving in with
Boone. He'll never notice. He has 7 bedrooms.

What was that she had told Mr. Berkley
about girls? She hadn't promised patience and
understanding, she hoped.

She quickly sent a reply that explained she
was working and if Violet needed to know
what that meant, she could Google afterbirth.
Her phone chimed a minute later.

OMG gross! I'm scarred for life!

Ruby finished her work, and when she left
the hospital, she was more than late. She drove
home to get changed and pick up Violet.

"He's going to make us listen to it twice because we're late," she complained when Ruby
walked through the front door.

"He knows babies are unpredictable. He'll
release you after one listen."

"I'm never having kids, by the way. Having them is gross, and then all they do is eat,
poop and cry."

"Don't forget when they get older and spend all your money on makeup they don't need to wear and tell you that your hair is embarrassing to be seen with."

"Exactly. More reasons never to have them," Violet said, following her upstairs. "But really, your hair was super embarrassing that day. Your appearance affects my life. Never forget that."

"I'm going to wear my hair in pigtails tonight. Will that be a good look?"

"Yeah, sure. It would look *great*. If you were three. Which you're not. You're, like, twenty times that."

Ruby gasped. "Someone needs her mom to sign her up for some math tutoring. Sheesh!"

Emmy answered the door when they finally arrived at Boone's. She and Violet could have been sisters in their black leggings and pale pink T-shirts with an elephant on the front pocket. Every shirt bought saved an elephant or something like that; at least, that was what the girls told Boone to convince him to buy them three each.

"He's getting a little anxious. Good thing you guys finally made it," Emmy said.

"Babies arrive when they want to, not when I want them to," Ruby reminded her as the girls took off ahead of her, their heads already together and surely planning something to drive her and Boone crazy.

Boone was waiting in his media room above the garage. His relief was visible when she walked in. He pulled her against him and kissed the crook of her neck.

"I thought you were never going to get here. This album has been cued up for two hours just itchin' to be played."

"Well, let's hear it. Violet has been waiting all week for this."

"I'm going to count how many times you say *pickup truck*. Each one will cost you a dollar," Violet said from the couch.

"I don't remember inviting her. Who invited her?"

Violet stuck out her tongue, and Emmy vouched for her. "I invited her. I wouldn't survive this without her."

She and Emmy both had their phones out and were giggling about something. They took a selfie, and Emmy encouraged Violet to send it to "him." Ruby wasn't aware of a "him" that Violet sent pictures to. She needed to schedule a phone snoop ASAP.

Boone got everything ready and clapped his hands to get the teenagers' attention. "No recording of anything you hear tonight. I do not want to find out things were leaked on

Facebook, Twitter, Snapchat, Instagram, Vine or whatever other social media sites you two spend your lives on. Understood?"

"I'm pretty sure we aren't into music piracy, Dad. Chill."

"Chill." Boone stared at Ruby. "That's your daughter's influence."

"Well, your daughter just told mine to send a picture of them to 'him.' That's her influence."

Boone frowned. "Who is this 'him'?"

"Oh my gosh, play the music. Please!" Violet groaned.

Boone had finished his album over a month ago. He had slaved away day and night in the studio. None of the three ladies in his life got to see much of him during the making of it. It was finally mixed and whatever else the producer did to it, and now Boone was giving them the first listen.

"I know it's not Pink Floyd, but try to keep an open mind."

"I also want a dollar for every reference to boots or T-shirts," Violet said before he pressed play.

"Good call," Emmy said. "My mom's album mentions lipstick, like, five hundred times. I should have thought to say that before she let me listen to it."

"Are you two extortionists done? Can I start now?"

They set their phones down and gave him their full attention. "Yes."

"I wrote a song for each of the three of you. Let's see if you can figure out which one is yours."

The music started, and Boone pulled Ruby close while they listened. He was so proud of it that she knew it was going to be phenomenal. There was no doubt. When Boone Williams put his heart and soul into something, it was magic.

Ruby guessed the song "Don't Call Me Red" was about Violet. It had a million color references and was about the sassiest girl in Nashville. It was upbeat and fun. Ruby would have called it a toe-tapper, but Violet would have made fun of her. The girls laughed all the way through. Violet loved it for sure.

Everyone was quiet during "Too Late for Sorry." That was Emmy's song and got Ruby choked up. She could feel Boone's heart beating a little faster. This was his favorite song on the record and the one he needed Emmy to love. This was his way of asking for redemption. Emmy got up and kissed his cheek when it was over. "It's never too late, Daddy."

Ruby's song was last. It was called "No Misunderstandings" and was a fun ditty with the catchiest hook. It was all about him being very clear about the reasons he loved her. It was the song Dean wanted to put out as the first single and was sure to be a hit.

"I think country music is going to welcome you home with open arms," Ruby said, giving him a kiss. "As a non-country-music listener, I loved it."

Emmy and Violet gave him a standing ovation. He stood and hugged them both at the same time.

"You owe me fifteen dollars," Violet informed him. "I'm a little disappointed there wasn't a song about a waitress in Daisy Dukes who got her heart broken because she didn't like your truck."

"That's one of the B-sides," Boone said with a wink.

Violet tipped her chin down. "I have no idea what that means, which means that's a word from 1940. So, to bring you back to the present, I think you should know I liked *my* song the best because it's about me. I also love that you snuck in the blue horse for Willow and mom's green eyes and our old yellow house. It's like every good memory from Grass Lake in one song."

"We're going to my room now. Proud of you,

Daddy." Emmy gave him another kiss and took off with Violet in tow.

"I feel like we are way too lucky that those two are thicker than thieves," Ruby said as Boone sat back down next to her.

"It was meant to be. This is my family."

Ruby's butterflies went crazy when he talked like that. They had been dating for six months, and everything was going too well. She was afraid to acknowledge how perfect it was for fear that would provoke a reversal of fortune.

She kissed him instead. Kissing Boone was always the best way to kill the time. She hadn't been lying when she'd told Holly it was like seeing fireworks or stars, but better. With Boone, everything was bigger, brighter, stronger.

"How come only the girls get to have sleepovers?" he asked when he came up for air.

"Because we are teaching our girls that it pays to do things the right way."

"Sometimes being bad isn't so bad." He flashed her that grin and gave her those eyes that could convince her of just about anything.

"Stop trying to Boone me." She covered her own eyes with her hand. "I won't give in until you marry me."

"That could be arranged."

Ruby dropped her hand and waited for him

to start laughing. Only, he didn't. He looked dead serious.

Boone and Ruby had talked about marriage once before, only to express their fear about doing something like that a second time. Neither one of them wanted to be divorced twice. If they were going to get married, they both had to be one hundred percent sure that they were in it for life.

"What are you saying?"

"I'm saying I love you, Miss Ruby Wynn, and there is no one in this world I want to grow old with other than you."

"You're sure?"

"One hundred ten percent."

Ruby was caught off guard. Something that Boone was good at doing. He always left her feeling a tiny bit off balance. Enough so things never got too comfortable. She loved that about him.

"I love you, too," she said.

"So what are you saying?"

"Are you asking me?"

He slid off the couch and got down on one knee. He took Ruby by the hand and stared back at her with the most sincere look in his eyes.

"I don't have a ring because I wasn't planning this, but I have known for a long time that this was what I wanted. Marry me, Ruby. Let's make this family the real deal."

She believed him when he said this wasn't some impulsive decision. They had both felt the shift. The fear had lifted some time ago. Ruby knew without a doubt that he was the only man for her.

"Let me be clear so there's no misunderstanding," she said, taking his face in her hands and pressing a chaste kiss on his lips. "Yes. I will marry you."

He jumped back on the couch, peppering her with kisses. "Let's not tell the girls. Let's surprise them with a destination wedding," he said.

"Someone really has been thinking about this."

"Only since I kissed you in your kitchen back in Grass Lake."

"Only since then?" Her heart fluttered at the memory.

"What can I say? You Rubied me."

CHAPTER THIRTY-THREE

MARY ELLEN FINISHED proofreading this month's Parenting Advice column and emailed it to Holly. She liked to get them one week in advance, but Mary Ellen always sent it two weeks ahead just to be safe.

This month's article was on the importance of having a fire safety plan. She shared with the good readers of the *Gazette* how her family ran fire drills four times a year. Her children might be small, but they could be taught to army crawl to the door, to check for heat with the backs of their little hands and to get outside as quickly as possible. They knew to meet by the oak tree in the front yard. The last time they practiced, everyone made it out safely in less than three and a half minutes.

The twins were napping peacefully, so she decided to go grab the mail. Keith was watching some hockey on the TV. He was allowed to watch only when the kids were sleeping. Monitoring their screen time was very important. They were not going to have children who were addicted to electronic devices.

The new neighbors were out watering the landscaping they had put in for spring. Sandy and Eugene were ideal neighbors. Their two boys were in elementary school and so polite. They had a dog, but they seemed to be good about keeping it leashed at all times. Her girls were allergic; she couldn't have some mutt charging at them if they happened to be outside at the same time.

They had bought the house from the Davises about a month after Ruby and her troubled daughter moved out. It was quite a change from living next door to renters, who were always a little shady.

She opened the mailbox and pulled out the small stack of envelopes. Bill, junk mail, junk mail, junk mail. On the bottom was a square envelope addressed to her and Keith in beautiful calligraphy. No return address, though. That was odd. She didn't have any family members celebrating anything important anytime soon. She couldn't imagine who it was from.

The envelope was thick and sturdy. It was obviously very expensive stationery. She didn't want to tear it, so she waited until she got inside and could use her letter opener.

It slid across the top like a hot knife through butter. Inside was a beautiful invitation on luxury card stock. This was no generic paper. This was custom. Whoever sent this was trying very hard to show off.

Mary Ellen sat down on one of the stools at her spotless kitchen island. All the lunch dishes were washed and dried, and the ingredients for stuffed peppers were set out to make things easier on her when it was time to start dinner. Mary Ellen was proud of her cleanliness and organizational strengths. Who wouldn't be?

She read the whole invitation. Twice.

They met.
They fell in love.
They're getting married.
You're invited.
Please join Ruby and Boone
as they become Mr. and Mrs.
The plane leaves BNA
June 2 at 3:00 p.m. sharp
for Turks and Caicos.
Bring your passport.
And a bathing suit.
You're welcome.

Mary Ellen felt faint. Today, according to the date circled on the calendar hanging on the wall of her kitchen command center, was June 1.

Leave it to Ruby to wait to the last minute to send out an invitation. Clearly she was still having trouble keeping her life in order. But she was marrying a music icon. Boone was back on the radio and his first single had been sitting at the top of the charts for weeks. That made Ruby someone Mary Ellen needed to be nice to.

"Keith!" she screamed loud enough to wake not only her children but also all the sleeping children in Grass Lake. "Grab the suitcases! I'll get the passports! We're going to a wedding!"

* * * * *

LARGER-PRINT BOOKS!

GET 2 FREE
LARGER-PRINT NOVELS
PLUS 2 FREE
MYSTERY GIFTS

Love Inspired®

Larger-print novels are now available...

LARGER-PRINT BOOKS!

GET 2 FREE LARGER-PRINT NOVELS PLUS 2 FREE MYSTERY GIFTS

Love Inspired.

SUSPENSE
RIVETING INSPIRATIONAL ROMANCE

Larger-print novels are now available...